# The Dragon Inside
## Book 1
## Becoming the Dragon

Alex Sapegin

D0630215

# CONTENTS

# CHARACTER LIST

Andrew Kerimov — the main character

Olga Kerimova and Irina Kerimova — his sisters

Iliya Kerimov — Andy's father, a scientist

Helen Kerimova — Andy's mother

Bon — Andy's dog

Sergey Usoltsev — a bow master and Andy's teacher

Ms. Nichol's – Andy's teacher

Alena, Mark, George (Troll), Vera, Egor — Irina's friends, Tolkieneers.

Sasha and Sam — Andy's friends

Arist — a mercenary leader

Chutka, Gichok — mercenaries

Grok the Magician

Jagirra (Jaga) — an elf , herbalist and magician, Karegar's "wife", takes part in Andy's ritual to become a dragon

Karegar – The Black Dragon

King Hudd — The King of Rimm

Nirel – An elf and a master of torture, working for The King of Rimm

Master Hugo — a master of torture

Countess Vinetta Menskaya – beautiful countess admired by many for her beauty

Alo Troi – instructor at the school of magic, imprisoned and tortured by Nirel

Count Ludwig Ramizo – the head of the foreign relations house

Namita – the younger daughter of King Hudd, age 14

Taliza – older daughter of King Hudd

Migur – loyal executioner of King Hudd

Sanchez – guard in the dungeon of King Hudd

Polana – a girl Andy believes is not local, with chestnut hair. Andy feels attraction for her.

Grom – The god of earth and metals, who gave his people the ability to see iron in the earth

Nirada – The goddess of beauty and fertility

Targ – a god similar to the Viking's god Loki, the god of deception

Enira – A larga, the daughter of a royal magnate who fell in love with the Lord of the Sky

# PART 1: PORTAL VOYAGER

## N-ville, Russia. Andy.

"I'm heading out! I won't be back 'til late!" Andy's mother grabbed her purse from the coffee table and threw her cell phone and keychain into the side pocket. "You've got this, right?"

"I got it, Mom." Andy frowned. "There's food in the fridge, pizza in the freezer. Feed Olga, get her dressed and ready, then make sure Irina takes a warm sweater, a coat and bug spray with her to her game. Did I forget anything?"

"Don't go into your dad's study. He's downloading something; it'll freeze the computer. You know very well, he'll be fuming about it until next Christmas. Are you going to Sergey's house?" Andy nodded. "Then take Olga to Grandma's. Okay, bye." Helen kissed her son on the cheek and slipped out the door. The company minibus had already honked a couple of times.

The clatter of claws on parquet came from the living room, and Bon scrambled into the entryway with his leash in his mouth.

"You've already gone out boy! You woke me up at the crack of dawn." Andy said to the pup. Bon sighed loudly and wagged his tail, showing he wouldn't mind going for another walk. "All right, fine. You talked me into it, you smooth-talking devil. But just to the bakery."

Andy took the leash from the dog and hooked the carabiner to his collar. Bon leaped joyfully in circles around his owner.

"Quie-e-et!" Andy snapped at the dog. "You'll wake the girls."

He needed to make a trip to the bakery anyway. Olga and Irina wouldn't eat breakfast on a Saturday without cinnamon rolls, and they were out.

Andy preferred sausages or bacon in the morning; Bon did, too, but the pup rarely got them.

*** 

Andy bought the cinnamon rolls at the bakery and a carton of milk at the store next door then headed home.

He was wide-awake with nothing to do, and he looked resentfully at Bon. "Why wake me so early on a Saturday, Boy?" The pup only wagged his tail in response.

He was struck by an old urge to jump on the computer and play some of his favorite online games, but soon an inner voice reminded him, "Don't go in your dad's study. He's downloading something; it'll freeze the computer."

"Ok," he said to himself. "Forget the computer."

Andy hadn't played computer games in more than two years, and he'd done just fine. But sometimes, something would come over him, and he'd want that escape into another reality.

He sighed loudly, making Bon turn to look at him as if to say, *Are you copying me, Master?* Andy smiled as he reached up to scratch a little scar at the base of his neck—courtesy of a lightning bolt, no less—a sad reminder of the danger of standing under trees during storms. For more than two years, Andy had been branded with the scar just above his right shoulder, but the memory of that fateful moment was as fresh as if it had happened yesterday…

\*\*\*

His homeroom teacher, Ms. Nichols, had long promised to take their 6A class on a field trip to the woods, and that day was finally here. After an hour of belting out songs on the bus, each kid singing at the top of his lungs (out of tune, but with feeling), they arrived. Mother Nature's wonder spread out before the young tourists in all its glory. The weather was beautiful—not a cloud in the sky—and the birds were singing. There was fresh May grass growing and no mosquitoes.

The idyllic scene was ruined, however, by signs of human neglect. Litter was scattered everywhere, and the strong smell of a public toilet came from the thick brush at the end of the field opposite from the river. To make the best of things, the children spent the first half-hour picking up paper, plastic bags, cans, cigarette butts and other trash from the meadow. Certainly, no one thought of going into the river where broken glass glittered near the shore.

Andy sadly recalled the days when he and his mom had visited his Uncle Rob. They had walked in the forest, collecting mushrooms and pinecones. *Now, that's a place of open spaces and natural beauty!* Towering cedars three arm's lengths around, their tops disappearing into the sky; even rows of round hilltops going off into the blue distance; and not a single tin can for hundreds of miles. He had longed to share that with his classmates.

The day went by fast, but starting around lunchtime, a gloomy haze curled up on the horizon.

"I love May's first storms!" one of his classmates shouted.

A strong gust of wind lifted last year's dead leaves into the air, and a clap of thunder, like the rumble of empty barrels, made them all duck.

Ms. Nichols began herding the whole class back to the bus stop, but the wind picked up, and the storm worsened. One flash of lightning followed another. There was still a half-mile to the bus stop when the heavens opened and soaked Andy and the others. Miserably, the class huddled under trees that at least gave the vague illusion of shelter from the rain.

Andy chose a young oak with sparse spreading branches. He had just gotten situated under a thick branch when a close flash of lightning blinded him. When he came to, he was already on the bus...

***

Andy's friends were waiting for him when he arrived home from the hospital. They all gathered around, filled with questions. First on the list, had the lightning awoken anything supernatural in him?

*No!* he thought gloomily, *I can't read minds, see the future or communicate with the spirits of the dead. What a crock! I was struck by lightning and don't even get anything out of it!*

It wasn't long, however, before Andy learned the lightning had left a rather unusual effect behind. As soon as he sat down at or lingered near a computer, it would slow down and freeze up. The television flickered with static if he came within five feet of it. Andy was forced to withdraw permanently from his lifelong love of gaming. He could never have expected such a cruel blow from Mother Nature. A scar on his neck was one thing—complete with bragging rights and a sort of war story—but to be sentenced to life without computers? That was punishment fit for the wretched.

When it became clear he could no longer use a computer, Andy fell into a deep melancholy. He felt his life was over and transformed almost overnight from a happy goofball to a pensive guy with an intense, piercing gaze.

In time, he realized he had no choice but to accept his new life and rediscover the world around him. Books (so many books!), his bicycle, rollerblades, the gym in the evening, and, oddly enough, even a passion for cooking...

***

One afternoon, Andy was idling around the house alone. His younger sister, Olga, was at daycare, and his older one, Irina, was at a friend's house. His parents were at work and he was starting to feel restless. In order to distract his mind and save himself from an attack of melancholy, he decided to leaf through a cookbook. Then the idea occurred to him to try cooking something—all by himself.

His first attempt at a meal was an eggplant-based lasagna, constructed mainly from leftover veggies in the fridge, and the result was mouthwatering! For a long time, his mother couldn't believe he had prepared something so delicious on his first try. She had expected him to be like Irina, who was capable of producing passable scrambled eggs at best.

For the next month, the family spent all of their spare money on various groceries and ingredients so Andy could prepare new and exciting culinary delights. Olga, a very picky eater, suddenly devoured the dishes her older brother prepared, dirtying both cheeks in the process and gaining three pounds as a result. Irina threw her diet out the window and joined her younger sister in the feasting. They teased each other about who could put on weight the fastest.

And there was no question their parents loved Andy's cooking. His father joked that his son could make a salad out of nothing. Still, Andy soon tired of his cooking phase and took to new hobbies, such as renovating the guest room to make it livable again. The added upside was his own space, since sharing a room with his little sister had become awkward and sleeping on the living room couch wasn't very appealing either.

Next, he tried sports to distract his ever-busy mind. He retrieved an old bicycle from the garage and fixed it up, and repaired some broken roller blades. Andy began to spend all of his time outside, convincing his friends, Sam and Sasha, to join him. Instead of *Counter-Strike* and *Call of Duty*, Andy persuaded the boys to experience skating in the park and the real-to-life world of paintball.

It was after one particularly grueling game of paintball that Andy first encountered Sergey, and his life took yet another unexpected sharp turn.

***

Sergey Usoltsev was a local celebrity and known eccentric. Old lady from next door used to mutter about him as he walked past. "What can you say about someone who collects old bows and restores them? What a ridiculous way to spend money, and on such useless things!"

Andy and the guys were coming back from the latest game of paintball, and Andy was distracted by some large welts on his backside, courtesy of Sasha, the sharpshooter. He continually stopped to rub them, slowing their pace, and as they plodded along, a sound like *donn* followed by a biting *click* caught his ears. Andy turned his head when he heard it again—*donn, click*. Sam saw Sergey first and tapped Andy on the shoulder, pointing past the fence of a two-story house. A tall, hoary-haired man with a wide chest and chiseled arms stood in the yard twisting an M-shaped bow in his hands. After looking around, he pulled an arrow out of the ground, raised the hand holding the bow and deftly set the arrow on the bowstring. He pulled it back almost to his ear and fired. The bowstring let out a ringing *donn* and *clicked* against the thick leather glove that he wore on his left hand. In a flash of feathers and with a dull thud, the arrow pierced a wooden pole dug into the ground 50 feet on the other side of the yard.

*That was awesome!* Andy thought to himself. Sasha and Sam stood with their mouths open. Like a whisper of olden times and epic heroes, it wasn't something you saw every day. *I would love to learn to shoot like that!*

The boys waited ten minutes for another show, but the man pulled the arrows from the pole, went into the house and didn't come out again.

*** 

The next day, Andy stood at the intricately carved wicket gate and rang the bell. The archer from the previous day appeared.

"What do you need, son?" he asked, glancing at the boy.

"My name is Andrew! Teach me to shoot like you do!" Andy blurted out, looking the man in the eyes.

"I don't take apprentices!" Sergey answered and slammed the gate.

Andy thought for a minute and settled down on a little bench near the gate. He had firmly made up his mind to learn to shoot a bow; he just had to get his future teacher on board. When it grew dark after a few hours, Andy finally got up from his spot. Sergey hadn't deigned to leave the house again.

*** 

The next day, the bench was once more occupied by the stubborn boy. This time, Andy brought a couple of books with him to help stave off boredom. All day, the homeowner showed no signs of life, although the tulle curtains did flutter from time to time.

*** 

On the third day, Andy repeated the whole process. He had decided patience was the key to success. New books helped the hours go by.

"What are you reading?" someone said from behind his ear.

"The *Land of Crimson Clouds* by Arkady and Boris Strugatsky," Andy answered and raised his eyes from the page. The archer stood at his gate.

"And the other one?"

"Yurii Kachaev, a historical book. There are a couple of stories in it: *Above the Forest Ridgepoles,* and *Beyond the Whistling Arrow of the Chanyu.*"

"Aren't you sick of hanging out by my gate?"

"No, my father has a large library. It'll last me a long time. I'm not bothering you, am I? Or are you worried I'll rub the paint off the bench?"

"Oh, for goodness' sake! Would you like to come into the yard and drink some tea?" the man unexpectedly offered, and for the first time, he smiled.

"I wouldn't say no to that," Andy answered. "Although I'd like some Fanta even more..."

The man opened the gate and let Andy into the yard. "So, you want to become a bowman?" he asked.

"I want to become a bowman, and maybe try to make my own bows."

"But can you stand the training? I won't coddle you," the archer said, again smiling with just the corners of his mouth.

"Yes!" Andy declared.

"Well then, come in!" The man opened the door to the porch for Andy. "My name is Sergey."

"Andy." He reached to shake the outstretched hand.

*** 

That was two years ago. Andy smiled thinking back.

"Tell me what you know about bows and shooting them," Sergey said as they sipped on their tea.

Except for Robin Hood, Andy couldn't think of anything, so he said so. Sergey winced visibly at the sound of the name and launched into a lecture on the topic of bows.

"Robin Hood, *indeed*! What stories they tell you young folk! The English bowmen were beating the French at the Battles of Crécy and Agincourt... That's all nonsense! At Crécy, they knocked out the horses and forced the knights to the ground, and then the tired Frenchmen were massacred. King Phillip should've been beheaded for organizing a battle in such a way, but the knights did right, you know. One must always listen to his commanding officer.

"What's an English bow? Even a Western European bow in general?" he continued. "A piece of wood remade and fashioned accordingly. That kind of bow was made from one piece of a certain kind of wood. Most often, they used elm and yew, but they made use of ash and hazel, too. To have such fine material as yew available and not bring it to perfection was the height of extravagance on the part of the Europeans. The English could shoot their bows just over a hundred yards, with the record-holders hitting the target at about 220. When firing at random, without a target, an arrow fired from a recurve English bow could reach almost 550. And that's the last good thing one can say about recurve bows. They didn't do well with moisture, always lost the battle in heat and cold, and God forbid you should drop such a bow in the water!

"No matter what the Europeans said, Eastern bows outperformed their English counterparts in all respects, and bowmen in the East were much better than the English. I'll give you a couple of examples: a randomly fired arrow from a Russian compound bow can fly up to 875 yards. In Russia, there was a measurement used for distance called 'arrow's flight' or simply 'flight.' It dealt not only with how far an arrow flew but how far it could fly and retain its deadly force! It wasn't all that much, around 240 yards, but still not bad. You can up and do that right now if you like; it was nothing special.

"Tatar, Arab and Turkish bows surpassed European bows by far, both in efficacy during battle and in technical excellence. And there were no English or Italian yews there! They had to bring the materials they had readily available up to standard. The same Ugrians or Hungarians—the 'threat of Europe' of the tenth century—were knocked off their chain-mail-clad cavalry by Mongol bows at the Battle of Mohi.

"But...back to bows. An Eastern compound bow can withstand cold, heat, or moisture; if you had to, you could dip it in water, and it wouldn't lose the battle! See..."

Sergey ran into another room and returned with the bow Andy had seen him use. "It's an exact reconstruction of a compound bow from the tenth to eleventh centuries. It consists of two wooden planks glued together lengthwise, on the inside."

He ran his finger along the inside of the bow. "A juniper plank planted on fish glue; here and here, there are sinews. If you took the string out now, the sinews would pull the bow the other way. This bow has been glued with boiled birch bark.

"Later on, people began to strengthen bows with decorative bone plates. They made plates of iron, too, but that was at the request of the epic Russian warriors of old. The strings were different, too. In the West, they generally made bowstrings out of hemp. In Russia, they used silk or animal tendons. A string made of specially dressed dorsal skin was considered especially chic. The Arabs preferred to use the dorsal skin of scrawny camels for this purpose. The bowstrings prepared by special methods could withstand heat and moisture. You could fire an arrow in the rain!"

Sergey kept going into the other room until an entire collection of different kinds of bows lay on the coffee table. The lecture had a lasting effect on Andy. In an hour, he'd learned more about bows than he'd read in books from first through sixth grade.

*** 

Sergey began Andy's training with breathing exercises. Then came the development of his shoulder girdle, strengthening exercises and various tasks designed to improve his ability to judge by eye, and his hand-eye coordination. The lessons were interesting. Andy's friends showed up just to listen to the lectures on bows and ancient weapons. Sergey had a large selection of books and materials on old weapons that started with ancient Egypt and ended at the beginning of the twentieth century. In fact, the tutor had developed a whole philosophy on the lore of archery and spent a good deal of time edifying his young pupil in it.

It was six months before Andy picked up a bow for the first time, and still, he didn't get to shoot it. Instead, his tutor asked him to fit it with a bowstring and slowly pull on it to the point at which an arrow could be shot from it. Then he had to return it to the starting position in an equally slow motion and continue doing so for endless hours until his hands began to quiver.

***

One day, Andy came to Sergey's class with a puppy on a leash. Much to his relief, the dog's presence was met favorably. Sergey scratched and rubbed his shaggy sides and pet his wide forehead. He then told his student to fully accept his responsibility for another and learn to take care of his four-legged friend.

The puppy was a hand-me-down of sorts from Andy's older sister, Irina. The impulsive girl was prone to bursts of compassion and love for her fellow creatures. She fed stray kittens in the alley and pigeons and sparrows in their backyard. And when she found a little, lost puppy, she brought him home, intent on caring for him the best she could. Unfortunately, although she had the best of intentions, her interest in these new projects tended to fade quickly. Before long, she had abandoned the puppy to his own devices, which often consisted of leaving puddles and piles behind him. These, Irina flatly refused to clean up, and although no one wanted to take responsibility for Bon, they couldn't bring themselves to cast him back out on the street. Finally, their father, Iliya, delegated Bon to Andy and severely reprimanded his impulsive daughter, forbidding her even to go near other animals. "Love them from a distance," he instructed.

In a year, Bon shot up from a funny little puppy to an enormous canine, something like a cross between a crocodile and a puffed-up suitcase, weighing over a hundred pounds. Andy was Bon's mother, father, and kind master all in one, and, in Bon's eyes, the only commanding officer above Andy was Iliya. The hearty, big-boned man commanded respect by his appearance alone, but with a mastery of three languages and an advanced degree in physics, he was an intimidating figure to both man and beast alike.

Bon was a cooperative and loyal companion, always at Andy's side. During Andy's training sessions with Sergey, the canine behaved himself nicely and was never underfoot. Sergey adored the dog and even took care of him a couple of times when Andy's family took vacations to the seashore.

***

Andy returned from the bakery to a ruckus that included the strumming of a guitar and the sound of many voices. The entryway was full of backpacks and various kinds of gear. He then realized they'd been descended upon by the "Tolkieneers," as his father called them. Iliya was irate about his daughter's new obsession with elves, reconstructions, and cosplay, considering it all foolishness and nonsense. Irina and her equally odd girlfriends were learning Qenya and ordering custom-made elvish-style dresses online. They spent hours on the internet meticulously searching for the best fashions for role-playing games. Mom and Andy had no problem with Irina's new obsession and actually found it mildly amusing.

"Oh, Iliya," his mom tried to reason, "let them have their quirks."

"Andy?" Irina appeared in the entryway. "How about making something yummy for breakfast?"

"Yeah, right," Andy retorted immediately. Judging by the shoes left in the hall, there were at least five people over. He had no desire to feed that crowd.

"Ande-e-e-e, dear..." Irina pouted. "I've talked up your talent in the kitchen so much, they're simply drooling in anticipation. Now, they're going to think I'm just a bragger whose word is no good. Come on, be a dear. Do it for me? Pleeeease?"

Her palms together in a supplicating gesture, Irina gazed sweetly at her little brother and batted her long eyelashes.

Andy silently contemplated his sister. *When did she have time to do her makeup?* he thought. *Fifteen minutes ago, she was sleeping like a log!*

"You *are* a stupid bragger, but I'll do it this once," Andy relented. "But you're cleaning up!"

"You're the best, Bro! No doubt about it!"

***

While Andy clunked dishes preparing breakfast, a serious argument broke out in the living room as to whether a modern person could be transported to a fantasy world and how amazing the possibilities would be.

*What's the fuss about?* Andy thought. *This portal voyager will probably end up knifed upon arrival, and that's it, the end. Or worse still, he would be captured and sent to work the streets or to a harem. What, you think they'll be waiting for you there with open arms? Get real!*

In the end, the debating parties agreed that taking a stroll in another world would be awesome.

No one paid attention to the argument Alena, Irina's friend, put forward. She suggested the inhabitants of another world may not know of Qenya and may have another way of living.

"Don't they have enough local mages there already?" she asked. "What's more, they handle weapons from childhood, not just during role-playing games."

The debate quieted down for a moment, and then someone apparently said something that made the whole crew burst out laughing. Bon, intuitively realizing Andy was super irritated by the loud sounds coming from the other room, trotted over to the door between the living room and kitchen, stuck his head into the room and barked deafeningly. He stood there a few more seconds to make sure his interference in the conversation had the desired effect, shook himself, turned around and laid down on his rug near the kitchen door.

"Good job, Boy!" Andy praised the dog and tossed him a piece of ham. The treat didn't reach the floor.

"What was that?" Andy heard the question rolling in from the other room.

"That mutt will cure your hiccups in a hurry! Hey, Troll, you look a little pale after that. You okay?"

"Peachy. I almost pooped my pants." Andy heard this unknown "Troll" answer, and a new outbreak of laughter nearly shook the walls. "It's a good thing I went at home this morning, or I would've had a hard time keeping clean!"

Andy glanced at the dog in a conspiratorial manner and pointed to the room. "Bon, sic!"

Bon got up from the rug and headed toward the room to lay down the law. Andy followed on tiptoe to watch. A mirror hanging on the wall in the entryway gave him a great view of the unfolding events. Leaving her half-finished juice on the table, Olga followed her brother, determined to join in the fun.

The room was full of guests. Andy recognized two of them. There was Alena, Irina's friend, and next to his sister, perched on a high-backed chair, sat Mark, the tow-headed fellow currently seeking the role of his sister's boyfriend.

*Naive guy, you're clueless*, Andy thought pityingly. *Irina changes gallant knights more often than she changes her clothes, and you, along with the crowd, will get kicked to the curb, as soon as the next fad comes along.*

Next to Alena, on the sofa, sat a long-legged beauty he'd never seen before. She was an eye-catching brunette with short hair and a plunging neckline on her fitted blazer. In the armchair by the window sat a strapping, ham-handed young man with a shaved head. *Troll!* Andy guessed. There were no other candidates for such a moniker. In another armchair, with his back to Andy and a seven-string guitar resting on his knees, sat a long-haired young man, the one who called Bon a crocodile.

While Andy eyed the company, Mark scooted closer to Irina and tried to put his arm around her. She recoiled, just slightly moving her shoulder away from the suitor and directing her gaze toward the long-haired Legolas facing her from across the room.

*Mark doesn't even stand a chance!*

As soon as Bon entered the room, the laughter quieted as if he'd waved a magic wand. The canine inspected the whole party, let out a snort of disgust and then, baring his formidable teeth, delivered another strong round of intimidating barks. He focused mostly on Troll, growling at him to boot. When he had given the bewildered crowd a second contemptuous snort and licked Irina's hands, he retired to the entryway.

"Troll, did you get what he was saying to you?" the long-haired youth called out.

"I can't even imagine…"

"That demon—by some divine error called a dog—just let you know not to defile other people's homes with your presence!"

Andy left his lookout post and entered the living room, capturing the Tolkieneers' attention. Irina subtly shook her fist at him, knowing very well who had unleashed Bon on them.

"I need volunteers," Andy announced. "Two of you move the table in here and set it," he nodded in the direction of the round table in the corner, "and a couple of you wonderful 'elves' can serve the fare that some other helpers can bring in from the kitchen. Don't be afraid of Bon. The dog's been fed. Just don't be loud, or he'll get nervous!"

*** 

"Oh, wow! The food is so good!" Vera, the brunette, exclaimed, before licking her plump red lips with the end of her tongue as she stabbed the last morsel on her plate with her fork.

Before they began serving, Irina had remembered her manners and introduced the guests to her brother.

"Irina, where'd you get a brother like that?" asked George, AKA Troll, still chewing.

"You'll make a good husband someday!" Vera said, casting a soulful look at the chef and winking at Irina. "You can do everything; your wife won't have to go near the stove!"

Andy feigned confusion. "But why would I need a wife who won't do anything?"

"What do you mean! To carry her in your arms and bring her breakfast in bed of course!" Vera got up, walked over to him, leaned over and wiped a drop of sauce from his chin with a napkin. The subtle odor of expensive perfume engulfed him. Her décolleté, with its milky-white, firm looking, inviting little breasts, was right in front of his face. She ran her slender fingers mischievously over his shoulder.

Andy's jeans suddenly became several sizes too tight in the crotch. It was too late to extract his eyes from the quagmire of her bosom.

"Oh! This colt's become a steed already!" Vera noticed the awkward fit of his pants. "Irina, you said he was just a little boy! Some little boy! Take a glance at his fly! Just look how he's staring! And his shoulders are so wide... Troll, hon, this guy will soon rival you!"

Vera messed up Andy's hair flirtatiously and kissed him on the top of his head, making him turn as red as a lobster. They had more than gotten back at him for his antics with Bon; they had ridiculed him. The gang around the table laughed.

Thinking quickly, Andy said, "Vera, how many days does your game go?"

"Three. Olga didn't tell you?"

"I've got a proposition for you. You know, this game you're playing...let them play for a while. You give me a couple of private lessons in domestic life, and I'll carry you in my arms and bring you breakfast in bed. I won't let you near the stove. What do you think?"

The room broke out in another burst of laughter.

"Troll, look, you've got competition! The boy is about to steal Vera right out from under you!" Egor, the long-haired youth remarked, choking on his laughter.

"Yeaaaah..." Vera drawled. "Kerimova," she said addressing Irina, "you and your boy are cut from the same cloth; you've got razor-sharp tongues."

The landline on the coffee table jangled. Irina waved her hand for silence. She answered the phone. "Hello...yeah, Dad...fine...I'll check...Andy can bring it...I'll tell him. Bye."

"What's up?" Andy asked his sister.

"Dad's boss showed up and asked to see his work on the new apparatus, but the documents with the color bar test patterns are here at home. Can you take them? And I can take Olga to Grandma's."

He'd take them; what choice did he have?

"What does your dad do?" Egor asked.

"He works with high-voltage magnetic fields and resonance phenomena. Something like that. It's all mumbo-jumbo to me," Irina said. "Point-like variation in the metrics of space. He's trying to create teleportation. He says they've made some headway. Can you imagine? A quick 'Zooomph!' and you're in America! Whoever paves the way with that kind of thing will be raking in the dough!"

"Has the government really forked over the funding for that?" Egor asked in surprise.

"You expect that from the government? No, a very wealthy investor is financing the whole thing. There's a lot of money tied up in this research. When Dad got picked up by this investor, his salary increased ten times."

Irina ran into her father's study and came back with a black folder of documents since Andy couldn't enter the office when the computer was running.

As Andy tied his shoes in the hall, Bon seemed to go berserk. As he stood to leave, the dog bit into Andy's pant leg and wouldn't let him out the door. When he managed to trick the dog and slide out the entrance, the dog sat back on his haunches and howled at the top of his lungs.

Everyone was surprised. "Does he always behave like this?" Egor asked Irina. She shook her head, her eyebrows slightly raised in concern.

"Hmm," Egor reflected, "it's as if he can sense some trouble coming..."

***

Iliya's office was on a former military base on the other side of the city. Andy had to change buses to get there since there were no direct routes. The first part of the route was on an old Korean-made bus. At the back sat a boisterous group of four guys dressed in imitation gangster-style clothes. They wore the typical baggy rapper pants, bandanas, baseball caps and sweaty untucked t-shirts with chunky chains around their necks. Andy turned toward the window. He never liked posers like these, imitating African American rappers and clinging to a subculture that wasn't theirs. One of the guys took a laptop out of his bag, and Andy soon heard the sound of passionate moans and groans coming from the speakers. The group guffawed at the on-screen action, with the whole bus privy to their comments. A couple of passengers reprimanded them, to which the young hoodlums responded with a round of profanity.

*Jerks!* Andy thought and decided to put a stop to the anarchy. He offered his seat to an old lady and used the excuse to move closer to the group. *Let the good times begin!*

The moans began to fade at the most interesting moment, and then completely fell away. He knew the laptop's screen showed nothing but flickering ripples.

"What!" he heard one boy squawk. "We haven't finished the film!" Next, came a torrent of comments and ideas on how to restore the frozen video. They passed the laptop between them, trying to revive it, but it showed no signs of life. Andy stared out the window so they wouldn't know he was grinning mischievously.

The cure-all fix came next—a power reboot. They turned the laptop off and on again; it started up normally for a second, giving them hope, and then the screen immediately turned back to ripples, followed by a fade to black. Frustrated to their wits' end, the boys decided any attempt to revive the computer was worthless. It had flat-lined.

"Stupid piece of crap!" its owner furiously threw the computer down on the seat. "'Made in China.' Cheap garbage!"

"Sell that thing for scrap metal," one of the hoodlums said sagely. "And maybe next time, don't get one that's made in China."

Two stops before Andy's, the group got off the bus and left the laptop on the seat. *It's a nice laptop,* Andy though. *The Chinese aren't so bad. I'll give it to Irina. She can reinstall Windows on it herself.* He deftly snatched the abandoned property.

***

Andy sputtered in a thick cloud of diesel exhaust as the bus rolled away. After ten minutes of leisurely walking, he came to the old concrete guardrail of the military base.

*Now, where is that hole in the fence I know so well?* The wall was there to keep folks out for their own good. Andy bypassed it and headed toward the former base headquarters.

"Builders have been busy here! They've cluttered up the whole grounds," Andy mumbled, walking around strange, latticed construction and bizarre 10-foot-long cast blocks. Every 20 feet or so, he had to jump over thick, high-voltage cable harnesses.

A sharp pain in his head stopped him short in the middle of the grounds. He found himself enveloped in St. Elmo's fire, surrounded by a rumble like a low-flying jet. Everything grew dim. The savage pain drilled at his temples, and Andy grabbed his head.

*I have to get out of here!* He didn't know where to go. Suddenly, an instinctual internal voice cried, *Anywhere!* He took a step, and the earth pulled away from under his feet. His face met the branches of a coniferous tree…

***

"Mr. Kerimov, perhaps in the meantime, we can warm the equipment up? How much longer will it be?" The investor's inspector was anxious.

"I requested the machine, but you decided there was no rush and arranged an inspection of the complex." Andy's father cast the inspector a hostile glance.

What in the world did they send him for? He hasn't got the slightest clue what's going on, yet he expects a report. He's putting on airs as goodness knows what…

"You're allotted sizable funds; the administration is interested in the quickest possible results. Money should be making more money, not settling into useless scraps of iron!" That comment had set Iliya off from the beginning.

*What a jerk! No one ever promised a quick turnaround! The project's preliminary duration estimate was five years. It has been three. What's the point of running in circles? The administration can send all the Poindexters and pencil-pushers it wants; that won't speed up the work. We have already reached milestones that other countries are still struggling with, accomplished at least enough for two Nobel prizes. Investments in science should be made with long-term returns in mind, not instantaneous gratification.*

"I admit that was a mistake" The inspector's words brought him back to the conversation. "But just think; I don't have a heap of time, only a handful of hours. I understand, of course, that a few hours on site won't enlighten me about your work, but I have to present results to the higher-ups. Even if the progress is minuscule, funding for your project next year depends on it. Opponents to our projects will seek to decrease investment in this area at the next board meeting, so it's in your best interests to shut them up! And there's no need to furrow your brows at me; I'm not responsible for our current difficulties!"

Iliya simply exhaled through his clenched teeth. *It's just like some of the bosses to abandon research halfway through; it's happened before.* The whole group was scattered then; people got out of science and went to work as janitors. A couple of the promising ones moved to America, obviously not to sweep the streets.

*What a pain it was to find a new group of colleagues! And now, to throw it all away again? Not on your life! If they were so ravenous, let them eat 'til they choke!* The equipment could be run on idle. The inspector would jump for joy.

"Denis, start the device," he commanded his young assistant.

"Starting up, sir."

The lights in the building flickered. The walls vibrated slightly; the diesel power plant's axles began to spin. The operators took their places in front of their computer screens and control monitors. Testing began.

"The shielding of the external electromagnetic circuit and peripheral field are activated."

"The external circuit; we're at 30 percent power, sir! The accumulators are in start-up mode; 50 percent, sir. The internal circuit's at 50 percent power. It's going into idle mode, sir."

"Metamaterial and dielectric polarizers deployed. Electromagnetic blocks activated."

"We have quantization…"

"What are the guards doing?" the external video surveillance guy suddenly broke out, breaking the strict communication protocol in panicked exclamations "There's an object on the active field! I'll kill you, you—"

Iliya cut him off. "What's going on?"

"Unauthorized person on the site!"

"Visual on the main screen!" Iliya cried, his blood running cold with a terrible apprehension. *Oh, God!* In the middle of the grounds, dropping his papers and grabbing his head, stood Andy! Iliya's son bent forward. He took a step and then…

"Holy mackerel!" Denis gasped in awe at his screen. "The transfer chamber's showing zero, and there's some kind of trick on the external field!" The main operator hit the red emergency abort button to drop the load and deactivate the device.

It was too late; an oval-shaped "window" appeared before Andy, through which Iliya could see a coniferous forest stretching back to the mountains in the distance. Andy took another step.

"Nooooo!" Iliya threw himself at the screen as if that could stop the boy. "Andy-y-y!"

When Andy disappeared from view, the window closed and a round shockwave spread from the very center of the grounds, sweeping over the accumulators in its wake.

An oppressive silence hung over the operator's room, broken only by the quiet sobs of the project's leader, on his knees in front of the main screen.

He could be anywhere…

\*\*\*

"Momma!" was the only thing Andy managed to spit out before his chest snapped the first twig at the top of the pine tree. After that, all of the sensations a slipper experiences came toppling down on him. His body snapped the thinner branches and banged flatly against the thick ones as he fell about halfway down the trunk, where he caught a fat bough in the crotch. It diminished the blow of the teenager's weight and bent, breaking from the trunk. Several more branches later, Andy crashed to the ground. One of the several large pine cones hurled from above with him landed right on his head and knocked him out.

Not one thought—only the pounding pain in the back of his skull pulled at Andy in the darkness. A wave of a thousand shivers ran over his body, returning the feeling to his numb limbs. His nose itched, making him sneeze, although chills swept over his whole body in a chaotic wave. The feeling of bugs crawling all over his arms, legs, and face grew stronger. *Ow!* He felt he'd been stabbed with a red-hot needle in his right nipple. He howled in pain, giving his sleeping brain a kick. Red-hot needles swept over his whole body in a burning wave. *Ow! Stop!* Consciousness came flooding back as if someone had flipped a switch in his head. Andy opened his eyes and tried to sit up; he hadn't the strength to stand.

His jaw dropped at the sight before him, but he closed it right away so no ants couldn't get in. Thousands of them scurried over him and around him, similar to the red wood ants he was familiar with back home but were twice as big and, by all appearances, meaner. And with that thought, a few of the little buggers chomped down on his wrist. His arm burned as if from a stinging nettle. Instead of a bite, a couple of drops of blood appeared on his skin.

*Brutal little pests! Hold on you! What? It's lunchtime, and you've already decided on the menu? I'd like to know how long I was laying here before they decided to bite me*, Andy thought.

Judging by how actively the ants moved, his appetizing carcass was to be the main course, and they weren't in the least worried by his objections.

*There are a lot of them, and only one of me—and all I can do is hobble like an elephant!* His sudden movements angered the ruddy things, and with tripled energy, they took to stripping the fillets and other parts.

*What are they doing, the little beasts? It hurts!* Andy tried to flick the hungry things off him. *You don't like that, nasty creeps?* The creeps didn't like it; furious ants started dumping formic acid on him, and their cousins, slightly bigger, with big heads and powerful mandibles, joined the red pests.

*I have to get out of here, pronto!* The acid in his many abrasions didn't just hurt; it burned and itched.

*Oh, great!* Some of the pests had wriggled their way to his "sacred" parts. Andy patted himself a couple of times in the area of his crotch and stumbled to his feet, then almost tumbled right back down. His head exploded in sharp pain, everything swam before his eyes, and a nauseating lump welled up in his throat. In the next second, his stomach turned inside out, he doubled over, ridding himself of his half-digested food.

Realizing their lunch might run away at any moment, the ants sent their bigheaded fellow tribesmen to the front and went on the offensive, attacking Andy's legs and hands, which were stuck firmly to the ground. Andy suddenly forgot about his nausea and headache and began to knock the little aggressors off his arms and legs with a vengeance. The bites of the bigheaded ones were more painful by far, stabbing their jaws two or three millimeters into his skin; they didn't waste their time on anything less.

Staggering like a drunkard, going from one tree to another in a zig-zag and grabbing onto every oncoming trunk in order not to fall, Andy left the banquet hall full of disappointed ants. The stream he crossed stripped the insects of any hope of pursuing.

"Well, Dad, look what you've done! The teleporter!" Andy said. "It's brought me to the ends of the earth. Interesting... Am I the first 'teleport-onaut' or were there other experimental subjects, and where did they end up?"

He could imagine endless scenarios for "teleport-onauts" but they all had one thing in common—flying to space was nicer than falling from a cedar tree. Neil Armstrong triumphantly declared "One small step..." but Andy only had time to screech some profanity before hitting the ground.

*It's a good thing I didn't land over the crater of a volcano! A fried naturalist isn't good, neither are drowned men eaten by sharks or gnawed on by crabs at the bottom of the ocean. Now if only specks weren't flying before my eyes and my head didn't hurt, I'd be swell!*

Andy stopped near a gigantic pine tree, so big that if it were cut down, a couple of pianos could easily be set on the stump. *A sequoia!* he decided. *I've read about this kind of tree, but where was it they grew again? Irina blabbed on about different parts of America...*

A whole forest loomed behind the first woody titan, their tree tops tickling the clouds. Which national park? Yellowstone? That didn't sound right, but his head hurt, and he couldn't think. So, he was somewhere in the wild United States.

*The pest!* Andy slapped himself on the back of the neck, squishing the latest ant in an entire mob of hungry insects that had set out on a journey on his clothes—or what was left of them, to be more precise. *Strange, flesh-eating ants didn't live in North America, their habitat was in hot climates, wasn't it? Stop.* Andy glanced warily in all directions. *How could I have forgotten about other predators! Olga enjoys watching animal shows; we have a whole collection of disks on that topic at home, including one about Yellowstone grizzlies, wolves, coyotes and mountain lions, a long list of "cute" creatures I wouldn't want to meet—and there are also rattlesnakes and various spiders. Yikes! Now, I have to watch my step, too, so I don't step on some creepy-crawly!*

His headache slowly faded into the background, and the nausea stopped tormenting him. Andy paused near a cluster of large boulders and decided to check his pockets for potentially useful items, anything that might come in handy for survival in the wilderness.

*Hmm, fairly scant.* His wallet with a $10 bill. Shoelaces: one pair. A thread wrapped around a piece of paper and a needle to go with it; he was prepared in case a button came off. A pocket knife, made in China. A mechanical wrist watch; he didn't have a digital watch for obvious reasons. A keychain. No matches, no documents. The entire description of his "riches" took up less than a paragraph. Some Robinson Crusoe I am. Of the whole list, only this little knife could be considered a useful acquisition. The rest is junk.

"W-a-a-i-a-i-ai, w-a-i-a-i-ai!" Andy heard the strange sound coming from deep in the woods. Glancing around with a start, he hastily stuck his meager belongings back into his pockets. He had no desire to meet the author of the wood song and needed to think about where to spend the night. No matter how he tried to spin it, he would have to crash under the stars for who knew how long. Andy looked at the enormous sequoia and crossed out the idea of sleeping in the redwood grove of the forest. True, there was no underbrush, and he could see for a hundred yards in all directions, but the ground was littered with old wind-fallen trees. The main disadvantage was that the knots only began to appear on the trunks about ten yards up. It would have been useless to try to climb the trees without claws. And a night spent on the ground, more than likely, could end in the belly of some native predator. He had to search for another place, and another place might be downhill.

He knew the direction of the mountains, their snowy tops shining, the yellow-green wall of the taiga stretched in a dense carpet. He had managed to glimpse that in the instant he'd been falling through the cedar, but had no idea what might lay in the other direction. *If there's no place safe here, perhaps it's worth a look in the opposite direction?*

Once he had made up his mind, it was as good as done, and in a few minutes, Andy was heartily trekking downhill. It was in his best interest to move his feet along quickly since the memorable "w-a-a-i-ai" rang out a few more times from his right.

***

He froze—and just in time. The gaping drop-off under his feet could have been the final and fatal obstacle for a speed-walker who forgot to look down. Andy estimated the distance, judging by the looks of it, at 200 feet. Had he fallen, no one would have been able to collect all his bones in a million years. He would have become the Humpty-Dumpty of the Yellowstone Canyon.

A fantastic view opened before Andy from the height of a bald peak. It was a green sea of deciduous trees stretching over the horizon, the foliage overlapping the wide light-blue ribbon of a river. In the center, between a rocky precipice and the river, rose a perfectly round hill.

About 50 yards below Andy, a fairly small half-circle rock shelf about 5 yards across protruded from the solid wall of basalt-like a little tongue. *I found a place to spend the night!* He just had to descend to it and have a good look at everything from there.

He found a good spot for the descent 200 yards to the left of a convenient little trail to his intended sleeping spot. True, he had to huff and puff as he climbed the almost vertical wall to a height of over 20 feet, but no grizzlies or other predators could climb up there.

When he finished, his fingers were insanely sore, and his knees shook. *Clinging to the slightest cracks and supporting myself with my feet on the tiniest ledges—what a rush!* The question now, of course, was how would he get back down from his chosen patch of rock, but he would sleep on it.

*** 

It got dark fast. The last ray of daylight went out and, bypassing the evening twilight, the night came into its own. A myriad of unusually bright stars appeared in the sky. A nearby constellation stood out like the bright beam of a street lamp, and he noticed yet another oddity—there was no milky way in the sky, no Ursa Major or Ursa Minor.

*Perhaps I landed in South America, not North America? What else can explain this completely unfamiliar pattern of stars?*

Andy settled between two large stones still radiating daytime warmth. *Warmth is great, but how am I supposed to fall asleep?* The moon came out, casting a brilliant glow around itself in the sky, and the nocturnal world came to life no less fervently than the daytime one. The world around him immediately took on dark shadows; crickets and cicadas chirped with all their might; an owl hooted in the woods; and from below, came the sounds of animals calling out to one another in screeches, whistles, and howls. Some formidable creature let out a "sneeze" heard around the world. The Eastern horizon lit up, and …

*Impossible!* Andy scampered to his feet. His sleepy stupor vanished. *How is this happening!* In violation of all astronomical principles, there arose in the dome of the sky a second celestial body. The second rising body reminded him of an image of the Earthrise on the moon. Eyes open wide, everything else vanished from his mind as Andy stared at the exotic view. *It's not a satellite; it's another planet, blue and full of life!* The white spirals of cyclones and the azure of oceans were visible to the naked eye. He could make out the vague outlines of continents in spots.

"So much for that! Not Yellowstone, not South America," Andy whispered, swallowing bitter tears. He sat down on the nearest stone. "Where am I, Dad?"

*** 

He froze like a popsicle; the milky cloud of fog that covered the forest and the rock shelf dragged its damp and chill all along his body. Andy had slept for two hours at most when a loud "mrooouuwn" made him clamber to his feet. *Who wouldn't be sleeping at this hour?* The nocturnal brutes had already disappeared into their holes, and the day-life had not yet crawled out. The murky veil of fog hid everything within 30 feet of his shelf. Andy picked up a hefty rock and threw it at the spot where the outline of something living could be seen. "Mraa-uu-w" came from below.

*Look at that! Hit the target on my first try!* Something large slipped under the ledge? follow by f heavy sigh came from under the ledge.

***

A slight breeze, like a playful puppy, began to break the fog into pieces and carry it off to the west. The first rays of light from the sun painted the world below in rose-colored hues. "Mrown. Mreoow," the visitor made himself known.

Andy lay on his stomach, carefully crawled to the edge of the rock shelf and looked down. "Eeek!" he exclaimed when his eyes met a pair of yellow eyes with vertical pupils.

He recalled a scene from Lewis Carroll's story about Alice in Wonderland. "The wide, wide grin means the Cheshire cat's in!" The member of the feline family that had settled down beneath the shelf was like the famed Cheshire cat's older brother, only quite a bit bigger—about the size of a tiger or lion. Its grin from ear to ear revealed an immense mouth, strewn with fearsome triangular teeth like a picket fence.

"Mrooowr," the Cheshire meowed. "Mram…"

"Uh-huh, and good morning to you. Have you lost something here?"

"Mrrrrow," the Cheshire meowed once more and started licking its right side.

"Me? No, man, I disagree! I'm not lost, and why eat me?"

*Why not?* The Cheshire stared at him quizzically. *How would you like to see yourself as stew meat?* Andy's mind raced as it imagined a conversation with the cat, but he had trouble picturing himself as stew meat. *Everything here is so mean and hungry! Did you learn that from the ants?*

"Mrru." The cat tilted its head to the side.

The Cheshire came out into the sunlight, stretched all its limbs out by turns and gave Andy a frisky look. "Come out!" it seemed to say. "Let's play!" Andy imagined what any such games might end with and decided to cancel all play dates.

"Sorry, cat, but I'll be better off at home! I'll remain intact!" Andy informed the feline.

The tailed creature didn't seem to take offense. Home was home, and he didn't have anywhere to hurry off to either.

"Maybe you could leave me alone?" he asked the Cheshire.

"Mr-r," the cat quipped and, turning back to the woods, growled loudly. "Mr-rr-uun!"

"So, you've rejected me? Is that right, whiskers?" The cat did not react at all to this last harangue. An hour later, the bushes on the edge of the clearing began to flutter and revealed new members of the feline family—a sleek momma and two kittens. *Terrific...*

***

When they had surrounded the ledge according to all the rules of siege craft, the Cheshires went off to relax, romping around in the small brook that flowed along the edge of the clearing. *They are hot, you see! But aren't I hot, too? Soon my tongue will be like a dry sponge.* The two kittens, which were no smaller than a large lynx, seemed to be chasing butterflies. But, from time to time, they glanced in the direction of the precipice to see if the prey had decided to come down yet.

Andy climbed right up to the wall in an attempt to spare himself from the heat of the day in the skimpy shade of the rocky ledge. It didn't help much. His stomach growled loudly enough to rival the kittens below. It periodically distracted them, causing them to look up curiously. First one, then the other, as if teasing him, would go over to the brook and loudly lap at the elixir of life. Andy could only swallow greedily and dream of a drop of rain. He didn't notice when he started to doze under the hot sun.

Someone tried to wake him, stubbornly tugging at his pant leg. At first shyly and carefully, then with all its strength. The r-r-r-rip of tearing fabric rang out. Andy pulled his leg back and opened his eyes. *What is this?*

On the edge of the rock shelf, as big as medium-sized dogs, sat several little griffons. *Did I sleep so long that scavengers appeared?* The griffons couldn't be anything else. Interesting creatures, Mother Nature had had some fun putting the head, neck, and wings of a vulture together with the body of an orange cat. There were a few other differences—the fingers of their paws were long and fit for grabbing onto thick branches and shredding the bodies of their victims or other carrion with their imposing claws. Another difference was in the way the tail was built. It started out just like a regular cat's tail, but about 5-7 centimeters from the base, it turned into a wide fan of long feathers. After all, they couldn't use their paws to stabilize and steer their flights.

Andy didn't have the strength to marvel at this new wonder of nature. Thinking for a moment, he grabbed the nearest stone and flung it at the beasts. He missed, but the rock flying by made them open their tail fans and shove off to the nearest tree. *What's going on below?* The Cheshires were darting around along the cliff wall, trying to find some point at which they could climb up to the ledge. The griffon's presence seriously upset them, since they had invested so much time and energy into keeping watch. They opposed giving up their prey to this brazen feathered scum.

"Mr-a-a-w!" the dad of the little family joyfully exclaimed when he saw Andy. *He's alive!* Now he could calm down and continue his pleasant bath. The griffons in the tree cawed repulsively.

Andy backed away from the edge of the rock shelf and occupied his familiar spot near the wall, leaning his upper back on the rough stone. He was between a rock and a hard place, literally. One more day of sitting under siege like this and the beasties from the tree would undoubtedly peck him to death; he simply wouldn't have the strength to resist. He heard the sound of wings. A few more griffons straddled the upper branches of their sturdy roost. The new arrivals started cawing with the previous residents.

The Cheshire on the ground growled threateningly and threw himself at the tree. The griffons looked at the enraged cat as if he were a halfwit and relocated to a slightly higher spot, emptying their bowels in the process. It didn't land on the cat—he managed to dodge in time—but the tree now stunk like a public toilet. A scuffle broke out in the tops of the branches. The griffons who had migrated from the lower tier tried to take a VIP spot, but they were stopped by their counterparts who had occupied the roost first. The scuffle turned into a savage battle, feathers, and clumps of fur flying in all directions. The kittens below egged the fighting half-birds on with their mewing. The adult Cheshires didn't even deign to glance at the ruckus. The battle ended with the expulsion of five of the fighters. The dozen that remained settled on the branches and took to pruning their feathers and licking their wounds. A silence fell over the clearing.

Andy closed his eyes. *What will become of me now? Where will I go if I survive the siege? How can I live if it turns out there are no people in this world?* Too many "ifs."

He heard the sound of flapping wings again. An impatient griffon had landed on the rock shelf, reassured by Andy's stillness. A sharp wave of the hand and a heavy stone with a hearty smack cleared the careless creature off. Its offended caw was interrupted by its death yell from under the paw of one of the kittens. The rest of the griffons squawked indignantly, but no one else dared make an attempt at the prize.

\*\*\*

Nothing at all happened the rest of the day. The approach of evening sent the griffons off for the night; the Cheshires lay down under the shelf and quietly purred to one another. Andy stared silently at the rising of the blue planet and prayed that God might send him relief from his suffering…and at least a glass of water. His tongue swelled up in his mouth, his lips cracked, the walls of his stomach seemed to chew on one another. The Cheshires were just fine; they had scarfed up the griffon; the momma had gone into the woods and brought out a rabbit, also devoured with pleasure. Andy wouldn't have turned down some roast rabbit legs, all the more so because, by the looks of it, the local rodents weighed about 45 pounds. *Dang*, he wondered, *what do these cats need me for if the woods are full of games?* The cats didn't hurry to answer his question.

He dreamed of Germans. Deutsche Zoldaten in field-gray uniforms. It was a phantasmagoria of historical images from films about World War II. The Nazis set up a field kitchen under the ledge to make buckwheat porridge with stewed meat. The fat cook whistled a happy tune and banged a rhythm on the boiler lid with a ladle. Two platoons of soldiers joined hands and led circle dances around the kitchen, clinking mugs of beer and blowing the white foam caps. Each new round began with the distribution of sausages and pouring the white foamy beverage into outstretched glasses. One sergeant built a whole orchestra of crickets and, picking up a long stick, was conducting before the black musicians. Mugs and sausages in the soldiers' hands were replaced with wooden spoons, and the soldiers, removing their helmets, lined up in front of the kitchen. The happy cook in a greasy apron and crumpled cap dished out to each one a kindly ladle of the nourishing porridge.

The Zoldaten waved to Andy invitingly, yelled "Kom! Kom!" and extended a helmet full of porridge to him. The cook smiled a wide, fatherly grin from ear to ear. In the next second, the cook's eyes turned yellow, and a Cheshire cat was looking at him, dressed in the German field uniform. "Kom!" the cat said sweetly and threw the de-plumed griffon into the pot. The soldiers built a fire and stretched out their chilly palms to him...

Andy awoke curled up; it was below freezing. A chilly wind chased dark clouds around the sky, and the freezing weather made his jaws chatter. *How lucky are those sitting in front of a campfire now, the one that's happily illuminating the slope of the bald hill?* Andy stopped shaking; for a moment, he felt a sensation of warmth. *Fire! If there was a fire, that meant there were people!* He almost danced for joy. On the wave of positivity, the Cheshires seemed like such a small detail, merely a pesky obstacle. Andy lay on his stomach and glanced under the ledge; all four fascists were still there. They just needed helmets on their heads to complete the picture.

"Meow," the dad meowed in a questioning tone.

"I'm freaking out," Andy answered and spat at the dad. The wind carried it away, which was a shame because the spit was so full of poison that the Cheshire would have died instantly—even though it wasn't meant to be. "Die, slime bags!"

"Mr-r-r."

"Yes, you!"

The Cheshire didn't seem to take offense at the comment, but its face showed that someone would answer in full the next day for the nighttime awakening.

A strong gust of wind rustled the crowns of the trees; lightning flashed in the sky. The first fat drops fell to the ground. The downpour went on for an hour, and Andy quenched his thirst. *God granted me water. Now I ought to find a way to save it.*

But he was frozen to the bone and couldn't wait for the sun to rise.

*** 

The first rays of sunlight hadn't yet touched the rocky shelf when the flapping of wings rang out, and the first griffon landed on the roost tree. A half an hour later, the whole top was littered with the cawing crowd—at least forty of them. The griffons, by all signs, were discussing the prospect of sharing lunch with the Cheshires. There were two possibilities: either "lunch" would die and pass entirely into the hands of the half-feathered vultures, or they would have to settle for the leftovers from the lords' table, which would be a completely undesirable turn of events for them. Andy pictured a third possibility involving two protruding middle fingers and some choice words to boot.

The Cheshires below became flustered and began sniffing the air excitedly. With a husky meow, the female herded her kittens and tore off out of the field, glancing up with a sorry look. The head of the family also ran off with his offspring and better half. Just as the tip of his tail disappeared into the bushes, a whole herd of large animals entered the clearing, cutting through the thick underbrush with their chests. The griffons left their roosts with a repulsive squawking, screeching and the loud flap of wings. Andy stared wide-eyed at this new marvel of nature.

The animals looked like the result of some mad scientists' experiment in crossing an elephant with a giraffe. They had large bodies like elephants, long necks, and elephant-like heads, only of smaller proportions. That was where the similarities ended, and the differences began. They had no tusks, but the males' heads were crowned with sharp, 3-foot-long horns. Their long trunks were covered in sheets on the outer side that resembled the scales of an armadillo The scales covered the entire length of the trunk with overlapping edges. Especially tough, thick scales covered the lower fourth.

*Interesting. Why? Perhaps nature will reveal the secret to me sometime.* The new animals' feet were more like those of a camel, but a lot thicker. Their thick, short fur with tiger stripes let them blend in excellently behind the hazelnut trees.

"I hereby dub thee 'Eleraffs!'" Andy said triumphantly, and as quickly and quietly as a fly, got down from the ledge. He hadn't the slightest difficulty getting down. *Shouldn't have worried.* He had to hurry; the Cheshires could come back at any moment. The farther away he got, the better. A big, wrinkled Eleraff looked his way, carefully inspected him with its little eyes, and whistled softly, after which it turned toward the nearest tree and began munching on the highest leaves. The ritual of his being accepted into the herd had taken place... *Well, maybe not so much a ritual and not exactly accepted, but permission from the monarch to follow them had been granted. He was no danger to them, and so be it!*

The herd turned in the direction of the bald hill. Andy trudged along behind them, following their tracks, not getting too close and not too far behind. His path led to the place of the nighttime bonfire...

***

"What hard luck! Oooo..." Andy moaned, and darted into the bushes, breaking off a big burdock leaf along the road....

Following the Eleraffs turned out to be convenient and relatively safe. In about three hours, the mass of forest was left behind, and the animals stopped in a wide meadow to the right of the bald hill. The giants didn't trouble over which trail to choose; they just paved a path where they pleased. Predators preferred to get out of their way sooner rather than later. Andy wasn't the only "barnacle". Behind the herd of Eleraffs, small herds of goats and antelopes followed, small wild pigs grunted off to the sides, and colorful birds that resembled terrestrial blue-tits swarmed on huge piles of manure.

But one thing kept him from letting his guard down completely. Along the way, the herd stopped at a meadow circled with trees full of ripe fruit. Andy picked the spiky, fuzzy fruit, which resembled a southern peach. He had observed the Eleraffs and other herbivores stuffing their faces with the forest delicacy and decided to have lunch. He lacked the strength to resist his empty stomach, which emitted a gigantic portion of gastric juice at the sight of food. He savored the juicy flesh, gnawing on it once he had ripped off the rind. The "peach" tasted something like a cantaloupe and was just as sweet. In the center, it held a bilobular pit that resembled a cute little butt.

As he finished his fifth one, frightened bleating broke out on the edge of the meadow and, breaking through the thin undergrowth, a curly-horned antelope from the same cohort of "hangers-on" to which Andy belonged leaped into the clearing. With a snarl, a dark brown Cheshire shot through in pursuit.

The sharp-toothed cat did not have time to do anything else. At the sound of its snarl, one of the horned male Eleraffs turned around with shocking speed for such a heavy body. The folded trunk whistled like a whip and hit the cat's back with the outer, armored side. The Cheshire was thrown back 20 feet, right at the feet of a female Eleraff with a cub. In the blink of an eye, the cat was trampled into a bedside rug.

From that moment on, Andy never left the Eleraffs' side. The incident with the antelope and the cat showed very colorfully that hungry predators were carefully observing the "hangers-on," and although they were not visible, that did not mean they weren't there behind the thick underbrush. After so much grief to avoid ending up in some stomachs, he had no desire to turn up in others.

The only thing was, he shouldn't have picked those "peaches." The seed in the middle that looked like a butt turned out to be a real pain in the butt. In an hour, Andy's stomach churned mightily, and on wobbly legs, he took to occupying the bushes. He had had three such "outings" in the last couple of hours. He had not yet sat down when a humongous something entered the clearing. Miraculously cured, Andy flew up the nearest tree like a bullet; he couldn't remember when he had managed to pull up his pants and button his fly.

The small herbivores dashed out of the clearing from all sides, bleating, and squeaking. In some places, the bleating turned into death rattles as they met skulking predators in the bush. The Eleraffs formed a circle with the females and young in the center. The males stuck out their horned heads and swung their trunks threateningly. Finally, the "something" stepped into the open field from behind the crowns of the trees, and Andy got a look at it.

*A saber-toothed tiger! But what a tiger!* Terrestrial relatives of the saber-toothed beauty could only run away from this fellow, curling their tails behind them in fear. More than anything, the tiger reminded him of the Smilodon, now extinct on Earth. It had a reddish-brown coat, a short tail, and powerful paws. At the shoulder, it was no less than six-and-a-half feet high and about a dozen to fifteen feet in length. The predator's mouth was crowned with fangs a foot-and-a-half long. *How much does it weigh?* Andy wondered, examining the predator from 50 feet up the tree.

With a guttural growl, the tiger began to circle the bunch of Eleraffs; the youngsters and females whistled and trumpeted in alarm. The males whipped their trunks. They swayed their heads from side to side and threateningly lowered their horns to the ground. All of a sudden, the tiger leaped forward and immediately back again. A young Eleraff took a step forward and tried to provoke the beast with its horn. The tiger dodged with its whole body, crept forward and delivered a blow with its fangs into the base of the Eleraff's neck. After that, it jumped back to the edge of the clearing and lay down under a tree. Its hunting was done; it had only to wait for the victim to bleed to death. Bright crimson blood splashed jerkily from two deep wounds on the victim's neck. In a few minutes, the wounded male's legs gave way, and it fell to the grass that was already soaked with its blood.

The herd, trumpeting and whistling fiercely, slowly quit the meadow. The tiger remained calmly where it lay; the rest of the herd didn't interest it...for now. The sound of flapping wings came from above; a griffon landed on the branch next to Andy; several more circled in the sky. *The scavengers have come; they're everywhere!* Next to the griffon, a regular vulture saddled the roost, a cousin of the terrestrial scavenger. Staying in the tree any longer became dangerous, and Andy, getting down, followed the herd of herbivores out of the meadow. The tiger cast him an indifferent glance. *Why would it want the tough-trimmings-two-legs when there was a mountain of fresh meat available?*

Following the retreating grass-eating giants up the hill, Andy stepped on a round flat boulder. Something clicked loudly under the stone, a bright flash blinded him and, in the next instant, he collapsed into the hole that opened up underfoot...

# PART 2: BLACK DRAGON

## The Northwestern border of the Kingdom of Rimm, the Wildlands.

"Chutka, eet, what was that?" the man, shaking like a leaf in the wind, asked his heavy-set young counterpart. The carnivore's guttural roar continued to echo through the woods.

Chutka ran his palm over his bushy beard and cast a scornful glance at the young man. He was tall and thin like a beanpole. Gichok looked nervously from side to side. The end of the broadsword he held firmly in his right hand shook like a rabbit's tail. *Meat! Spineless meat!* Chutka thought. *What in the name of the goddesses brought you to the hunters? Seeking wealth and women?*

"Sul is hunting," Chutka answered, loading the bundle of ropes onto his back. He headed for the camp.

"S-sul?" Gichok went pale. "Don't they live on the steppes? Which is far away?"

"May-a far, may-a not. Look alive and chop; he won't eat you!"

"Why not?"

"He stinks from meat that's soiled itself!" Chutka laughed aloud and gave the cowardly Gichok a firm pat on the back. "He's like a high-born, 'Let's have only fresh, clean meat; you'll just do for feeding the yella flies'. You're yella yourself, inside and out!"

Gichok, calmed by the fact that no one would eat him anytime soon, began chopping through the thick underbrush of creepers and hazel, cursing like a sailor. "How long must we keep on feeding the horseflies and mosquitoes here, eet? Maybe a dragon'll join the party?" he asked, turning toward Chutka.

"May-a join, may-a not," Chutka repeated his tall-tale embellishment. "You'll hang about here until Grok the magician says enough or until you get eaten up by midges. Sul's the one who's squeamish about ya, but midges are keen on manure!"

"Tfoo on you!" the young hunter swore as if spitting and immediately got a telling blow to the back.

"Shut your trap and chop. What Grok says goes! You took the money, so no gripin', Little Hunter. Pray to the goddesses or beg the One God, that a dragon'll join us, or instead of a dragon, Grok'll gut YOU! Got it?"

Gichok nodded.

"Now you've got it. Hack more lively; no yapping!" Chutka bellowed.

Gichok shut up and took to it, frantically swinging the long knife. Chutka stayed back a bit; he had no desire to come under the wide swing of the double-sided blade. The pair continued in silence right up to the camp.

"Did you set the 'spider's web'?" Grok the wizard asked Chutka right away. He employed the squadron of hunters. Chutka nodded.

"Look," Grok added, "if you damaged the weight-bearing threads, I'll have your hides!"

Arist, the commander of the small squadron, approached the magician. He was just as heavy-set, big-boned, and broad-shouldered as Chutka. A dreadful scar intersected his crooked face from his left eye to his chin; his neat beard barely overlapped it. Arist's ice-blue eyes, the depths of which hid a malignant cunning, gazed perceptively and carefully, noticing every detail and every movement.

"I'll have my own peoples' hides, thank you, and let's get one thing straight right now, Grok: I'm in charge here! If you don't like something, let me know. A bozl should have but one head! If someone else starts commanding them, not only will we not zapag a dragon, we'll become side dishes for Sul, the mrowns, or long-maned wolves! You pay; we execute. If anyone doesn't do it right..." he glanced at Gichok, who lowered his head and cast his eyes downward. The tips of his ears became crimson. "...I'll stuff his ears down his throat! You've already scared my people. And frightened people are not hunters, more like shadows in the woods."

Grok turned to Arist and pursed his pale lips into a thin strip. His glare bore holes into the old hunter. Arist calmly returned the magician's piercing gaze. Grok, in his dark frock with his pale face, shaved head, and crooked nose, looked like a servant of the goddess of death, Hel. His unblinking eyes added credibility to his "servant of death" image.

"E-e-excellent, you've vouched for your people, most esteemed Arist. I'll ask you in case I need anything," the magician hissed and cast a glance at the long-suffering Gichok, who had instantly changed the color of his face from red to deathly white and started trembling slightly. Something flashed with a blue light inside the magician's tent; he turned sharply and set off to check on his artifacts.

Arist heaved a long hissing sigh. The struggle with the magician was hard on him. In the last seven days and nights, he'd gained many gray hairs and many times cursed the day he'd agreed to take the job. They had been enticed by the idea of easy money, but as they say, "Set foot in the swamp, you'll feed the troglomp."

The contract had been signed, and the magician had furnished a handsome advance payment. The hunters had been out of work for a good while and were glad of the order. Now, they would have been glad to return the money, but the hired man's code did not allow any backing out.

"Go on, chop wood for the fire and help the others strip the deer," Arist told Gichok and, with a wave of his hand, sent him away. Happy to be as far away as possible from the magician and the squadron leader, Gichok practically skipped toward the fire and the porridge-boiling hunters.

Arist turned to Chutka. "What do you suggest?"

Without a word, Chutka ran the edge of his finger across his throat. The commander shook his head.

"The code. Your people would slaughter you for it later."

"Then there be only hope in the dragon, may-a he'll eat the turd. I'll give it to ya straight; I'll shed no tears!"

Grok exited his tent and headed directly to the conversing pair.

"You've come from the burial ground. Did you see anything strange?" he asked Chutka.

"No. Like you said, we didn't go on the hill. So?"

"Strange. The 'tracking frame' registered the use of magic in the area. You're sure you didn't see anyone?"

"What's there to see? We hung the tubes with gluten and stretched the 'spider web' over 'em. By the goddesses, who'er enters that hill is caught!"

The magician nodded his approval and turned to Arist. "Your repose is over; gather your people, Commander. Set Watchmen at all the snaring spider webs. A dragon will fly in soon. The black lizard won't miss the spells of the guardians of the burial ground. Yes, and I almost forgot, let the 'web-men' come to me for the negotiated artifacts." The magician issued his instructions and disappeared into his tent.

Chutka and Arist glanced at one another.

"The wait is over," the commander said quietly and, already with increasing volume, went to rouse the bozles.

***

# The Marble Mountains, No Man's Land, the Valley of a Thousand Streams, Karegar, Jagirra.

"What are you laying around for, you old fart!" the grouchy voice of Jagirra, herbalist, and magician, interrupted the dragon's afternoon nap.

Karegar opened his left eye and looked at the woman who'd awoken him. *What now?* She was standing with her hands on her hips as if she were getting ready to chase after a little man rather than a dragon. And she didn't look anything like a highborn Snow Elf; she was a country wench in a traditional peasant's apron embroidered with red roosters, but with a stature above and beyond that of a mere mortal. Her posture, her expression, the turn of her head, her enraged glare—all of these made him put his tail between his legs.

"Open your shameless little eyes, black lizard!" Jagirra continued in just as agitated a tone. She grabbed a towel from her shoulder and swatted the dragon on the nose with it.

"You old hag!" Karegar opened his eyes and lifted his head from the hot stones. The name "lizard" had offended him.

"WHAT? Who are you calling old hag?" Jagirra's eyes blazed with a raging fire.

Karegar backed away; he'd crossed the line. He'd let it slip before he knew it. Jagirra just might send a fireball flying.

"Come here! I'll show you old hag!"

It might have been an amusing sight for an on-looker—an enormous black dragon backing away from a sleek female figure brandishing a rolled-up towel before his nose. Soon the dragon's back hit the cliff; there was nowhere to retreat. He had to pull his shoulders and neck in to hide behind his wings. Jagirra might have seemed funny only to those who didn't know her. When angry, she could smash a decent rock to bits or burn a reinforced border fort to the ground in a couple of moments. It had happened. Karegar, without too much effort, could recall five or so such times.

He had had time to study the she-elf over the course of two thousand years, and today's mistake was an unforgivable error on his part. He sat on his tail and put out his front paws.

"Ok, I'm sorry! Let's get it over with. I'm not a lizard or a fart, and you're not an old hag."

"Just try calling me that again, and I'll tie your tongue in a knot!" the elf mumbled, calming down.

"I've heard, too, that Rauu are the very picture of imperturbability. 'Icicles,' they call them." Karegar couldn't resist teasing. The storm had passed, and he once again lay down on his bed of stone, resting his head on his left front paw. Jagirra perched herself in the curve of his elbow. It made a sort of deep warm seat, and she pet the dragon on the forehead... Karegar couldn't count the number of times they'd been alone together like this, just talking, or even more often, letting themselves be silent. He enjoyed the capricious woman's company; apparently, the feeling was mutual. Sometimes, Jagirra would fall asleep in the embrace of his arm-seat, in which case Karegar would feel afraid to breathe lest he wakes the sleeping herbalist.

"Idiots say so, and you're repeating like a parrot."

Karegar twisted his neck and looked at her.

"What are you looking at?" Jagirra was braiding her hair.

"You know," Karegar began, "For a thousand years now, I've thought of you as..." here he faltered, not knowing how to continue.

"Cat got your tongue? Spit it out! After 'old hag' I can handle anything!"

"As my wife..." the dragon finished his sentence and stuck his head under his wing. If he were capable of blushing, his black scales would have turned crimson.

"Ye-e-es," Jagirra drawled. "Been thinking about that for a long time, have you? They say dragons don't suffer from dementia! But I've got a loon."

"That's just like you," Karegar lifted his wing a bit and said from underneath his webbed covering as if hoping his wing would protect him. "You chase me off like a country wench does her wandering husband. I can't even wave my wing one too many times without your permission! Don't fly there, stop scaring the herds here, ladies are bathing there; don't peek! What do they call it nowadays? Under your thumb!"

The herbalist bent over in a fit of uncontrollable laughter. Karegar sighed heavily and put his head back down on his left paw. He would have stamped any other woman out ages ago—he had no particular deference for human or elf life—and would have lived peacefully, but all his rage passed and turned into a puppy's desire to wag its tail before this woman.

"Now that's a good one! I'll forgive you 'hag' for making me laugh so hard!"

"Oh, thank you. Tell me again why you woke me up?"

Jagirra abruptly ceased her laughter and glanced at the dragon with a serious look. He immediately felt guilty.

"Did you fly to the Bowing slope?" she asked.

"I was hunting."

"What, you're too lazy to use your 'true' vision?"

"Just tell me what I've done wrong."

Jagirra shook her head. "Some country wenches were gathering berries in the wood, and then you show up with your hunting. Anyway, from your type of sport, Tria, Trog Sosna's daughter-in-law gave birth right there. It's clear, you're the Master and owner of the valley and the mountains around it but couldn't you have dragged this elk to your cave instead of ripping its head off alive? And then what? If you would look with your true vision, you'd see people and would have thought twice before carving up that elk!"

Karegar cast his eyes down. What rotten luck. But ultimately, he wasn't a hand-fed pet; sometimes he craved fresh blood. The fact that humans went gallivanting about wherever they pleased was their problem, not his!

"And who was born?" the dragon asked tactfully.

"A boy, they're naming him after you. There'll be another Regar in the valley!"

"There's already at least five. Brog has a daughter called Regara, and I can't count all the boys by that name!"

"You should be happy! People love you! They call the valley 'Karegar's Valley!'"

The dragon winced; the herbalist's last words cut him to the quick. They dredged up ancient memories from the back of his mind.

"It's already been called that for a very long time," he carefully set the she-elf down from the curve of his elbow.

A cave filled with black blood and dead children spread before the dragon's eyes. The little dragons weren't yet three years old. They had put his daughters to sleep with black lily dust, then cut their heads off. He found the killers. The Forest Elves hadn't had time to get far. They hadn't time to kill anyone else. Karegar set upon the pointy-eared camp like a hurricane of wrath. Irru attacked the camp from the other side. His wife had come back from the hunt and, seeing the demolished nest, tore off in pursuit. Not even smoldering twigs were left of the camp; the wind scattered the thick ashes... Irru, in her grief, lost sight of her senses and two days later was burned up in a violent attack of dragons on the Great Forest. The elves, it turned out, had attacked not only his valley, but other valleys too. Karegar remained alive, but after the attack he lost the ability to wield magic, descending to the level of a third-rate human wizard-wannabe. The war had wiped out the dragon population. The Great Forest ceased to be, becoming an idle wasteland, but the Light Forest remained, for the time being... Karegar tried not to think about what would happen later on.

The last true bloods had left Ilanta. They had left one "minor" working portal, fitting it with "closing" loops, and sealed the rest. What happened at Nelita remained a secret. *Why hadn't the true bloods and the few dragons that had left with them come back?* The goddess Nel's Night Eye didn't hurry to reveal the secret. The "minor" portal turned out to have a surprise—it could only be opened from Nelita. The tracking beacons would register all attempts to open the portal, but there still had not been a single attempt. One such tracking beacon lay in the dragon's cave, which had never once lit up green. Inside the portal, no one activated the spell's security complex, which was set to true bloods. Once every couple of months, Karegar would fly to the portal, as if that would open it and dragons would start flying through the gates. But hope lingered in his soul that someday exactly that would happen.

The war had ended almost three thousand years ago; he had been alone for a long time since. Until one day, Jagirra came to the valley. She managed to rouse the solitary dragon and once more imbue him with the desire to live. Since then, a lot had changed, but his home had not been called "Karegar's Valley" in almost three thousand years...

"I'm sorry," the herbalist's quiet voice called him back to the moment and made him put away his inveterate pain for a time.

"You can't bring back the past, but tell people not to call the valley that. Tell them I asked..." Karegar stepped from one leg to another and stretched his neck like a dog.

"Okay."

A slight peep came from inside the cave.

"What's that?" Jagirra asked, surprised. Karegar jerked the ends of his wings, the dragon's equivalent of shrugging his shoulders. "I don't know; I'll go check it out."

After a few seconds, the dragon shot out of the cave.

"The tracking beacon! Someone's activated a portal to Ilanta! I'll fly over and take a look. I'll be back by morning." He threw his wings open wide, pushed himself off the ground with all four paws and rocketed into the air.

*** 

Four hours later, Karegar was already making his third circle over the bald hill that hid the ancient portal in its depths. He hadn't seen any sign of digging or attempts to get inside it. *Perhaps the magical guard perimeter lost the energy from the spell it contained? Or the digging sites have been masked over with sod?* The dragon switched to true vision; there was no magical activity! *Why then did the beacon blink? Maybe my tracking beacon's broken?* Little did he know, even activating the exit point portal on Ilanta would trip the beacon. No one had tried to come through from Nelita, but a certain guest was having an unwanted adventure under the hill...

Karegar decided to inspect the hill once more, set a course with his wing, and descended, flying over the very tops of the trees. Something white flickered behind him and entangled his hind legs and wings, sharply pulling him backward. Karegar roared angrily and pressed his wings flat against his back. Breaking branches, he crashed to the ground, which quaked slightly with the blow of the dragon's body. A bald man in dark garb leaped out of the bushes and ran to where the dragon fell.

***

*How much more of this!* The lone thought played over and over in Andy's head. Finally, the slanted tube he had so unfortunately fallen into ended and his legs crashed into a plaster lattice in a cloud of dust, pebbles and dry leaves. He tumbled out into a room of gargantuan proportions.

Flying in a curve for another several feet, Andy landed on his back on the gigantic skeleton of some kind of animal. The bleached bones couldn't withstand the new load and with a terrible *crack* collapsed like a house of cards. The cloud of dust that was stirred up as a result covered the former skeleton and the human figure that was trying desperately to extract itself from the heap. A rumbling echo rang through the hall, and it was impossible to sort out the crackle of bones from the sounds of stones that continued to fall from the hole in the wall.

Getting out of the heap and covering his face with what was left of his t-shirt, Andy ran off in the opposite direction of the dust cloud. The adrenaline rush was slowly passing; the hurt and injured parts of his body began to let him know they'd come to harm—in some places, a sharp pain; in others, a dull stinging ache. His whole back from his neck to his tailbone screamed in agony from the multitude of cuts, and a couple of small splinters were deeply embedded in the muscle tissue just above his right kidney.

"Aw man...," he moaned, almost swearing, and stepping to the side to search for a relatively clean patch of floor. When he found it, he carefully removed his t-shirt and twisted it into a tight whip, laid down on the surface on his stomach, put the shirt in his mouth and, by feeling around, began to extract the foreign objects with his fingers. Tears gushed from his eyes. He was all alone; no reason to be shy.

For lack of alcohol or another disinfectant, he had no choice but to take his chances. He lay down on his stomach, put his t-shirt in his mouth, which soon got all chewed up and saturated with saliva, and put his arms behind his back to extract the splinters with his fingers. *Some surgeon I am!* After the "surgery," which seemed relatively successful, he lacked the strength to move. For another twenty minutes, he lay crying. He felt sorry for himself.

*Why did all this have to happen to me? Why couldn't the stupid Tolkieneers from Irina's group have gotten thrown into this land? They would have been ecstatic!*

"Why me?" he cried as loud as he could, touching his lips in despair and hitting the floor with a fist, which raised a small cloud of dust. The cry bounced off the walls and came back to him in a multitude of resounding replies. No one was ready with the answer.

*What had he done to offend the powers that be, for them to make fun of him so? First, they pet him with a bit of lightning, then decide that's not enough, so they add an other-worldly excursion? But I'm lucky no one has gobbled me up, and I haven't stepped on a poisonous snake. That "peach" could well have been the last fruit I ate in my life. On the other hand, what does luck mean? Luck would have been not walking through the experimentation field, or even better, not going to my father's work in the first place.*

***

When the cold of the stone began to take its toll and his adrenaline had waved bye-bye, he carefully sat up. Trying not to move his shoulder blades or back too much, he was finally upright and wiped his wet face with the t-shirt. He squinted at his surroundings. *Enough with the wet eyes, tears won't solve your problems.*

*They will answer me. They will answer for everything. I will make this sucky world face the music, just you wait!* Andy didn't yet know who "they" were and how exactly he would make them face the music, but he firmly made up his mind to survive. He would survive despite everything, no matter what it took.

"Where've I ended up this time?" he posed the philosophical question to the emptiness.

Silence reigned in the place, disturbed only by the broken crumbling of pebbles still sprinkling from the hole in the wall. The room he'd found his way into was enormous. Andy raised his head. A cupola glowed with a soft, subdued light. The floating specks of dust danced in the air like a myriad of little stars.

"About 250 feet…" he measured the height of the cupola by sight. "Probably about 350 from wall to wall."

It turned out that the bald hill hid an ancient structure. The walls were ornamented with bas-reliefs, but a thick layer of dirt and dust covered all the surfaces, keeping him from examining them more closely. In the thick dirt of the room, the unnatural cleanliness of a high arc stood out; it looked as if it were cut from one solid piece of crystal. Sparks of reflected light played along the arc; a pale purple light illuminated the crystal's thickness from within.

A mountain of bones towered before the arc, bones so big one might surmise they belonged to a dinosaur. The vertebrae of the tail Andy was sitting next to stretched in a row at least 25 feet long. *How did that paleontological exhibit get in here?* He couldn't see any doors or passageways. *Did they fly in?* This last thought had barely just formed in his brain and spread over his cerebrum when his eyes, just ahead of his brain, caught sight of the oblong bones lying to the right and left of the skeleton he'd destroyed. *Well, well!*

Andy stood up, a wave of dull pain running along his spine as he did. *Okay, I can handle that; I can walk and jump.* The position of the bones was very similar to the frame of bat wings or a pterodactyl. "How about that!" The local flying creature's wingspan was about 65 feet. *Some pretty formidable birds hang out in these skies!*

Andy walked up a little closer. It was a wing all right. He stood there snapping his fingers pensively and staring straight ahead. There were griffons in this world, so logically he had to accept the idea that this mountain of bones was, at one time, a dragon. But it was somehow difficult to believe that this dragon flew. The wingspan was too small for such a bulky, cumbersome beast, unless...

Unless there was magic here. If so, everything would fall into place. A dragon's flight, the lighting in this place he was in, the question that had already bothered him—where did the light come? As far as he could remember, there hadn't been any windows on the hill. Batteries? What enormous volume they must have to be working still after all the time it took for this layer of dust to form! It had obviously been quite a while. Automatic electrical power? Ha!

"You're not thinking in the right direction, Andy Dip-head. You've got to think about how to get out of here, not about how the lights work!" the unfortunate traveler scolded himself. "I've got to take a look at this wonder of nature's mind."

Andy walked around the dragon. The monster lay before some kind of pedestal or alter, its head resting on it. Although, calling a skull with five-foot-long teeth a "head" seemed inadequate.

"Whew! Now that's big!" Andy said, drumming on the dragon's tooth with his fingernail. The dragon's jaws also bore two pairs of upper and lower fangs about 16 inches each. The skull itself was of a conical form and got wider toward the eye sockets. Both sockets were tilted forward, so there was no question of whether it had binocular vision. A collar of bone about a foot and a half long protruded from the back of the skull, covering the base, which divided into two cones that became 3-foot-long horns. The horns faced backward and ran parallel to the fifteen-foot-long neck. *This "birdie" didn't peck at seeds—it pecked at those who pecked at seeds—Eleraffs, for example.*

Andy turned to the altar and almost fell, getting his foot tangled in a chain that came out from under the dragon's right paw.

"Well now, let's see..." he bent and tugged on the chain. Clanking against the stone in protest, a real round "pancake" with a blood-red stone in the center appeared from under the creature's paw. It was something like a medallion, perfectly fit for a dragon, the right size, and everything, about a foot and a half across. Andy pulled the circular object toward himself, not the least bit surprised by the weight of it, and picked it up—25 pounds, give or take. He spat on the metal and rubbed it with the edge of his t-shirt. The clean part shined with a dark yellowish color. That explained the pancake's heaviness; it was made of gold. Was the stone a ruby? Andy lifted the object up and watched the light play within the gem. *Was the dragon "whacked" here because of this gold? Maybe someone had... but no, there are no other bones around, no signs of violence.* He crossed out the possibility of a dragon slayer.

The medallion suddenly flashed yellow and strange runes lit up on its surface. The crystal arc started humming like a swarm of angry bees. Its pale purple light changed to a bright neon color. Andy got scared and tried to toss the heavy circle away. No such luck; the medallion melted onto his palms.

The arc's fluorescence grew brighter; Andy's startled fear turned to full-blown panic. Not knowing what to do, Andy slammed the yellow thing on the altar with all his might. This junk, this circle, this amulet, medallion, whatever it was, detached itself from his hands. Bits of the skin off his palms remained on its surface and fell to the ground by the dragon's head, clinking victoriously.

Andy sputtered from the pain and shook his hands back and forth at the wrist. A couple of drops of blood had gotten onto the woe-bringing golden circle. A dark red beam of light shot from the ruby to the ceiling.

In the next instant, he felt as if his chest was being slammed by a sledgehammer, his feet lifted off the ground, and he felt himself soaring in the direction of the opposite wall. He didn't make it all the way there; he landed 30 feet from the take-off point, then skidded another 15 by inertia.

The arc had stopped glowing, and the red beam from the ruby disappeared. The question *What was that?* somehow immediately took a back seat to the exclamatory maxim *Run like heck! You didn't believe in magic? There's proof for you! Is it alright that it'll leave its mark on your ribcage?*

The air over Andy lit up, his ears perked up at the sound of a very high-pitched, borderline ultrasonic, screech. The outlines of some kind of pentagram formed in the air above him out of nowhere. According to all indicators, the magic had decided to finish him off.

Andy couldn't manage to pick his butt up off the surface it had polished and get out of there, no matter where. The pentagram suddenly glowed, the bright light slashing at his eyes and the ultrasonic screech turning to a rumbling hum that made the walls shake. His body was overwhelmed with an incredible weight, pinning him to the floor. His arms and legs felt nailed down with invisible nails, and Andy could only stare at the pentagram descending upon him.

"Aahhh!" he writhed with his whole body. "Let me gooo! I don't want it! What is it? I'll tear you apart!" Instead of his cries, a muffled rattle escaped his throat. The desperate attempt to free himself from the pentagram's hold had no effect. It finally touched his body, and the glow went out as if it had never been. The weight lifted, and Andy sprang from the ground to his feet in one movement.

Rage and a readiness to kill whatever might cross his path bubbled inside him. He grabbed a large thighbone of the dragon and began to destroy the remains of the skeleton with it. A few minutes later, all that remained intact was the skull. Wiping the ample sweat from his forehead, Andy looked around.

The room had changed. The dirt and dust buildup from many centuries had disappeared, and the room shone clean. Only the ruined skeleton, fallen stones under the hole in the wall, and dirty, bloody Andy, himself, spoiled the magical transformation. The coat he'd been holding was left somewhere in the ventilation pipe as he slid his way in here and his t-shirt was in rags, but his shoes looked good as new.

Andy shifted his weight from one leg to another and let the enormous bone fall from his hands. It was strange; he wondered how he had been able to smash the skeleton. Looking at the bone he was gripping in his hands, he questioned why it had been stronger than the others. Andy looked at his hands and kicked the bone that lay on the floor—an ordinary bone. He was suddenly ashamed of what he'd done to the dragon.

He turned from the destruction to find a way out of the room. He walked along the walls, examining the bas-reliefs and stone carvings as he did so. The stone images took his breath away. Dragons, people, judging from the long pointed ears, elves, and other creatures were depicted in full detail. The tiniest details were carved with meticulous precision.

***

How much time Andy spent immersed contemplating the lives of the winged race and the other stone characters, he couldn't say. He tried to turn away from the walls, but involuntarily, his gaze continually fixated on one or another of the carved images or bas-reliefs. He soon came back around to where he had begun—pretty hard to find any doors or other rooms. Either they weren't part of the project, or they were scrupulously masked, which was most likely—maybe even by some magical password or passage only by aura. Andy scratched his scar. *I could fail to find my way out of here until the second coming; then my skeleton would take its place beside the dragon's mashed-up bones. How cute. The composition would be called...*

"It won't be called anything! I'll get out the same way I came in!" The thud of pebbles falling from the ventilation hole had pulled him out of his thoughts and given him an idea.

*Easier said than done. Let's say I can get to the hole by climbing on the arc. What then? Then the challenges begin. How can I climb up the inclined tube? I don't have claws! Think, man, think!*

"What are you smiling at?" Andy kicked the innocent skull in frustration. Its teeth clanked noisily; the reflection of the internal violet light from the arc glinted across the fangs.

"Sorry, man!" Andy sat down in front of the dragon's skull. He had no claws, but he had a substitute... "Can you share your chompers? I need them more than you do!"

The fangs really didn't want to come out of the skull. The second stone he used to try to pry them out was shattered to pieces with no success. He had one fang at his disposal; ideally, he would need three more. Andy struggled with them longer than he had spent smashing the skeleton. The fangs were in there good and tight.

They were sharp, and the inside edge was finely serrated; it cut no worse than a knife. *I could cut my palms to shreds on these!* Andy cut a few strips of fabric from his t-shirt with his pocket knife. Now, he just had to wrap the bases of the newly acquired climbing devices in fabric, and he could get going. He'd been there too long already...

***

*Punch a fang in. Pull yourself up. Left, right, pull yourself up.* Small crumbs and sand fell on his face. "Dang! It got in my eye again!"

Andy punched a fang in deep with his left hand and got situated a little more comfortably, then wiped his eyes with his right hand. He didn't know whether he would make it out or not, but the dirt, clay, and sand would last him the rest of his life if he did. *Crunch.* The fang in his right hand hit something hard in the dirt wall and broke. Andy reached for a replacement in his belt. Three teeth left; he had to be more careful.

The walls of the tube glowed with a ghostly light as if glow-in-the-dark mushrooms or phosphorous microorganisms lived in the depths and on the surfaces covered in dirt. Sand and little clumps of earth periodically fell on his head from above, and the little bits scratched his stomach, drawing blood.

*Punch a fang in, pull yourself up. Now the other hand, pull yourself up. Halfway there.*

All kinds of stupid thoughts came to mind. Andy wondered whether he'd have a blister on his belly button or whether his belly button would be completely wiped into oblivion. Cowboys get blisters on their butt cheeks, and his situation was a lot worse than horseback riding. *Fifty yards down, fifty to go.*

He saw his coat hanging there. *Punch a fang in, pull yourself up. Right hand, pull yourself up. There's my little coat. Did you miss me?* He took hold of it and brought it with him, clenching it in between his teeth.

Another landing on the dragon's bones would certainly end badly, if not fatally. *I shouldn't have smashed the bones. Not worth it! Don't spit in the wind, especially if the wind is a dragon skeleton.*

Roots, just like live tentacles, strove to hook onto his belt and prevent him from crawling up and out. They grabbed his hands and tried to poke at his face. It was no use; the robot Andy had become had a job to do. *Punch a fang in, pull yourself up, punch the other one in, pull yourself up.*

Three-quarters of the way—the finish line... He sure couldn't take a final sprint, but no big deal; he would go by the Olympic principle, *It's not whether you win or lose, but how you play the game that counts.* He wished he could fix the fangs to his legs; his arms were already shaking quite violently. He caught his breath and kept going—punch, pull; the other hand, pull.

Andy got another portion of moist earth in the face. *Good thing I shut my eyes in time. How much dirtier could I be? I'm already like Winnie the Pooh when he jumped in the mud before flying up to the honey!*

It was hard not to mispronounce the poem with the coat collar in his mouth: "It's a very funny sought that, if Bears vere Bees, zey'd build zeir nests at ze bottom of trees. And zat bein' so (if ze Bees vere Bears), We shouldn't have to climb up all zese stairs!"

*Interesting,* he thought, *what kind of "bears" or "bees" dug out this "burrow?"* Maybe they hired a red-eyed rabbit to do the job? *'If I know anything about anything, that hole means Rabbit,'* he further quoted the childhood classic in his mind. *'...And Rabbit means Company....'* Anything was possible. Momma "Cheshire" brought a bunny from the woods the size of a large dog. God-forbid he should meet such a fellow in the tube or one of the "bees" he was wondering about.

*If they have rabbit like that here, what kind of elephants do they have? The size of a five-story building! And the fleas on these "pet" elephants would be the size of a car. Jump-crash, jump-crash, the jumping cars on the backs of friendly giant elephants....*

He bumped his head on a big boulder. *Stop. I made it, I made it!* Andy better secured his footing and began to look for the gap between the boulder covering the hatch and the edge of the tube. There were no traces of one. *How did so much dust, dirt and leaves get in here? Open up!* Andy hit the stone with all his might until his knuckles bled. He heard a *click* above his head, and the boulder rolled to the side, revealing the opening and the darkening sky overhead. *Evening already?* The wind blew into the tube and howled above it; the moving roof sprinkled bits of dirt into the hole. Not waiting any longer, Andy climbed out of the trap. With the speed of the guillotine, the huge boulder rolled back into place, almost squishing his feet.

Andy lay down on his back. His arms were stiff and seemed to buzz like a transformer. *How much distance did I cover climbing up?*

*About a hundred yards? I should probably get to the river and wash myself off...*

The sky brightened. The light blue edge of the rising planet appeared over the horizon. Andy sat up. *What should I do now? Go down to the woods and look for the tallest tree I can find?* Staying on the hill seemed like an incredibly bad idea. Andy would have to go out to the dark forest stockade anyway; better to do it sooner rather than when the nighttime creatures came out to hunt. He could orient himself by the light of the fire between the trees. Suddenly he stopped. *You idiot! Fire! There are people there!*

His exhaustion lifted, and he bolted downhill, hurdling over boulders, bushes, and fallen trees. If he had tripped at that pace, he would have been shattered to pieces. He raced, dodging in and out between the trees, not noticing the underbrush and cleverly threading through the thin trunks of the dense hazelnut trees. The fire was close by already.

Andy ran right into some cords that hit him in the chest and blocked his way. He grabbed one of the fangs from his belt and began hacking away at the ropes. *Faster, faster! What's this? A net?* He stopped at the very last second. *What kind of people are they? Have you forgotten everything you were thinking about portal voyagers?*

Trying not to make any noise, Andy stepped back. His left leg tangled in the mesh of the sticky net. A couple of improvised dagger strokes, and his leg was free, but with a thin ringing sound, the thick thread that connected to the net's mesh snapped.

An eerie roar came from somewhere off to the side. A dark shadow Andy took for an uprooted tree in the twilight suddenly grew larger. People began to scream excitedly; he heard snippets of orders being barked here and there. Shadows broken by the fire began to move and quiver in different directions. The dark shadow to the right stretched upward and lifted off the ground; wide wings opened on the background of the starry sky.

"A dragon!" Andy froze in a stupor. The powerful beating of the enormous wings pushed Andy back with gusts of air. He stumbled on one of the cords and, stepping carefully about to avoid falling, scrambled into the clearing and right into a pale-faced guy in a black frock.

A punch in the jaw snapped Andy out of his stupor. The thug put his foot in Andy's stomach and let out a guttural cry. His face was distorted into a repulsive grimace. If Andy hadn't studied hand-to-hand combat with Sergey, as well as archery, everything would have ended here. The lessons weren't very systematic, as opposed to the shooting lessons, but it was some kind of self-defense. Instinctively, Andy jumped back slightly and tightened his stomach muscles to absorb some of the energy from the blow.

All the same, he lost his breath for a few seconds, and a bloody film covered his eyes. A knife glinted in the man's hand. He again cried something out to the others; people stopped.

Andy took a long step forward to meet the hand that suddenly brandished a knife and, as Sergey had taught him, knocked the knife away. He leaned his torso away from another possible blow and, crouching, struck the guy in the liver with his right hand. The man wheezed. Andy felt something warm on his hand. His enemy seized the hand that hit him and squeezed it like a vice.

A lump of bile welled up in Andy's throat. He had stabbed the man in the liver with a long dragon's fang. *I KILLED him! What now?* The pale-faced man wheezed and collapsed to the ground. Andy stared in horror at his bloody hands.

A blow to the back of his head caused a whole host of various-colored stars to appear. The stars went out, and everything went black…

***

# Northwestern border of the Kingdom of Rimm, the Wildlands.

"Take it easy, little fellow," Chutka muttered between clenched teeth, hiding a lead mace-and-chain in his sleeve. "No point in flailin' yer arms around here." He kicked Andy with the toe of his boot, sending him collapsing to the ground in a heap. "Arist, what'll we do? The dragon got away! Grok, the magician, is already telling Hel off; he'll have a dark afterlife."

The seven hunters stared silently at the two bodies lying on the ground.

"Eet, were'd he come from? He sailed in from nowhere, like a morning fog!" Gichok's voice put in. "Chutka, you didn't knock him off by chance?"

"What? He'll be back on his feet by mornin'." Chutka squatted and turned the stranger's body face up. Then he started. "A lad!"

The rest of the hunters' faces showed surprise and disbelief in equal measures. They questioned how a boy had taken out an experienced mage, and so quickly, that no one had had time to blink an eye.

"What are you gawking at!" Arist took the lead. "Chutka, Drai, run to the magician's tent, look for some notrium shackles. Grok should have some."

"Why?" asked Titus, a hunter with a narrow, pockmarked face.

"Because the lad is a mage. Or d'ya think Grok was walking about without a defense amulet?" Arist called their attention to an entire bundle of chains with various amulets around the dead magician's neck. "Besides an amulet, Grok always kept a shroud on him, and it'll be a fine day afore ya break through 'er. Yer hand'll sink in, and you're the one who'll go limp then! And the lad sent him to his maker in three seconds! Explain that t'me? If he ain't a mage, I'm Madame Dora from the public haus in Pulha!"

The hunters chuckled at their commander's crude humor.

Drok was overweight and clumsy, with the sloping mustache of a southerner. He poked the boy with his finger and waved in the direction of the hill. "The little wizard chopped up the spider web and cut the anchoring ends that were holding the dragon," he explained in gestures.

Arist gave the remaining hunters work to do: Gichok chopped sticks; Titus and Drok wind an entire spider web into a roll; Taylor, a former legionary, searched Grok's pockets. The commander himself squatted down near the boy, knocked senseless by Chutka, and retrieved two more dragon fangs from Andy's belt. He held them in his hand and contemplated. The boy was somehow strange. His camisole was sewn from some sort of thin fabric; he wore tight pants made from a dense sackcloth. Arist inspected the boy's hands. Peasants' calluses were absent, although he saw characteristics typical of professional archers: thickened skin from the protective thumb ring and abrasions from the bowstring on the pointer and middle fingers of his right hand. The former foreman was well versed in deciphering such details. The boy had a well-developed frame and muscles, was built proportionally correct, and had the wide shoulders of a bowman.

Arist continued the examination. He had an even, oval face and hair cropped short. *A nobleman, perhaps. It was most likely, but what had he been doing in the woods like that, obviously for more than one day?* He was ragged, dirty as an urban pauper, swathed in cuts and bruises, with his hair covered in white cobwebs. Just then, Gichok tossed a new handful of dried sticks onto the fire, and the blaze flared up, shedding light on the field. Arist frowned in surprise. The boy's hair wasn't entangled in a cobweb—it was gray....

*** 

Behind Arist, Taylor let out a choked wheeze. Sensing danger, Arist threw himself on the ground just as he heard the resounding slaps of bowstrings against leather gloves. Gichok screamed, and in the next second, the scream became a death rattle. Drok fell to the ground on his back, and Titus lay beside him. *Forest Watchmen! But why? Why were they shooting them down?*

"Don't shoot! Arist show yourself!" The old hunter heard a familiar voice call. Arist stood up. No sense in jerking about, they had taken his men completely by surprise. A stately man in Watchmen's garb entered the field. He wore high soft boots, a green, loose-fitting camisole weaved of dense fabric, and pants of the same, with a wide belt wrapped several times around his waist. A short sword was attached to his belt. The watchman was holding a small, cocked crossbow with a short bolt.

"Hands in the air. Higher. Don't move, or one of us will send you to the great beyond. You see how nervous they've become; they killed all your men!"

"Dimir!" Arist recognized the watchman's voice. He used to be a hunter until he disappeared a few years ago. "What do you mean by this? What did we do?" he ran his gaze over the field of lifeless bodies. Titus had stopped writhing and was eternally quieted. The watchmen had the notorious habit of coating their arrow tips with poison.

"There's only one punishment for poaching on the land of the Duke of Lere—death!" Dimir said, squinting contemptuously and brandished his weapon.

"What duke? What are you saying! These are no man's lands!"

"You're mistaken. A week ago, His Majesty, in exchange for services to the crown, bequeathed these lands to the Duke."

"But we're not subject to the edict! We've been in the forest for two weeks! According to the code, a watchman has to warn a free hunter first if laws are being broken or if rules have changed!"

"Consider yourself warned." Dimir grinned. Muffled laughs were heard from behind the brush. "We have no problems with you personally, but you made such a bad choice of employer, Arist. You're losing your grip. You didn't know the Duke had offered a reward for Grok the magician of 200 Imperials? That's a decent amount of money for you. Grok owed him—owed him quite a lot."

The commander shook his head; Dimir's message was news to him. It was useless to argue or try to prove anything to the Duke's Watchmen; they did everything just like that. Just try to find some wiggle room, and you'd be shot full of arrows. They had almost certainly covered the base camp as well. Confirming the hunter's worst fears, three watchmen appeared on the field, one of them bearing Drai's head in his hands. Arist closed his eyes and said a silent prayer to Hel that she would grant his bozles a light afterlife; they didn't deserve to die like that.

If the hunters had known these lands had been given to Duke Lere, they never would have agreed to such a job just for some stupid perks. The Duke was known for his cruelty toward trespassers. *But Dimir, how could he? He was a former hunter!* Arist watched as Dimir's men patted down the dead hunters' clothes, ripped away their belts with knives. They then took Arist's belt, confiscated his steel and flint, and collected the remaining dragon fangs. Deft hands grabbed the small dagger from his boot.

"How is it that you, Arist, failed to protect your employer?" Dimir asked, grinning malignantly. The hunter shrugged. Dimir snapped his fingers and pointed to the mage. Two watchmen walked up to Grok's body and cut off his bald head, immediately placing it in a dense sack. Dimir explained, if caught dead, the duke would pay 150 Imperials—still not bad.

"And who is this?" The crossbow turned toward the boy.

"A stranger, he came from the woods. He's the one who killed Grok." Dimir raised his right eyebrow skeptically. "We thought he was a mage."

"Dorit, come here." Dimir turned to the bushes. The branches rustled and a thin, short figure stepped onto the field. "Have a look. Is it a mage?"

Dorit removed her fur-lined hood and cape to reveal a yellow-haired gnome. Her short hair was glinting like fire, she leaned over the stranger and whispered something.

"He's been stunned very badly; his aura is barely intact," Dorit said in a melodious voice, concluding her examination. "He might have been knocked into permanent foolishness."

"That's not what I asked you," Dimir interrupted her.

"Calm down. He's a mage. I haven't figured out his elements; everything's topsy-turvy with him. Targ himself couldn't make sense of it!"

Dimir nodded and pointed at the half-dead guy. "Put him in the master shackles, the ones we prepared for Grok."

The same watchmen who had cut the mage's head off deftly clamped the metal bracelets onto the unconscious boy's wrists and ankles, and threaded them with a thick chain. They produced a rideable reptiloid from the bushes and strapped the boy's unfeeling body to the lizard's back.

"What do you need him for?" the gnome asked her boss.

"We'll sell him tomorrow on the road, get a couple of gold coins in the common purse."

Dorit nodded in agreement.

"We're done here! Let's go!" Dimir cried to his subordinates, once they had plundered the corpses and destroyed the special hunters' crossbows and tackles. A couple of men collected the knives, daggers and broadswords in a sack. The gnome picked up the third dragon's fang, which had fallen to the ground from Taylor's hand. A gust of wind brought the smell of smoke to Arist's nostrils; they had burned the base camp.

The squadron of Watchmen disappeared into the darkness of the forest. Arist remained alone on the bloody field. *The pigs! How could they!* It would have been better if they'd killed him...

A callused hand lay on the hunter's shoulder. Arist turned. *Chutka! Alive!* But how he had changed! He looked...older.

"Let's go, Commander. Mustn't a-stay here, mrowns'll smell the bloode. We won't be aible to defend us'selves, the two of us!"

Chutka pulled the commander along by the hand, as one would a child. Arist, lacking any will of his own, not heeding the roads at all, followed the bozl. "Not all is lost, Commander! I'll now surprise ya!"

Chutka led him to a small clearing where, tied to trees, two reptiloids stomped the ground. It turned out the sly hunter hadn't fulfilled the commander's order to fetch the shackles but instead started going through the mage's tote bags, thereby getting his hands on something that was nothing to sneeze at. He grabbed the totes and snuck out of the tent, intending to bring the thing back to his commander. Then he had seen Drai's feet lifted off the ground and some unnatural adornments appear on his chest. Chutka plopped down to the ground and crawled away from the camp. The reptiloids, smelling strangers, broke the pegs they were tethered to and rushed to the woods, where our hero intercepted them. There were 300 weighty Tantrian pounds and a couple of purses of jewels in the leather totes. The mage had been a person of means.

"Where shell we a-go from here, Commander?" asked Chutka, climbing into the saddle.

Arist thought for a moment. "North, to the vampires. One former hunter owes us big time, don't you think?" A desire for vengeance burned in his eyes.

The bozl's lips stretched into a gap-toothed smile. He too could almost taste revenge. "We'll exchange this purse of jewels for Dimir's head."

The two reptiloids, despite the dark of night, carried their riders to the mountains.

# PART 3: FIRE OF THE SOUL

## Raston, the capital of the Kingdom of Rimm. Nirel.

*...Therefore, Duke Lere represents the most compelling threat to the interests of the forest. He has a policy of centralizing management of his dukedom and reacts negatively to any interference in his affairs. In the last several years, the number of royal officials in Lere's dukedom has decreased two-fold. All the posts that have become available during that time are now occupied by people loyal to the Duke personally.*

*The king has no reason to trouble him—a third of the Duke's revenue goes to the treasury. King Hudd's attempts to decrease treasury spending on border security by transferring those functions to landowners have allowed the Duke to increase the standing number of his personal guards to 15,000 or 20,000 men—almost comparable to the royal army. What does the Duke need that kind of force for?*

*All expenses for maintaining the personal guard are covered by the Duke's personal funds. Check all possible means of income, post-haste. Does Tantre have anything to do with this?*

*Lere's actions are aimed at supporting the urban population, large and mid-sized manufacturing, and artisan guilds. The burgeoning development of skilled craftsmanship and the creation of workshops is possible due to the introduction of a new tax collection system in the dukedom. The per-head tax has been changed to a capitation tax; the workshops and guilds send a firmly fixed percentage of the profits: a tenth to the Duke's treasury and one-twentieth to maintain the internal and municipal guards. There's a road toll and a merchant fee...*

There was a knock at the door. Nirel ran his hand over the paper and the ink faded. The newly written text was replaced by another.

"Come in!" Nirel said, standing up behind the desk. The door silently opened, and a freckle-faced kid in the light blue uniform of the Royal House of Heralds and Messengers entered.

"Sir," the herald bowed low before the head executioner of the Kingdom of Rimm. "Master Hugo requests your immediate presence in the fourth cabinet of the courthouse."

Nirel smiled in comprehension. Apparently, Hugo's interrogation method was not yielding the necessary results. He needed urgent help of the magical kind. He often needed help to break through the mental barriers of his subjects, but the subject was reduced to barely functioning. Nirel was called when the information was needed, and the person was not.

He commanded the herald to wait and began to gather the necessary instruments in an unassuming valise, casting sideways glances at the mirror on the wall. Just as he thought, the herald had crept toward the desk and was staring at an unfinished letter. *Well, well! How rude it was to read other people's love letters! So young and so curious. Who's compensating you for your curiosity?*

Countess Vinetta Menskaya had a string of admirers; tomorrow— possibly even today—the court would learn of a new devotee to her beauty. Nirel welcomed the idea of wooing the Countess. She was not bad at all, even to his picky elf's taste. It was highly possible, of course, that the scenario would lead to some tension with Duchess Reirskaya. The jealousy of the king's eldest daughter would add a certain spice to the situation. A woman in love could become a great source of information, especially one like her; he just had to think a few steps ahead.

"Let's go," Nirel commanded bluntly and, letting the boy lead, left his office.

***

Stepping along the dark underground passageways of the palace complex, the elf swore silently at the king's stinginess. *What kind of king has money for amusement and women but can't spend a pittance on magical lanterns for the underground corridors?*

The courthouse met the elf with silence. Even the clerks, it seemed, were not walking but hovering above the floor in order not to disturb their reverent awe before the law. Nirel snickered. Dark deals were dealt while the law kept silent. He knew all the ins and outs of the royal judicial machine and the cost of any given service.

Accompanying Nirel to the cellar entrance, the herald bowed and departed to attend to his own affairs; he hadn't the slightest desire to descend to the executioner's lair. A pair of royal guards silently stepped aside, allowing Master Hugo's assistant to proceed to the fourth cabinet. The smaller torture chamber was known by this unassuming title.

With an ear-splitting metallic screech, the doors of the antechamberslammed behind Nirel, and he stepped into the brightly lit torture chamber. The ineradicable stench of singed flesh, blood, iron, and excrement assailed his nose. Master Hugo lounged in a comfortable leather armchair. The old man appreciated comfort, and at his request, resting corners had been installed in all the torture chambers. The investigator's clerk was napping behind a desk, smacking his lips sweetly. The Master's second helper, Journeyman Migur, was going through the inventory spread out on a shelf. In the corner, a brazier crackled with coals.

At the center of it all was a bloodied man who lifted a glance at Nirel as he entered. Recognition flashed in his eyes, and his lips pursed, but Nirel, stepped quickly toward the chair and interrupted his exclamation with a punch to the temple. *He was a mage! Targ take him! The guy recognized him as an elf.*

Nirel switched to true vision and examined the mysterious mage. The aura of the person limp in the chair dimly sparkled with a violet light. He was a sharp-wit! This wouldn't be so easy to crack. Sharp-wits could block and intercept painful sensations.

"Why didn't you send for me right away?" Nirel looked at Hugo. The investigator blinked his pale eyelashes in surprise. "It's a sharp-wit. Didn't you know? You should be grateful he didn't have time to work his mind magic! Who is he, and what are you keeping him for?"

"Alo Troi, an instructor at the school of magic. He's been invited by the rector from Tantre," the clerk roused himself from behind the desk.

"We now deal with instructors?" Nirel said in surprise.

"Yes, especially those who attract the interest of foreign reconnaissance representatives."

"Tantre?" The clerk nodded.

Nirel wanted very badly to swear. *They had no concept of discretion! They let simple clerks in on state secrets, then, later on, they would be pulling their hair out over leaked information!*

"Master Hugo, I kindly ask all present to quit the premises and that Hurga the orc be summoned to aid me. I'll have to crack him the hard way."

The investigator nodded and with a wave of his hand ordered everyone to leave the torture chamber. He was partial to the idea of his journeyman guarding his little secrets with such great care. Nothing could be dragged out of the mute, dim-witted orc anyway.

"Call me when you're finished," Hugo added, closing the door.

Nirel roused the mage by dousing him with cold water from a barrel nestled in the corner of the chamber.

"Elvish dog," Alo Troi pronounced in a hoarse voice, and spat on the floor, blood and bits of teeth flying out of his mouth along with it. "You won't get anything!"

"Now, now," Nirel slapped the mage on the cheeks and jerked his head up by the chin. "You'll beg me to kill you. I'll turn you into a whimpering dog and make you kiss my feet."

It was very difficult to work with mages like Alo Troi, but the elf knew of a way to get to sharp-wits. The trick was not to give them a chance to block the pain and to thwart all attempts at suicide.

The iron door gave a shrill scrape, and an enormous orc entered the chamber.

*\*\*\**

The guards at the chamber door soon grew tired of recoiling at the piercing, inhuman cries. When the cries finally ended, the orc stepped into the corridor. He murmured something unintelligible and, with a slight bow, accompanied Hugo and the clerk into the torture chamber.

The investigator was delighted to see the mage, swimming in a cold sweat, trembling with fear and horror. *Nirel has a knack for convincing the stubborn ones.*

"I'll tell you everything! Everything!" the victim cried, choking on his tears and glancing in horror at the smiling assistant.

*\*\*\**

## The Northwestern border of the kingdom of Rimm, the Northern trade route, the Happy Horse Inn.

Yawning, Dorit descended the spiral staircase to the first floor. She was sleepy; the idea that gnomes were tougher than draft mules was a myth. Sleepless nights took their toll on them as much as they did on humans. The room was empty except for a boy—the waiter—sleeping behind the corner table with his shaggy head on the table's chipped boards. Metallic tapping sounds came from the direction of the kitchen. The cooks had awoken and were preparing for a new day. They were scraping the old ash off the stoves and butchering fresh meat in the backyard. Geese cackled; a piglet squealed.

Dorit went to the stables where the boy had been left tied up in a cage in the corner. She had lacked the strength and desire to check on him during the night, and with Dimir's permission, put off the task.

Cautiously stepping along the dirt floor, Dorit approached the cage. The prisoner came to. As soon as she walked up to the iron door, the boy bared his teeth and threw himself at the lattice door with a guttural growl. The gnome recoiled. Howling and snarling, the prisoner continued to throw himself up against the metal door, foaming at the mouth.

Dorit couldn't believe that this had been a person. Discovering who he was and where he was from was apparently impossible. Who knew what had made him this way? A blow to the head or a death curse by the magician he had killed—perhaps both. In any case, in this cage before her was…a beast. A strong, intelligent beast, with active, budding magical powers, but a beast nonetheless. *What a shame.*

"How's the boy?" Dimir met her with the inquiry as she returned to the inn. He was sitting at a table in the corner, sipping beer from a large mug. He looked collected and all business, his face freshly shaven, although he had gone to bed last night later than anyone else.

Dorit shook her head. "Not well. It's as I feared."

"He's become a fool?" Dimir took a swig of the foamy beverage.

"Worse—an animal! We should have finished him off yesterday."

"Who would have known? And I thought he might be a nobleman; he's got the right stance for it. We could have made a killing for saving him. If he were an outsider or a peasant, we could have sold him to the merchants..."

Dimir placed an empty cup on the table and looked across it at the woman.

"I'll have gabar," Dorit replied.

"Another beer and a goblet of gabar," Dimir said to the waiter who had just appeared. Taking the empty mug, the man disappeared into the kitchen. A junior waiter returned in a minute with a new portion of beer and a tall goblet of the thick gnomian booze.

The Watchmen took gulps in silence. Dimir let the lady quench her thirst first, and then, when she had put the goblet down, posed a question. "Can we sell him?"

"At the price of an animal," she answered bluntly.

Dimir nodded in agreement.

"Why did you let Arist go?"

Dimir's eyes glowed with a dark flame. His hands clenched into fists; he leaned over the table and fixed a heavy stare on the gnome. "He'll die there, with no weapons, no riding animals... he can't even light a fire. He will be food for the mrowns or the wolves.

"How long I've waited for this day! Now, I just have to find his little brother, Ludvir, and throw him in the woods naked. No, I'll cover him in dung and tie him to a tree—leave him as a tasty morsel for the midges! I'll never forget that Ludvir cast me, alone, into the Dark Impenetrable Forest when my error had caused a black sul to break from its cage and get away. I was just a boy; it was only my fifth hunt! No, their accursed family will answer for everything! I'll tear the Rondors to pieces, all of them!" Dimir fell silent. His face was red; his eyes flashed.

*Oh, merciful Gorn! Why have you sent me a commander obsessed with revenge?* Dorit thought. *I need to transfer to another squadron before this crazy man leads us to our deaths!*

Dimir moved closer to the lady gnome and grabbed her by the shoulder. As if he read her mind, he whispered in her ear, "You can transfer to another squadron if you fear I've lost my head. But if you even think of talking, I'll kill you!"

***

The rest of the watchmen woke up around lunch and came down to the dining room. Dorit dug around in her bowl with a spoon; she wasn't hungry. Leaving her favorite pudding untouched, she went to the stables. The prisoner met her with a growl, but he no longer threw himself against the door of the cage. The little beast's hands were bloody. Apparently, he hadn't stopped trying to break the shackles.

She heard steps behind her. Den and Turin, young men who had signed up to be watchmen three weeks ago, walked into the stables. The little beast moved back into the corner and hissed at the Watchmen threateningly. Den kicked the cage. The predator in human guise instantly clamored to the cage door and grabbed the watchman's foot with his hands, then sunk his teeth into the guy's calf. Turin, punching the boy's head, tried to extract him from his friend's leg. Den wailed and swore like there was no tomorrow.

"Get away!" Dorit pushed Turin aside. A magical flame with a braided trail spread from the gnome's open palm and struck the little beast in the chest. He let go of the watchman's leg and went into convulsions. Den fell to the ground and clutched his leg, bitten to the bone.

"What's going on here?" Dimir burst into the stables, throwing the gates open wide. Dorit pointed to Den.

"Our hero made the acquaintance of the little beast. The numbskull!"

"What an interesting case..." An elderly man with a long white beard appeared from behind Dimir. A medallion of the House of Mages of His Royal Majesty hung around the newcomer's neck, sparkling with rubies. His right hand clutched a long staff topped with a mountain crystal. All present bowed low; the little beast growled threateningly. The mage turned to Dimir. "Are you selling him? I'll pay you 15 golden pounds."

"Sold!" Dimir agreed immediately. Fifteen pounds was an excellent price, ten times more than they had hoped for. "Let's head toward the dining room; we'll take care of the payment there and celebrate our transaction."

***

The stables filled with people. Several folks from a caravan headed by the royal mage joined the Watchmen. They had been staying at the inn for a short repose. Now, cages with various animals were fastened to the caravan's wagons. Five of them contained several dozen wild gray orcs, hunched up. Separate from the others, was a double-cage made of notrium. In the closest cell to the stables, lined with different colored cords and bits of leather, sat a small, wrinkled female shaman.

The watchmen and their willing helpers backed the snarling and scratching beast-boy into the corner of the cage with wooden rods. The members of the caravan grabbed the shackles by the chain and dragged him out. Then the unexpected happened. A horse harnessed to a wagon with a cage containing three long-maned wolves neighed and reared up on her hind legs; the cage turned upside down. As it hit the ground, the doors opened, and the wolves burst out.

Frightened, the caravan members dropped the load they were carrying and ran into the stables. The little beast darted off. The chain broke and slipped through the rings that attached it to the shackles. Sensing that he was free, the two-legged beast growled furiously and threw himself at the wolves. The wolves responded in kind with all they had, and the orcs began to whistle and cheer. After a while, one wolf fell away from the yelping ball; its neck was twisted at an unnatural angle. Its dead, unseeing eyes stared at the sky. After another minute, a second wolf followed, its head bashed in by the metal shackle the boy was wearing. The third wolf, with its tail between its legs, took to its heels from the bloody, horribly bitten up little beast.

The main doors of the inn flung open, and the mage darted out. Instantly assessing the situation, he lifted his staff. The crystal began to glow brightly, and a blue light emanated from it to touch the boy's head. The little beast fell to the ground in a heap. Turin and the limping Den lifted the unfeeling body by the arms and legs and tossed him into a second cage made of notrium. A hefty man from the caravan quickly slapped a lock on the cage. The third wolf was long gone, off into the woods.

*** 

Dorit went back to the dining room. However, she wasn't able to finish her pudding. The main entrance opened to reveal Trog, the commander of a second squadron of Watchmen in Duke Lere's new lands. When he saw Dimir, Trog marched right up to the table the watchmen were sitting at. They greeted one another with short, firm handshakes, and Trog kissed Dorit's hand. He then plopped down into an empty chair.

"There's something going on," he began right away. "Yesterday, we were at the bald hill—" Dimir and the others snickered.

"We killed a magician there," Dimir interrupted Trog, smiling indulgently.

"He can go to Targ, that magician," Trog waved his hand dismissively. The royal mage sat down at the adjoining table. "A wounded black dragon was caught in a shooting spider web set by poachers at the Southern Slopes! Its wing was broken! You're a former hunter—"

"What!" the mage and Dimir exclaimed in unison. The mage moved over to their table.

"If you can catch that dragon alive at Raston, I'll pay you 70,000 gold pounds! I'm coming with you!" the royal mage said.

The room went quiet. You could hear the sounds of a green fly knocking against the window. The Watchmen commanders exchanged glances.

A burning greed for profit lit up Dimir's eyes. Had they turned the mage down, their own people would have torn them to pieces on the spot.

"You have a deal!" Dimir answered, swallowing, and shook the mage's hand.

***

Dorit led her reptiloid out of the stables, but suddenly, felt someone looking at her from behind. It was a heavy, penetrating stare that made her shudder. The gnome turned, and her eyes met those of the little beast, who had come to. Holding on to the cage door with his hands, the boy looked at her with the gaze of a human. There was no trace of the beast-boy left; she was sure. The great hate behind his blue seemed almost palpable, and it frightened her. The former beast's aura sparkled with all colors of the rainbow. The wounds on his arms and legs from the wolves were healed.

Trying not to turn her back to the cage, Dorit moved to the middle of the courtyard. The royal mage, who shared her observation and her efforts not to face away from the cage, had given back the boy's mind. *It almost would have been better if he'd remained a beast. Beasts don't seek revenge,* Dorit thought.

The drivers' cries and the whistles of the whips forced the boy to turn away from the woman. The caravan's first cartload left the courtyard headed south without the bearded mage.

***

Several large fires lit up the caravan as it stopped for the night in the middle of a field. The sentries quietly called to one another. In the sky, flooding the land with a ghostly glow, the nocturnal eyes of the twin goddesses twinkled. Gynug, unlike the human in the adjoining cage, couldn't sleep. The old shaman was looking over a string of bone beads. She knew what fate lay in store for them as intelligent prey for the royal hunt. Neither she nor the best warriors of the tribes entrapped in the cages would survive. The human boy rolled over to his other side in a feverish sleep. He was a mage. Humans like him showed great promise for the future in their schools. But this one was still inexperienced and untrained. *Spending his remaining reserves on the healing of wounds was utter folly for a mage in a cage of notrium!*

The little human moaned and kicked in his sleep. His knuckles hitting the wooden floor, the strange boy's hand lay palm-up before the orc shaman, having slipped between the bars of the cage. Gynug peered at the palm before her. *How interesting this one's life and fate lines are...*

"He'll avenge us! They don't know who it is they're trying to make into prey. Get back at them for us, boy. Your soul's fire shines very brightly; may it light our way to the goddess' judgment!"

The old shaman's cackling laugh resounded through the camp.

***

# Kingdom of Rimm, the northern trade route, Raston. Andy.

The wagon wheel bounced over another bump. The cage jerked to the side, and Andy was thrown against the bars for the hundredth time that day. He wanted to scream. Gynug muttered something guttural in the adjoining cell. Judging by her tone, it wasn't a couplet by Saint Augustine. They had been moving along at the pace of a running turtle for the second day now.

Three guards rode by the cage on reptiloids. "Hasses," as Gynug called them, were interesting lizards. From a distance, they looked something like horses, without their tails and with a flap of skin under their chins. But up close, they had long, powerful paws with retractable claws, strong, tight-knit scales, V-shaped heads on long necks and sharp teeth. There were no scales on their chests; instead, they had wide bone plates, freely stacking against one another and not interfering with their motion. Such plates could also be found on the animals' backs, peeking out from under the riders' saddles.

The last guard knocked on the cage with the shaft of his spear and laughed, seeing how Gynug recoiled. Andy spat after him and, as luck would have it, got him. It smeared down the laughing guy's shield hanging on his back. His neighbor clapped the floor approvingly with her palm a couple of times.

The guards were dressed in what looked like Japanese medieval armor of thick tanned leather. "O-yoroi." Andy recalled the name, learned from the books he, Sam and Sasha used to read at Sergey's house in his other life.

*In my other life...* The phrase forced him to freeze for a moment and look around. It was true; even if some unknown force carried him home this minute, that life would remain a thing of the past. He had died, surrendering his place to another creature, one with a wild beast inside, ready to kill people for his life and freedom, lacking in any regrets or emotional distress as a result of his actions. Andy hadn't considered why such a dramatic change in his values had taken place. He hadn't had time. If he didn't shy away from the effort of thinking about it, then he would probably be horrified at this change. But his flexible adolescent brain flexed into a bow and circumvented the slippery question of universal values. When he thought of the way these jerks had whipped a gray-skinned slave to death the previous day, Andy's hands clenched into fists, and a bestial roar bubbled in his chest.

Pushing all thoughts of his bright past and dark present out of his mind, he concentrated on the construction of the armor. The stomach was covered by four horizontal rows of plates, starting with the right side and going along the frontal surface of the torso to the left. The plates curved around the left side, and along the back, they went back the other way, not connecting to one another. A thin plate tied them together, fastened to the front and back edges by little hooks which were double silk threads. One pair had a loop on the end; the other had an oval-shaped bone button.

The chest and upper part of the back were covered with three rows of horizontal plates. A metal plate with a half-circle shape cut-out in the center provided extra protection to the upper chest. The cut-out allowed the wearers to move their necks freely. There was another one like it on the back. The spots where the hooks were fastened on—vulnerable to an enemy—were covered by two movable metal plates. The leather bits were decorated with designs of red diamonds. The armor's wide shoulder pads and thigh pads lent it a distinctive look. The thigh pads also protected the wearer's hips while seated on a hass. They were kept on by the string that ran throughout the suit of armor and covered both saddle-bows. The way the wide shoulder pads were fastened on, allowed the wearer to freely shoot from a bow despite the pads' bulky look, which was especially important given the fact that they faced the constant possibility of being attacked by bandits. When the guard raised his arm with a bow, the shoulder pad "curled" over to his back, not hindering his movement. As soon as he lowered the bow and began to take the reins, the pads would move back to their former places, covering the arms up to the elbow.

A tall, broad-shouldered man with a black mane of hair commanded the caravan. Gynug cast a fearful, sidelong glance at him and called him "davur." *Davur... hmm, davur.* It meant nothing to Andy.

The next day, with Gynug's help, he learned the language of Ryldan, or the Ryldanes, and he came to understand many words and phrases. They hadn't gotten to numbers and values; they would have to make due with some simple words. In the meantime, he had figured out that Ryldanes was the name the gray-skinned people called itself. The old woman almost drooled, swearing in her clicking and clacking dialect. An individual was called a Ryldor, and only the black-haired man was still called davur, although Andy could not see the difference between him and a Ryldor.

For his part, he classified her and her fellow tribesmen behind bars as orcs and hoped he hadn't sinned against the truth too severely. The grayish skin color, the strongly protruding upper and lower fangs, the pointed ears—these were some of the ways Ryldanes differed from humans.

"A-rei," the old woman cawed from behind him. Andy turned. Gynug indicated by gestures that he ought not to look at the guards; they didn't like it. Andy spit. *If they don't like it, that's their problem.*

"A-rei," the orc said again.

"Okay, okay, to heck with it! I've turned around, see?"

'A-rei,' she's butchering my name, he thought to himself in annoyance, turning away from the guards. Gynug smiled approvingly, revealing her sizable fangs.

"How many times do I have to tell you, my name is Andy! An-dee, got it?" He moved toward the bars that separated the cage into two cells. Just then, the wagon's wheel fell into a hole, and Andy hit his face on the cage door, slapping his jaws together loudly.

Gynug shook her head from side to side, grabbed a bit of chalk from somewhere under the scraps of hide, and in a few seconds of careful motions, drew a wolf on the cage floor. The orc was a good artist. The wolf had a grinning mouth, ears pinned back against its head, and hair standing up on the back of its neck.

"Rei," she said, pointing at the wolf.

"I get it, 'rei' means wolf."

"Ah," she said. The old woman's pointed to the chalk when she saw that Andy didn't understand. She grabbed a bit of leather with some white fur remaining and pointed at it. "Ah!"

"I get it, 'ah' means white!" To be more certain of his guess, Andy pointed to a white cloud. "Ah?"

Gynug nodded joyfully and pointed to the drawing of the wolf, then to him.

"'White wolf'" apparently? Fine, to heck with you all. I'll be a white wolf if you like; just let me be."

With that, the meaningful conversation was quieted for a while. Andy tried to think how he could ask the question that was tormenting him for the second day. He asked the orc for the chalk, and on his half of the cage floor drew a schematic of prisoners behind bars, then patted his chest, poked Gynug, and pointed to the other orcs. Finally, he shrugged his shoulders demonstratively as if to say, "Why?."

The old woman's eyes narrowed to thin slits. She looked at him for a long time, as if considering whether to tell him or not. She then took the chalk and drew several horsemen with bows and spears. Then she drew people running away from them.

"Gynug, Ryldan, A-rei!" her knotty finger with its calloused fingertips pointed at the running figures. The white chalk in the shaman's hands moved about as if alive. Using minute, separate clicks of the chalk against the thick wooden planks, she drew arrows piercing the running figures, adding a crown to one of the horsemen's heads.

"I get it. The royal hunt, and we're the prey."

Andy turned away from the old orc. The news didn't exactly shock him, but with every fiber of his being, he wanted to avoid trying a slave's shoes on for size, let alone the shoes of someone's prey. A wild wrath and hatred for everything around him rose up from somewhere deep within his nature. He suddenly remembered a nightmare he had recently in which he had twisted the necks and punched the sides of strange wolves with thick gray lion's manes. The thirst for blood he felt right now was surprisingly equal to what he had felt during the dream. His desire to twist the neck of the figure with the crown on its head overwhelmed him. He turned to Gynug and poked at the crowned man, then ran his finger along his throat.

Glancing at him, the orc moved back in fear, her back stopping against the opposite wall of the cage. Then her face smoothed back out, and her cackling laugh rang throughout the caravan.

*** 

Thick branches of tall trees spread to either side, giving way, and the caravan entered a wide clearing. In a few minutes, the wagon, and the cargo of animals and slaves were lined up in a circle, fencing off the center of the clearing from the forest. It was time for a rest and for lunch. From the central wagon, they unloaded onto a bundle of sticks and a sack with charcoal. No one entered the forest during the halt; they were afraid either of robbers or predators. They collected water in leather wineskins where a stream met a river.

Andy turned away from the orc and relieved himself through the bars of the cage. It was a bit tricky to do this while moving. He couldn't very well relieve himself onto the cage floor. The presence of females in the vicinity had an effect as well. Not all of his moral foundations had undergone cardinal changes.

Only his empty stomach saved him from a more embarrassing scenario. He flatly refused to eat the slop that was offered to the slaves. Just the odor made him want to vomit.

Soon, a pleasant meaty smell came from the center of the clearing. Andy's mouth watered; he closed his eyes dreaming of a big, beefy hamburger. Shattering his rosy dreams to smithereens, a piece of spoiled meat slapped onto the cage floor. Turning away from the moldy stuff, he looked down. Across from the cell stood a thick, Middle-Eastern looking overseer grinning impudently. A young guard without a mustache approached the other side of the cage on a hass. Andy kicked the rotten meat with his right foot with all his might. It shot at the overseer as if from a cannon and hit him right in the face. *Bull's eye!*

An alarm roared out the distress signal. The young guard grabbed a short javelin from a special quiver strapped to his saddle and jabbed it into the cage, aiming for the renegade slave. Reacting to the danger in time, Andy jumped to the side, clutched the spear with both hands and snatched it away from the unsuspecting guard. Screaming like a wounded elephant and rolling his bloodshot eyes, the enraged overseer jumped up and darted over to the cage—where he met the narrow tip of the spear in Andy's hand.

Cries rang out in the clearing. The guard unsheathed his sword, but he wasn't able to slash the slave with it. Andy stabbed the five-foot spear into the side of the hass. With that, the animal bellowed in protest and reared, throwing its rider off its back in the process. The orcs began to hoot merrily in their cages. The overseer uttered a strained, dying wheeze from under the wagon.

Abandoning their posts, two guards rode into the skirmish. These guys weren't about to repeat their colleague's mistakes. Death smiled at Andy in the form of two feathered arrows placed on bows.

Gynug curled up into a ball and cowered in the far corner, as far as she could get from the black-haired giant. Davur stopped two feet from the wagon, casting a cold, dead serpentine stare at the slave who had killed the overseer. Andy no longer cared where or how he died. He glared back at the commander of the guards. An elaborate tattoo decorated the man's handsome face on his right cheek. Another ornamental vine-like pattern crept out from under his chain-mail onto his neck. The backs of davur's hands were covered with a plethora of tiny scars.

He extended his right hand to the cage and indicated with gestures. "Give me the spear!" Andy looked at the man's outstretched hand, then at the tense guards, their bows stretched to their ears, and with one swift movement, slid his trophy halfway between the bars and broke it off, casting the pieces at the main guard's feet.

Davur's face remained unmoving, but a hint of respect flashed in his eyes—or maybe it was Andy's imagination. In the next second, a glass bulb smashed under the renegade slave's feet. The noxious smoke that came from it shrouded Andy. The last thing he remembered before losing consciousness was the frowning glance the commander cast at the guy with a medɹllion on his chest in the shape of an eight-pointed star. Gynug called him "gajeen." She had said he was a Ryldor and, pointing at herself and Andy, added that they, too, were gajeen.

\*\*\*

A sharp smell brought him around, and a hand with a dirty, smelly rag appeared before his eyes. A whip whistled above his head, and his back suddenly burned with unbearable pain. A lump welled up in his throat. Maybe that's why Andy didn't cry out. The second lash made him moan, at the seventh or eighth, he lost consciousness again.

***

The wagon wobbled side to side. The cage wobbled, and with it, the whole world. The alarm ringing in his head resounded with the sound of the wheels on the pavement. His whole back, from his rear end to his neck, stung sharply. His legs were limp. Biting his lips from the pain, sometimes until they bled, Andy wondered why they hadn't beat him to death like they had that orc. His hands were so numb he could not feel them at all, perhaps because he had been hanging by them. After the flogging, they hadn't put him back in his "home" cage. He was in a separate one, his hands already fitted with metal bracelets with a new chain. His legs were held by special constraints, bolted to the floor, with chains pulling outward to each side and upward into an "X". It was impossible to do anything in that position.

Andy didn't know how many lashes he received. By the time he came to, the caravan had left the woods and was moving toward a castle on a rocky cliff that jutted out over a wide river. A winding road led up to the cliff, and then turned to the left. With their right side facing the castle walls, the caravan continued to a small drawbridge across the wide, moat. From inside one of the narrow arrow-slit openings of the right flanking tower, the pointed helmet of a soldier gleamed in the sunlight. Despite the pain in his back, Andy examined the stone walls curiously. He had read a lot about the architecture of medieval castles but was seeing a real one for the first time.

The base of the walls was reinforced with powerful stone boulders about 20 feet high. Above that, there was masonry of red brick, but the total height of the walls was no less than 35 feet. Thin arrow-slit openings for archers decorated the top, alternating every ten feet with flat openings for crossbows, wider at the edges. At the corners of the walls, flanking towers protruded. A deep moat, dug out before the castle was built, curved toward the road in an arc and full of water. Behind it, forward-thinking engineers and construction workers had installed a palisade and equipped it with stakes like a porcupine. The same palisade was in front of the moat, too. The road ended at a high tower over the gates, adorned with quite formidable tar spikes.

The caravan came to a halt across from the gates, and two horsemen rode out from it. The pair crossed the drawbridge, and the metal gate lifted for the exact time it took to cross under it before closing with a crash.

Above the high parapet gallery, concealed by a wooden awning, the helmets of the castle garrison flashed.

Andy closed his eyes and tried to relax. It was all he could do. His mom used to go to yoga quite often and practiced autogenic training, so there was no shortage of literature—books and brochures—on these topics at home. He had periodically leafed through them—they were too tedious to read flat-out. Now, he recalled that information, and in 30 or 40 minutes, he'd begun to relax. Continuing with the methods described in the brochures, he estranged himself completely from the world around him and concentrated on his burning back. It was surprisingly easy; Andy noticed that in his new cage, which was made of simple iron, he felt much more at ease. The old cage had drained him of his energy and pressed on him with an unrelenting doom.

Now, the sensations of the world faded, and the darkness around him changed to whole gushes of rainbow light. A whole ocean of energy roared like a tidal wave, somewhere just beyond the borders of perception. With an overwhelming need, he reached toward that wave and felt a thin border pop. Energy crashed in on him, and acting on intuition, he divided it along the parts of his body, directing most of it toward his wounded back.

The wagon jerked, pulling Andy from his trance. The pain in his back was gone, and he knew the wounds had been replaced with young, pink skin. He was ravenous and prepared to scarf down even the slop that was offered to the slaves.

*** 

After an hour of waiting, the metal mechanisms in the tower began to screech, and the gates were lifted. The first cart in the caravan entered the fortress. The wagon containing Andy's cage ended up in a narrow stone courtyard before passing through a second set of gates to stop in a little peninsula of high walls. They took the castle's defenses seriously, apparently. Under the awnings, there were large cauldrons. Piles of firewood lay around. Barrels of tar stood next to the cauldrons. Pyramids of boulders had been carefully stacked by the walls. Order and cleanliness reigned. The garrison commander earned his keep.

From within the stone walls, the wagon rolled out to a wide courtyard, at the far end of which stood the dungeon tower. But something else caught Andy's attention. In the middle of a large square, between two tall pillars, a platform had been constructed with ramps attached to it. A blue haze hung in the air between the pillars. Below that, a dozen people in white cloaks with eight-pointed stars on their backs milled about.

The first wagon went up on the platform and disappeared, followed by a second, which repeated the fate of the first. *Teleport!* Andy guessed.

Soon, it was his own wagon's turn. The female driver gave the horses' crupper a jerk with the reins, and the wagon left the castle to appear suddenly in a wide square surrounded by walls of white stone. Soldiers wearing chain-mail walked along the pedestrian walkway carrying crossbows. Andy turned his neck to look the other way, as much as was possible in his state. Behind his back loomed a tall arc, illuminated with a bluish haze toward the center.

"Raston!" the driver said happily and spurred the horses.

The wide cobblestone road led down the small hilltop from the fortress they had just entered toward a large city surrounded by white fortifying walls. Curving streets were discernible behind the walls; the spires of churches or other buildings stuck out above them. Andy recognized them as temples. Clay roof tiles adorned the tops of the three- or four-story buildings, forming a carpet of red. Hundreds of little villas stood out like a green patchwork quilt.

The city extended in a care-free manner from the edge of a large lake or small sea, on which a multitude of sailboats scurried about. Long piers, covered on top by stockades, wedged their way onto the water's surface. Traveling along a road lined with trim, pyramidal trees, the caravan turned at a wide fork toward the grandiose castle visible at the edge of the city.

This new wall was not as impressive to Andy as the first fortress on the rocky cliff. The caravan crew squawked at the soldiers on the wall and in the tower over the gates. The gates creaked, and the carts, one after another, moved forward into the wide courtyard. A wiry man in a long black robe approached the head wagon and spoke with the head of the caravan guards and a young, vile-looking guy with a medallion around his neck. Apparently, he gave them valuable directions, because the guy jumped down from his horse and went to the watch room. The wagon drivers drove the wagons with the slaves along a path sprinkled with fine gravel toward some boxy construction visible behind the trees. The cages containing animals remained on the square.

\*\*\*

The structures turned out to be not all that boxy. Against the backdrop of the grand castle, the structures looked a bit homely. The carts rode up to the barracks and stopped. The door of the first building opened, and no less than fifty warriors spilled out. Decked out in chain mail with mirrored breastplates, each one carried a spear similar to a Roman pilum, and sheaths with short swords hung from their belts.

The warriors formed two ranks before another couple dozen eager soldiers joined them with enormous dogs on leashes. They took the orcs from their cages one by one and chased them in the direction of the structures. The dogs chomped at the bit to get off their leashes, and a slave had only to pause or stumble for a moment to receive a strong blow with the shaft of a spear. One idiotic orc contrived to push a warrior with a pilum and run off the other way. The dogs were released, and the runaway didn't get ten steps before he was knocked to the ground. Another four dogs joined the melee and tore the screaming orc to pieces in a second. There were no more attempts to resist or disobey. The warriors grabbed the dead body with a hook and dragged it away somewhere behind a barn. They poured sand on the blood stains.

Andy was the last one to be removed from his cage. The blacksmith pounded on the rivets of the shackles for a long time to remove them; they had chained soundly. A couple of men with mage's stars on their black camisole uniforms joined the warriors. One of them carefully examined Andy's and said something to his peer, whose eyes opened wide. He joined him in the inspection. The mages spun Andy like a doll and clicked their tongues, exchanging words periodically.

Soon, the captain of the guard grew impatient with the improvised medical examination and shoved Andy in the direction of the second building, which had bars on the windows of a familiar grayish color. About ten guards fell into formation around it. The mages walked behind them, still discussing the results of their examination.

A strong kick sent him into the small chamber, and the lock on the super-thick doors began to screech. The doors were upholstered with studded strips of gray metal. A pile of hay lay in one corner, a wooden pail with a cover in another. There was a teeny little window. That was all. Andy sat down on the hay. Mice began to squeak in protest from underneath him. He hugged his knees and began to ponder. *The hunt is at hand...* he surmised correctly.

***

## The Kingdom of Rimm, Raston. Nirel.

Nirel adjusted his handkerchief and walked away from the mirror. *Just what was needed!* A dark gray camisole with silver embroidery and metallic wristbands fit him perfectly; it didn't tug or pinch anywhere. Nirel slapped his feet into long, over-the-knee boots of soft leather and smoothed his hair.

Only the final touches were left. The elf donned a signet ring with a sparkling stone on the middle finger of his right hand and hung a sheath encrusted with silver ornaments on his belt. It contained a long knife that matched his costume. Entering the ball with a sword was only allowed for the members of the king's personal guard. The noblemen would have to make due with knives or daggers to confirm their status.

The invitation to the ball in honor of King Hudd's youngest daughter's fourteenth birthday caught him unawares; he wondered for a long time who might have assisted him in this matter. Getting nowhere, he quit the pointless task. It was a very good thing that he would be visiting the palace today. He had a lot of affairs that he might be able to manage while blending into the hum of the palace and he mustn't miss this opportunity to acquire additional connections among high society.

Only the final touches were left. The elf donned a signet ring with a sparkling stone on the middle finger of his right hand and hung a sheath encrusted with silver ornaments on his belt. It contained a long knife that matched his costume. Entering the ball with a sword was only allowed for the members of the king's personal guard. The noblemen would have to make due with knives or daggers to confirm their status.

"Get the bags," he called to a servant, and with a steady step, descended to the first floor of his dwelling.

***

The gargantuan double doors swung open, and Nirel stepped into the Ceremonial Hall. Two servants in full dress livery shut the doors and returned to their positions like statues, awaiting the next guests. The huge hall was full of courtiers and nobles from the highest society of the kingdom, and the ambassadors invited from other states stood out as separate little islands of people. Dressed in their best, guests were constantly whispering to one another, creating a ceaseless din in the room.

Nirel's eyes scanned the room's decorations. The walls were covered with wooden panels of stained oak. He wouldn't have noticed them were it not for the indescribable beauty of the carvings they contained, showing animals, birds, and plants. Many of the carved figures were adorned with precious stones and seemed alive. The leaves on the trees were lined with green malachite, jade, and rubies. The high ceilings got lost among fake clouds. The floor was paved with tiles of various colors forming intricate patterns. The multitude of magical lanterns ingeniously hidden among the panels on the walls and the cupola ceiling brightly lit the hall and created a calm, cozy atmosphere.

At the far end of the hall, there was a high platform with thrones on it. A golden embroidered wall hanging decorated the back of the throne belonging to King Hudd. It portrayed the state emblem—a Eurasian cave lion standing on its hind legs. The second throne was draped with a white sheet. Queen Omelia had died three years ago of an acute fever. The life mages turned out to be powerless against the rare illness. As per the kingdom's traditions, they had draped the throne to indicate that the king was in mourning and not seeking a second bride at this time. The elf supposed Hudd himself, through his agents and schemes, had sent his wife to Hel's judgment.

Nirel, hands clasped behind his back, calmly walked along the walls, responding to nods of greeting from a few courtiers. The head executioner was a fairly well-known figure. Many ladies' dark glances followed the debonair man as he went by. He had but to stand close, and their tightly corseted chests began to expand in trepidation as their fans fluttered three times more rapidly.

Once he had wandered about the room for a while, Nirel approached the state dignitaries, who were discussing various political news. He carefully listened to the topic of conversation and put in a couple of sharp-witted comments regarding the policies on Tantre, indirectly touching on Duke Lere. In passing, based on his experience with the same Tantre and the Patskoi Empire, too, he suggested a few improvements in the organization of their foreign policies.

The young man's careful words and poised manners were for the benefit of one person only—the head of the foreign relations House, Count Ludwig Ramizo. The count was quite interested in the suggestions raised regarding the duke. He asked for a more in-depth explanation. Nirel immediately started in on the militia that was growing much too fast, specifically Lere's personal army. He expressed amazement at the fact that the dukedom had not become penniless; maintaining such a crowd of armed people is quite expensive, and taxes were being paid promptly to the treasury.

Ramizo exchanged a glance with another official, who simply nodded in response to the Count's silent accusation, confirming the accuracy of the young man's statement. The Count raised his bushy eyebrows and offered the elf a more private meeting, perhaps in two days' time. He asked to be assured that he wasn't imposing too much on the young man's schedule.

Nirel began to wave his hands. "Of course not! I am available anytime." After a few minutes, under a pleasant-sounding pretext, he parted from the group.

*Excellent!* One meeting with an old diplomat and head of the Foreign Affairs House and all the expenses of this evening were worth it. He hoped the evening's activities would lead to the secret service of the Foreign Relations House overseas. After all, the Count wouldn't necessarily need to know who the secret service was working for.

***

Nirel was losing his patience. He had spent no less than an hour in the main hall, and neither the king nor the princesses had appeared. Just then, the tall double-doors spread wide open, and the audience, holding its breath, listened to the herald's loud voice announcing the entrance of the royal family. The orchestra began to play the state hymn of the Kingdom of Rimm, and the King paused at the doors to let the birthday princess go first. With his elder daughter on his arm, he slowly moved toward the throne. All the ladies bowed reverently, heads down. The Cavaliers bowed low at the waist.

His Majesty Hudd of Rimm was a short, stout man with a puffy, vicious-looking countenance that gave him away as a lover of wine. The king's large shiny eyes perused all the ladies bent before him, resting on those with a large chest and a low décolleté. The disgusting arc of his puffy lips lent him a capricious expression, and scant greasy locks of brown curls draped onto his shoulders.

*He could have washed his hair for his daughter's birthday ball!* the elf thought. The golden crown on the king's head looked as out-of-place as a saddle on a cow—too big and constantly slipping down to his eyebrows. There were several dozen faceted diamonds on it. His Majesty, like a crow, had a penchant for all things shiny.

King Hudd's daughters didn't look anything like their father; their height, figures, and faces were like that of the deceased queen. The younger one, Namita, as thin as a reed, with a barely visible chest, was dressed in an airy white gown. Strings of river pearls were interwoven into the birthday girl's dark hair in an intricate hair do. Her tiny, low-heeled shoes were covered in topaz. Her large brown eyes, like her father's, shone rapturously.

Taliza was the opposite of her younger sister. Duchess Reirskaya, the heir to the throne, had a figure that called to mind Valkyrie of the Vikings. She had a large round chest, a thin waist, wide hips and long legs. The princess' dark curly hair was interwoven with green ribbons that cascaded like a waterfall to her waist. Taliza's green dress with yellow trim was sewn by the most skilled tailors, hiding any flaws and accentuating the merits of her figure.

A small golden diadem with emeralds held back her hair to expose her face and green eyes that held a constant and penetrating gaze. Her plump lips parted to reveal pearl-white teeth when she walked by Nirel, who was in a low bow. The elf's sixth sense told him who had sent him the invitation.

His Majesty ascended the platform and plopped down onto the throne. The hymn ended. Congratulations and best birthday wishes began, along with the passing out of presents. Nirel stepped out to a wide balcony to get some air. He was tired of the pandemonium and needed to ponder the situation.

Things seemed to be going well. He had baited the princess, apparently; he couldn't explain the invitation to the ball any other way. They had met at a social gathering at the house of Count Lars four months ago. Nirel was, at that time, showing ostentatious signs of attention towards Baroness Von Ramm and had only politely bowed his head and kissed the Duchess' hand, not showing a personal interest in her in the least. Surrounded by crowds of suitors, the Princess must have been surprised by such a cold attitude, although she did not become angry about it. Their next meeting was at a hunt at Baron Von Ramm's. Being an excellent horse-rider and archer, Nirel shot all the prize hares and laid them at the Princess' feet, pronouncing her the queen of the forest.

Upon arrival at the estate, he had not permitted himself to show anything but friendly, neutral attention toward Taliza. He then saw sparks of interest toward him flare up in her eyes. Their third meeting threw dry brush on those sparks. The Princess became the unwilling witness to a duel between Nirel and the eldest son of Count Orkneisky, a reputed bully and a notorious duelist, who had already run through more than a dozen men, sending them to meet their makers. Only his father's influence saved the man from vindication by the relatives of the deceased and punishment by the law.

Arranging the situation by an insult to the count that drew his challenge to a duel was not a problem. Nirel reduced the man to bits in a matter of seconds, piercing him with sharp blades. The Princess gave him a bit of emphatic applause and a radiant smile; she had had quite enough of the now-deceased admirer. Perhaps it was by her protection that Nirel had evaded all consequence for the death of a high-born noble at the hands of a simple executioner.

And then he had gotten the invitation... He had to step carefully, so as not to inadvertently offend the girl. Love and hate were just one step apart, after all. He had to find out what she wanted and give it to her, creating a tie to himself as much were possible. The ideal outcome would be to become the secret lover of the heir to the throne, a behind-the-scenes advisor to the future queen.

Music rang out in the hall, along with deafening applause. Nirel returned to society; the ball had begun.

*** 

After three hours of various paired tours and dances with constantly changing partners, his feet began to ache. He was not able to ask Taliza to dance. The Princess was surrounded by such a crowd of high-born admirers that blocked access to him, according to "legend," the second son of Count Strino from far-away Meriya.

Nirel bent his knee, kissed his last partner's hand and retreated to the refreshment tables. Her Highness' frauleins walked by. One of the ladies faltered and almost fell when she tripped over the long train of her ball gown, but the elf caught her in time. She thanked her savior and disappeared into the crowd. In the cuff of his sleeve, Nirel discovered a small note with the words, *In one hour, first floor, near the statue of Hel—T.*

\*\*\*

Exactly one hour later, he descended to the first floor of the castle and, at a leisurely pace, walked by the statue of the goddess Hel. An inconspicuous panel on the wall behind the statue turned around. "Sir..." The face of the fraulein he had saved from falling appeared in the opening. Nirel slipped into the passageway that she opened. The woman turned a lever on the wall, and the panel returned to its place. No one had seen anything. "Please follow me, sir."

The palace turned out to be full of secret passageways. Through the twists and turns, Nirel walked behind the fraulein and admired her handsome figure; perhaps she had elvish blood in her.

"This way," she came to a stop in front of a small door.

Entering through the door, he found himself in a richly decorated boudoir. Thick candles burned in silver candlesticks. The walls were draped with scarlet velvet and decorated with paintings in heavy gilded frames. The scent of expensive women's perfume hung in the air. A wide four-poster bed with a silk canopy stood in the center of the room. A small bedside table held a shining bottle of expensive wine and a bowl of fruit.

A masked door quietly creaked open, and Taliza stepped into the room.

"This is for Countess Menskaya," the Princess said and slapped Nirel in the face.

*So that's who employed the freckled herald's prying eyes.*

"Why her?"

"She's so like you, Your Grace!" Nirel feigned guilt, bowing his head.

The princess walked up to him and placed her hands on his shoulders.

"I was just afraid..." he said.

"Of what? Tell me!" Her little hands slipped along his back.

"That you would reject me. Who am I to you? I'm the son, but not the heir, of a well-known count from a faraway kingdom. I preferred to love you from afar, admiring you as one would an elvish rose in his father's garden. I'm accustomed to realistic thinking."

The elf placed his hands on her slim waist.

The Princess laughed. "Idiot. I'm once more convinced of how silly you men can be."

Nirel wanted to answer, but a thin finger pressed his lips.

"You'd better pour me some wine, my knight."

Nirel uncorked the bottle and poured wine for both of them in wide goblets with long thin stems. He touched a small protrusion on the edge of his pinky ring ever so lightly, and a tiny portion of a love potion spilled into the princess' glass. The mix was extremely rare; one drop cost 20,000 gold pounds, more than a dragon's heart. Anyone who ingested it before making love would engender a constant need in their partner; no one else would ever be able to give them such pleasure. Nirel measured the dose as accurately as possible to create a bond and the desire to meet again. He had no need for a sex slave; that could turn into strong evidence against him.

He knew he was but one of many well-built, handsome men who had already visited her bed and that he meant nothing to her. His potion helped ensure a chance to capture her attention.

Taliza sat on the bed, accepted the outstretched goblet and took a sip. "My father is organizing a hunt at the wild park tomorrow," she said. "Will you be my companion?"

"I'm hunting already," he quipped, and pulled on one of Taliza's ribbons, releasing her gown.

"Careful with the goods," the princess laughed gleefully.

*** 

## Raston, the Royal Hunt. Andy.

Andy had gobbled up all the slop they gave him in the evening and the morning. Despite his expectations, his stomach digested what he had consumed. He had barely slept last night; as soon as he began to doze, something a lot bigger than a mouse ran by his legs. He opened his eyes and glanced around the cell. In the dim light of the night sky through the tiny window, he couldn't see anything, but sleep escaped him from then on.

After his morning meal, Andy felt a lot better. His back stopped itching, and his stomach growled less. He even got a chance to sleep a bit. The clang of the lock awakened him. Three gigantic guards stepped into his cell and slapped shackles on him to drag him outside.

*It's starting!* Andy thought, looking at the chained orcs and several unknown creatures resembling beast-like people. The guards approached and threaded a long chain between special rings on all their shackles. He was next to Gynug. They forced the "prey" toward the gates.

The bipedal herd, pushed forward by humongous dogs, jogged for a short time. In ten minutes, a 20-foot-high stone wall stood before the slaves. It had small gates with a wicket inside, which opened to the slaves.

*** 

On the other side, they found themselves in the care of another group of guards and a pair of mages. They removed the prisoners' shackles and ripped all their clothes off, before painting markings on the slaves' backs.

*They numbered us!* Andy guessed. The humans and orcs then ran in the direction of a dense thicket, in their birthday suits, to the accompaniment of jeers and whistles.

"A-rei," Gynug's disheveled head appeared from the bushes. He turned toward her voice, covering his manhood. The old woman extended a clump of grass to him. "Gav-gav arg!"

Gynug indicated that he should rub the herb on himself and sniffed the air. Andy took the herb and began actively rubbing it on himself. "I get it. This plant'll throw the dogs off our trail." All thoughts of decorum had gone to the wayside. He was soon covered in dark green blotches and smelled like freshly cut grass. Meticulously examining his green arms, legs, and torso, Andy recalled the masks and markings of the Special Forces teams back home. He grabbed a whole fistful of moist black soil and rubbed it in wide stripes on his skin. Gynug observed him and began to do the same. When she had finished, she went up to Andy and rubbed his back with the herb. Andy took the shredded bundle of wild plants and rubbed it on the orc's back.

The sound of hunting horns and the loud barking of dogs came from far away. A couple of orcs jumped out of the bushes, grabbed the old shaman under the arms and pulled her into the depths of the thicket. Gynug cried out and writhed in her tribesmen's hands, but they didn't even think of obeying her. Andy was left alone. Bending down and creeping right over the ground, he ran to the abundant, sprawling trees that reminded him of oaks back home. His right foot got caught on some kind of stick, and he tumbled head over heels. The hapless stick turned out to be a fragment of a spear with a narrow leaf-shaped tip. Apparently, it had been left over from the previous hunt. Taking the find, Andy took off up the nearest tree as stealthily as a cat.

His animal instincts kicked in; killing the wolves no longer seemed like a dream. Everything inside him naturally flooded with animal feelings, strangely mingling with his human intellect. Andy remembered that it shouldn't be that way; that didn't happen to humans. But his human psyche was quiet, buried deep. In order to survive and get his revenge, he needed a human's intellect and an animal that knew the woods.

The blast of the hunters' horns sounded; he could tell they were close. Andy flattened himself against a fat branch. *I'm not here! I'm not here!* he repeated the three words in his head like a mantra. The bushes nearby began to rustle and crack before a pack of hounds burst into the open air. They turned around a couple of times on one spot, sniffing, picked up the scent of orcs and dashed off in the direction of the thicket. They hadn't caught his scent. *Thank you, Gynug!*

A dozen riders followed the dogs onto the field. There were men and women in equestrian costumes with short hunting bows in their hands. Each one also had a long knife; the men had shoulder belts with swords.

The saddles were equipped with sheaths for javelins. Two of the riders had eight-pointed medallions bouncing on chains around their necks. *I'm not here, I'm not here*, Andy continued his silent mantra, clinging to the tree.

The jolly company wasn't in a hurry to leave the field. Servants in green livery appeared bearing tables and foldable chairs. The Cavaliers helped the ladies down from their horses and began to pour wine into goblets. *They're having a delightful picnic, the turds! I hope the ants eat you instead! I'm not here, I'm not here...*

The hunters' horns now sounded from all sides. An explosion came from the depth of the ticket, and the dogs screamed hysterically. He heard a human cry, and someone blew into a big hunting horn. He heard another boom, and the horn went quiet. A dog seemed to go mad, then came another boom as if someone had set off a grenade. The picnicking party darted from their places, knocking over the little table with wine and hors d'oeuvres. The screeching of the dogs was replaced with the hysterical cry of whoever or whatever had been blown to pieces. Yet another hysterical wail, full of pain, was followed by the sound of cheering.

Parting the bushes with his chest, at a measured pace, a hass stepped onto the field with a scruffy rider. The new hunter's clothes were full of holes, his cloak was smoldering, there were crimson scratches on his cheeks, and he had twigs and leaves in his hair. Despite all that, he wore a self-satisfied smile. On the end of a long rope trailing behind the hass, stuck with arrows like a porcupine, he was dragging Gynug by the feet.

*I'm not here, I'm not here...*

The hunter was met with gleeful congratulations and a full pewter trophy. One of the young men removed the orc's fangs and handed them over to his lucky companion.

The dogs started barking again nearby. The bushes at the edge of the field began to rustle before a tall hunter, dressed like a dandy, waved his hand. An orc shot onto the field. The handsome fellow took down his prey by throwing a heavy knife. Applause broke out all around, and the dandy walked over to the orc to extract his knife and then the orc's fangs. He returned to the party and presented these trophies on one knee to a buxom green-eyed huntress.

Andy was quivered with rage. *I'm not here, I'm not here...*

A new crackling sound came from the other side of the field. From his branch high up, Andy could see the dogs chasing another five orcs. The hunters hopped onto their horses and took off after the fleeing prey, cornering them against a 20-foot-long fence. The field was empty except for the happy hunter who had caught Gynug. He rode over to the tree, taking refuge in the shade from the oppressive sun.

A satisfied growl sounded from Andy's chest as the tip of his spear pierced the man's back. Gynug's killer stared in disbelief, wheezed and fell off his saddle.

Then Andy noticed a bow and a quiver of 20 arrows. He pulled the leather glove from the left hand of the man he had killed and removed the sling holding a knife from the man's belt. *Could I have killed so calmly like that, just one week ago, and then raided the corpse?*

Andy's concentration was broken in a moment, and he darted to the side. A javelin hit the ground right where he had been sitting. Flying over the bushes in a single stride, a horse jumped onto the field with an elderly mustached hunter on its back. He had a green, slim-fitting costume, a double-pointed hat with a long feather, and high boots. Andy leaped forward to take down the horse, which crushed the old man's right leg. Andy finished his enemy off with the sword, which then got stuck in the ground. An arrow whizzed past.

*Holy moly!* Lying flat on the ground, howling fiercely, he threw himself into the bushes, grabbing the bow and quiver as he did. Horns hooted behind him; dogs began to bark somewhere in the distance.

Tearing through the fallen trees and thick underbrush, Andy came upon two watchmen. The first stared at the strange black and green apparition with a knife and bow in his hands. He died in his stupor, and Andy turned to the second. With one big leap, he increased the distance between them and chose to retreat. The watchman grabbed a horn and blew, communicating the prey's location. A feathered arrow, quivering slightly, put an end to the man's career. *He should not have forgotten about the bow.*

"Aaah!" A sharp pain stabbed Andy's right foot. He had run too much, not carefully enough. A sharp little stone had pierced his sole. He wasn't giving up. *If I have to lose my life, let it be for the highest price possible!*

He heard the pounding of hooves from the field. He knocked the first rider off his saddle, dead from the arrow's blow. The second broke his neck, knocked from his horse at full-speed; Andy had put two arrows in his chest.

The familiar picnicking party appeared from the other side. *They surrounded me!* Andy turned toward the new danger and started firing his arrows, one after another. One of the riders took an arrow to the chest and fell from his horse. That was Andy's last stroke of luck. Blocking the green-eyed woman with his body, the dandy jumped forward. A glowing dome appeared in front of him, which swallowed all of the arrows.

From behind, a heavy net covered Andy. Busy with the riders, he had forgotten the Watchmen. They knocked him down and kicked him from all sides. A strong blow to the chest by the handsome fellow, who had hurried over, knocked the wind out of him and made him gasp for air. A second blow, and he lost consciousness.

***

"He shot at me, Nir, he shot at ME!" Taliza cried hysterically. Holding Nirel's hands, the princess was shaking.

"There, there. It's over now. Calm down, Your Highness. He's no danger to you now." The elf hugged the princess and stroked her hair as if she were a little girl.

"You saved me! You're a real knight, you risked your own life!"

"What are you saying? I wasn't threatened at all!" Nirel leaned away from the princess a bit and retrieved a handkerchief from his breast pocket, then wiped her tears with it. *Real knights don't hunt people, he thought. I'm not a mage, not a master, but I can do a thing or two!*

Taliza smiled, left the embrace that was so pleasant to her, and walked over to the boy, tied by his arms and legs.

"How many did he kill?"

"Seven people, Your Grace. Another four were killed by others, orcs," answered one of the watchmen who had thrown the net.

"It's a human, a boy!" she kicked him in disgust with the toe of her Morocco boot. "The horrid orc's brat! I want him to pay! Let him understand what a great mistake it was to fire at me! I want him to suffer good and long, so he'll know what he's done!"

"It's a barbarian, Your Grace. He doesn't speak Alat," one of the mages stepped forward from the princess' entourage.

"That's not a problem. I know a mage who can quickly teach the little beast to speak!" Nirel put in, and the corners of his mouth turned up into a slight, sly smile, which did not bode well for the boy.

"Do it, Nir!" the Princess commanded, turning to her lover. Nirel bowed, accepting the task.

Just then, the thumping of hooves came from the direction of the royal palace. A frothy stallion jumped onto the field.

"Ladies and gentlemen!" a herald called from the back of the snorting horse. "As a gift to His Majesty, a live dragon has been brought to Raston!"

# PART 4: BIRTH OF THE DRAGON

## Raston. Nirel.

The stream of visitors came to an end. The yard keepers entered the square in front of the caged dragon to clean the mess left behind. Many had come with spoiled fruits and vegetables; some brought rocks in their pockets, made bets on who could hit closer, and threw them. The winged creature growled and jerked, but the thick chains on its snout prevented it from opening its mouth and spitting fire. His Majesty, upon advice from the Head of the Treasury House, opened up his menagerie to the public. Ten silver coins got a look at the dragon, another five to throw fruits or vegetables at the creature, and the royal vendors peddled spoiled ammunition.

Visitors could order a table and drink wine, supposedly from the royal cellars, or taste some exotic dishes prepared by the royal chefs. They'd opened a real tavern near the beast. The treasury made 3,500 weighty golden pounds on the first day. On the second day, they made seven thousand. In the space of two weeks, the treasury made a hundred thousand. It wasn't a dragon; it was a goldmine.

Nirel looked at the dragon, trying to seem calm. He mustn't let his feelings show. Like all Forest-dwellers, he harbored an insane hatred for the winged beasts who destroyed the Great Forest and Mellorny Tree Crowns, but here, he might be misunderstood. For humans, the flying creature was nothing more than an entertaining attraction. Revealing his thirst for revenge would be giving himself away. *Close your eyes and slowly exhale, that's right, calmly now.*

Two weeks had gone by since the dragon had been brought in. It was time to get used to this—an ancient and now harmless enemy being nearby. The previous night, he had subtly hinted to Taliza that he would be fine with taking care of the dragon, once the people had had their fill of the funny beast. The princess promised to speak to His Majesty so that he might entrust the black beast into Nirel's loving hands.

An enclosure had been opened next to the dragon exhibit that contained yet another living attraction—a wolf-man. Shaking off his nervous irritation at the dragon, Nirel walked up to the fence, picked up an onion that someone had dropped and chucked it at the half-wolf. *Bulls-eye.* With a loud thud, it hit the scruffy monster's head and broke to pieces. The freak shackled in chains of notrium bellowed something incoherent; the shackles clinked dully. *Hmm, that's a little better.* There was a good pile of apple cores, stones and spoiled vegetables around the less-than-human.

Throwing something at him cost just a half a silver coin, a low price many boys took advantage of.

The sharp-sighted elf noticed that the half-wolf's right ear was coming off. Nirel called the caretaker over. "Re-glue the mongrel's ear and change the fur on the back and tail. That's coming undone, too. How often do you renew the muteness spell?"

"Every two hours, sir," the shabby peasant replied, bowing. Fawning in front of his bosses and the high-born nobles, the caretaker turned into a cruel tyrant with his subordinates.

"How much have you swindled today?" Nirel asked in a neutral tone. The caretaker went pale. "Don't be afraid, I'm not going to take your personal gains away. How about this—I'll look the other way from your petty schemes, and you'll repay me by your services. Is that a deal?"

The caretaker's pale color turned red. He nodded in agreement. Better that way than losing both his money and his head. Royal investigators have no great love for their neighbors. They take everything and then send you to the scaffold.

The shabby man turned out to be quite a sly character. Realizing that trade in sub-standard goods might bring great profit, he quickly worked out a deal with a couple of market traders who brought the fruits of their gardens to the city. Now, a third of the rotten food sold by the vendors was of questionable origin, not coming from the royal vendors with profits not going to the treasury. The average gain from the illegal trade was about 150 pounds a day. It was good money, even for a wealthy resident of the capital.

One of the vendors had ratted the caretaker out, a guy who felt he hadn't gotten his fair share of the profits. Nirel found paper laying on the floor near a desk in the Security House after the boss' clerk had stepped out. He read the report, slipped it into his pocket and threw it into the sewer on his way out. He had decided to take the shabby peasant under his control. The vendor fell violently ill.

"So, how much? You didn't answer my question," Nirel said.

"A h-hundred an' seventy, sir," the caretaker got goosebumps all over and began to tremble. He knew who Nirel was. The court was buzzing with vague rumors about him and the heiress to the throne...

"Well, well! I think some of your services might then be quite substantial!" Nirel flashed a dazzling smile at the hustler, who had gone white as a sheet and hopped over the fence.

The wolf-man turned around upon hearing footsteps. Andy's face and body were bloody and bruised. Dodging rocks in shackles had proved difficult. He glared at the elf.

"How's it going, little wolf? Cat got your tongue?" *'A-rei,' the White Wolf, now a royal attraction, famous indeed! Why should he speak with mere mortals?*

"I'll kill you," the boy wheezed, and the gray wolf's ear fell off. Nirel looked at the caretaker maliciously. He had been stingy with the glue it hadn't held. And they'd have to do something about the muteness spell, or think of something else; he learned to counter the spell too quickly. They'd have to work him over today, too. He didn't seem unhappy and suffering enough for Her Highness, who had visited him yesterday. "Do something about it," she had commanded her love.

Nirel turned to the obsequious caretaker.

"Two weeks have gone by, and nothing has changed. The same words. Remove the mongrel's chains and deliver him in one hour to the executioner's chambers."

***

## Raston, Nirel. Two weeks prior...

Nirel remained in excellent spirits. His meeting with the Head of the Foreign Relations House had ended brilliantly. It was a lengthy interview beside the burning fireplace with a glass of sumptuous wine and superb light hors d'oeuvres in Count Ramizo's personal office.

He had had to prepare himself thoroughly in order not to fall face-first into the mud. He needed to clearly formulate all the suggested innovations he had mentioned at the ball. He had to compose a detailed note with personal conclusions about the Duke of Lere. He had to add to the paper a host of comments on Meriya's political school and points of view on this or that issue that had led him to draw such conclusions, and to indicate his sources of information. Everything had to be done just so, shipshape.

Before leaving, he stood for a long time in front of the mirror and checked his aura disguise, which meticulously hid any traces of his origin. It turned out it was time well spent; he had had to undergo a magical verification three times on the way to the Count's office, and there was no guarantee that he hadn't been controlled in the office itself as well. The meeting ended with his being given the title of Independent Consultant. The artful old fox had picked up on the subtle court breeze that blew between the Princess and his guest. The Count took preventative measures, so as to please the heiress to the throne and his guest, galvanizing the position by procuring her father's approval of the young man's endeavor.

No one in the kingdom's inner circle had any doubts that Taliza would be a tough ruler, and no one knew how it would play out with this executioner.

***

Whistling a happy tune, Nirel went down to the lowest level of the dungeon for political prisoners. Hurga the orc stomped dully behind him.

"Which cell is Alo Troi in?" he asked the floor supervisor, who bolted upright. *He was sleeping, the cur!* Nirel thought, eyeing the red traces of his palm on the skinny man's right cheek. Blinking his beady, deep-set eyes, he glanced at the list hanging on the wall and pronounced enthusiastically, "In Cell Eight, Your Honor!"

"Open it!" Nirel ordered.

The long-nosed man took a key chain from his belt and began to amble off toward the cell. As he opened the door, Nirel walked through.

"Hello, Alo," the elf said joyfully as if addressing a beloved relative. The gigantic orc cracked his knuckles loudly as he slid through the narrow door after Nirel.

A primal fear flashed behind the prisoner's eyes when he saw the visitors. He curled up into a ball and cowered in the far corner of the cell. His thin, dirty feet scraped up against the rotten hay.

"Troi, my friend, I need you!" Nirel continued just as merrily. The prisoner's fear turned to horror.

"No, you don't! I've told you everything! Everything!" Tears ran down his sunken, scruffy cheeks. A fearsome trembling overtook him. *Ye-e-es, I have broken him thoroughly.*

"Hurga, aren't you ashamed? You've frightened the poor mage so? Bad orc," Nirel teased. The orc chuckled. "You're a sharp-wit, aren't you Alo?" The wretch quickly nodded in reply. "Excellent. We have a little task for you then, shall we?"

"What is it?"

"Oh, nothing at all, really. You have to teach a barbarian to speak Alat. He doesn't understand a word, the nasty thing. I'll give you one day."

"I'm dying! My brain is shutting down! I don't have any reserves left at all! I would have to formulate all matrices and embed them directly using direct visual and tactile contact. I would collapse from physical exhaustion before I had time to do anything!" the prisoner began to protest quickly, now addressing a topic that was in his element.

"It's your choice, my friend. Either you kick the bucket that way, or our little friend Hurga will have some fun with you. He's a very creative orc, and with him, you'll suffer a lo-o-ong death." The orc's eyes began to burn like a maniac enjoying the thought of his victims' torture. Troi began to tremble again.

"I... I'll try..."

"All right, you see, we can come to a reasonable agreement, no need for name calling. If you had just told Master Hugo everything right away, we never would've met!

"You're right, though, about your physical condition. The dungeon is not a spa, and the menu here shows it. But I'll think of something for you." Then, leaving off his jokingly affectionate tone, Nirel went on in a cruel, serious voice. "I'll give you two days, you scum, to eat your fill and formulate the transferable philo-matrices. On the third day, you'll have to pay for the food. If that barbarian doesn't start to speak Alat and you don't croak, the orc will have his way with you, got it?"

"Yes, thank you…"

Nirel left the cell, and the supervisor deftly closed the door and all the locks attached to it.

"Now you listen," the elf turned to the dozing dolt. "Starting today, feed the prisoner Troi as you would one of the guards, with all the rations of meat and grains. If you even think of disobeying me, I'll remember you sleeping on duty and your other faults, and Hurga will be happy to help me beat an understanding of discipline into your thick head."

"It will be done!" the long-nosed man shouted at the top of his voice. He wouldn't dare fail.

\*\*\*

"What did those orcs call this wolf-man?" His Majesty, King Hudd asked, wrinkling his nose in disgust.

"A-rei, Your Majesty," the head mage pronounced in a deep base. "In their language, it means White Wolf."

The king approached the orc's adopted son, who was stretched out on pegs. A swarm of flies and horse flies buzzed above him, crawling on his body, which had been covered in swine blood. The prisoner's dull stare became clear and looked the king up and down, then, resting on his crown with an enormous emerald in the center, flared up with malice and contempt.

"Flies. I thought he should suffer and feel pain, as Duchess Reirskaya had asked. How do flies help?" His Highness addressed his question to Nirel, who was maintaining a respectful bow.

"He's suffering, Your Majesty. A thousand flies and horseflies, stinging one all over one's body, brings excruciating pain," the head mage answered instead of the elf.

"All right then, but I would lash him or stretch him on the rack. They're the good, old, tried and true methods. Have you found a mage that can teach him to talk?" the King once again addressed the executioner.

"Yes, Your Majesty. In two days, the little wolf will remember how to speak in a human way." He bowed low again. "The mage needs two days in order to formulate special spells that can teach," Nirel added quickly, seeing a vein under the monarch's left eye begin to bulge and his lips purse.

"Great job, Nirel! That's quite fast, Your Majesty," the royal mage came to Nirel's aid.

"All right, I'll remember your words. In two days, the little wolf should understand human speech."

Nirel exhaled quietly; the danger had passed. The King nodded in response to the mage who whispered something in his ear and started to walk out of the executioner's chambers, followed by his entourage, some of whom spat on the outstretched boy with relish as they passed by. Near the gates, His Majesty suddenly stopped and added, "Enough with the flies. Give him ten lashes. I don't trust flies."

***

## Raston. Alo Troi. One week, four days prior...

Alo cowered in the corner. He hated himself but could do nothing with his fear. The elf had broken him, turned him into a cowardly dog. He couldn't even end his own life; he wanted to live.

Today, he would die but, thank the Twins, it would be an almost painless death. Without any magical reserves, he would have to pour himself into it. First, his legs would stop working, then his arms would go numb, then his heart would stop. Not all at once; over the course of about two hours, give or take. Those hours would be his last trial. They wouldn't hurt; one can't feel pain with almost atrophied nerve endings. He had just one regret—his family wouldn't know what happened to him. *Although, no... let them be ignorant. I'll simply disappear from their lives and not be too much grief for them. But if only I could see my daughter...*

After the elf left the cell, two guards burst in and changed the hay for a mattress, threw him a ripped blanket; and brought him a whole kettle of vegetables and meat. Not waiting for the servants leave, Alo threw himself at the food, burning his fingers and tongue. He shoveled the hot bits into his mouth and swallowed without chewing. The kettle was empty in a minute. The redheaded guard returned and, frowning, took the empty kettle, left, and slammed the door. Alo burped and leaned his back against the cold wall. The elf had kept his promise regarding the food; he was equally capable of keeping his promise regarding the long, painful death. The fearsome orc, who was completely immune to Alo's powers of suggestion, would break his bones with pleasure. A peaceful death was better.

Alo banged on the door and, ignoring the swearing and cursing of the supervisor, asked for writing tools. Remembering everything he had been taught and had taught to others, he began to work out the building blocks of a lingo-matrix.

Sometime later, the little window through which he received food opened, interrupting his work. *Evening already?* A bowl of piping hot porridge with butter and a big glass of juice slid through. When he finished eating, he knocked on the door and asked for a light to be put into the cell. He had a lot of work to do, and it must be done in under two days. The long-nosed supervisor swore profanely, but he granted the request. Alo wasn't the only one who feared the elf.

***

The two days went by in a flash. The former teacher decided that his last work should be the best he'd ever done. The paper was filled with the outlines of the matrices for spelling and verb conjugation. A matrix for the Younger Edda was scribbled at the end of the last sheet in black boxes and arrows with sequential descriptions and step-by-step "filling" of each of the cerebral bases. But he wondered if he would have the strength to realize it. If so, the barbarian would not only speak, he would read and write Alat. Alo laid the papers out in front of him and scrupulously recalled the sequence of actions and activations of the barbarian's cerebral points during the transition stages of the spell matrices and the direct transfer of information. Troi hoped that his bipolar would have at least a drop of reasoning and that his brain would be at least somewhat developed. Otherwise, it would be difficult, and all Alo's efforts would go to waste.

The door screeched insufferably again, and the elf entered the cell. His cold eyes focused on Alo with an icy gaze.

"Are you ready?" he asked.

"Yes."

"Good. What is your last request?" the elf asked as if Alo were headed to the gallows.

"Wine, a glass of red." Alo expressed his desire right away, knowing full well he would not return to the cell, no matter what happened. The elf nodded to the supervisor who took off like a gust of wind. In a moment, his hurried steps were heard; a guard came into the cell with a half-full wineskin.

"Drink up, and let's get going."

Alo took a few gulps, breathed for a moment and partook once more. "Enough!" the pointy-eared executioner snatched the wine away. "Shackle him and lead him to the courtyard."

The light of the sun caused a whole river of tears that stung Alo's eyes. After the gloom of the casemate cell, the world was full of bright colors and miraculously fresh air. Alo breathed deeply.

A door opened in the next building over, and three young guards, grunting as they tugged on a chain, dragged out a second prisoner who was resisting with his legs. Alo, squinting after them, tried to see who he would be working with. The boy was a bit taller than average height with broad shoulders but thin. The guards ganged up on him and grabbed his arms altogether; the blacksmith appeared out of the blue and slapped shackles on the barbarian. They dragged him to a high wooden platform and strapped him to a thick plank with wide belts.

"Why did they shackle him?" Alo wondered aloud.

"Just to be safe," the elf answered and gave the mage a nudge. "You're on. They're waiting for you."

***

The barbarian turned out to be a boy, unskilled, but a mage. *So much the better.* Alo placed his palms on the young man's temples and touched his forehead to the boy's. He looked straight into the stranger's dark blue eyes and dilated pupils. Alo fell into a trance, his lips already bearing the first activation spell.

He wasn't able to enter the other's mind on the first try; the boy put up a defense intuitively that shocked the mage by its strength, although it had been executed clumsily. Using a few distraction interweaves, Alo broke the shield. The internal world of the...barbarian...opened up before him. He saw all the boy's memories.

*Almighty Twins, merciful Intercessor!* Images of another world overwhelmed the mage. He tried to examine the strange carts, driving without horses, and the giant buildings—over 20 stories—and metal birds—*airplanes*, the strange word came. The man turned out to be a traveler from another world, something Alo had never even heard of.

The other world faded, and images of memories began to implode one on top of another. The boy covered his memories and put up thought shields. *Unbelievable—thought shields inside of thoughts!* Tongue-twisting words, revolving orbs of all colors and spiky balls flying here and there wouldn't allow the boy to concentrate. Once Alo built an impregnable fog, he bluntly burst into the other person's mind, which was lit by rainbow-colored lights, stripes, and waves. There were millions of interconnections of various concepts, images, ideas, and actions. *And I feared it would be a stupid animal.*

The latest thought hadn't yet had time to form when among the colors of the boy's mind a decoy thought of foreign construction broke out. The image of a predator, a tiger, appeared before Alo. Its fangs were bared, its fur was standing on end, and it had sharp claws. The foreign behavioral matrix grew from the cerebral connections and actively pulsated in the center of the section responsible for aggression. In order not to allow the predator to interfere with him installing his units, Alo pulled on the link that held the construction of the matrix and broke the bond. The beast dissolved like a cloud.

Another week and it would have grown into the behavioral centers, where it would already have been impossible to destroy. Even so, it had reached the boy. *Such matrices are found in the traps of ancient mages, but what was it doing in a visitor from another world?*

The boy would remember the rage and strength for the rest of his life. The beast was destroyed, but the memory of it would remain. While the stun of the beast's destruction had not yet worn off, Alo activated the keys to his prefabricated units and began the transfer of the matrices. The blow to his consciousness was so strong, he almost lost control, not only of the other person's mind but of his own.

A funnel formed before the mage's eyes. In an instant, the funnel turned into a tornado, sucking in images, language matrices and written word information packets at an extremely fast pace as the bipolar's brain ate up information. All the Alat matrices were absorbed into the funnel, and Alo activated the Younger Edda, which was swallowed up as quickly as it was activated. Personal skills and the ability to wield mana were drawn into the funnel. For now, only simple ones like a basic power over the elements, but there was no doubt that the entire rest of the mage's personality could be gobbled up just as quickly. Mustering up his willpower, Alo severed the contact and fell out of the trance.

He couldn't feel his body anywhere below the neck. The rest of his body didn't have long left. Andy—the strange name floated into Alo Troi's head—stared at him from the log he was tied to.

"I'm going to die soon. But I have one thing to ask of you. If you can understand me, blink twice," the mage whispered ardently. Andy blinked. "Good. If you are somehow able to survive, and you should go to Orten, tell my wife and daughter my last words. Tell them I love them, tell—"

"Address," the visitor from another world said in a hoarse voice.

Alo licked his parched lips and told him the address, gave his last wishes and paused. His forehead was covered in sweat. Gathering his strength, he continued, "Don't let anyone see that you can read and write."

\*\*\*

"Did it work?" the elf walked up onto the platform. Not waiting for an answer, he touched the mage under the chin. It was as if Alo had been struck by lightning. He saw the image of some battle...and...the elf's death...that he would die of— Alo came undone with uncontrollable laughter.

"Answer me!" Nirel punched him in the face.

"A fortune teller told me ten years ago that my gift of seeing the future would one day awaken; she was right! I get a real pleasure from knowing that before I meet my death, I've seen yours! If only you knew... how you're going to croak!"

"Tell me, you scoundrel!" the elf made a fist.

"His Majesty!" a herald's projected voice rang out. The executioner pushed the unfortunate mage away and ran to greet the King.

Alo's eyes glazed over; parts of his brain began shutting down. The end was near.

"Have you kept your promise?" King Hudd's voice reached him, obviously addressing the hated elf.

"That fat, puffed-up peacock is your king? I feel bad for you..." came a voice right near Alo's ear.

"Oh! Congratulations, Nirel. You've achieved your goal, and I commend you. Twenty lashes to the barbarian so that he might learn to respect the crowned heads."

He then heard the footsteps of many people and again the King's voice, but much closer now. "And this is the mage that taught the little animal to talk? What's wrong with him?"

"He's dying. He's a Tantrian spy, but we've forced him to work for the good of Rimm. And that wolf-boy—" the elf began to explain.

"You're the shameful wolf!" Andy interrupted him.

"It's very nice, isn't it Nirel, that someone over-achieved his goals? The little beast has quite a sharp tongue now," the king's falsely sweet voice came again. "I have a great idea. Glue some fur and a tail on the little animal. Let it be that he might feel like an animal in my menagerie. Put him next to the dragon. Oh, and don't forget the lashes. What do you think, gentlemen?" The court sycophants began all at once to assure the King of the brilliance of his idea.

Their voices got quieter and quieter... Alo saw in his mind a beautiful pair of eyes with a greenish rainbow around the pupils. Hel... She doesn't have blue eyes, cold like mountain ice; it's not true, what they say. The eyes of Death were loving and warm, like those of Alo's grandmother. They called and beckoned him to her, promising peace and solace.

"I'm coming to your judgment, goddess!"

\*\*\*

# Raston, the Royal Menagerie. Andy. One day prior...

The stream of visitors dried up. The supervisor locked the gates. The street sweepers came out onto the square in front of the cage and the enclosure. There were huge piles of rotten food everywhere.

Andy straightened his back and stretched out as much as the shackles allowed. Everything hurt. *Those accursed boys. I'd like to wring their chicken necks...*

He fumbled about around him until he found a whole apple among the corks and rotten fruit, almost untouched by the bad stuff. He rubbed it on the fur on his stomach and bit into it. He was hungry. The daily battle with muteness and the bruises and scrapes from fruit and rocks thrown at him took its toll.

The dragon's chains clinked in his cage. *How long had they been living next to one another already?* It seemed like an eternity, and there had never been any other life—only the enclosure and the cage, and the dragon next door, who turned out to be his friend. Sadly, Andy wasn't able to talk to him; no one removed the chains from his snout. Andy did the talking, and the dragon blinked, shook his head, wiggled his fettered wings or beat his tail.

His neighbor was larger than the skeleton in the bald hill. He was the size of two African elephants stuffed inside a black scaly covering. The scales were of various sizes—the size of a large dinner plate on his chest and stomach; the size of the palm of Andy's hand, on his sides, back, and neck. Occasional smallish spikes protruded along his spine in a single row, which split into two rows by the time it got to his powerful tail. They were about 6 or 8 inches apart there. His mouth, with its protruding tips of his teeth, commanded respect, as did the size of the retractable claws on his front and hind paws. And he had horns—quite formidable horns. However, his frightening appearance masked a kind soul.

As soon as Andy saw the black silhouette in the cage, vague doubts began to cloud his mind. He had seen this life form before somewhere, he was sure. Three days later, when the phony half-wolf learned to counter the muteness spell, they had their first conversation, most of which took place in gestures, signs, and various types of question-and-answer techniques. The rest of it was more fruitful; it confirmed the doubts that were tormenting Andy. The black dragon was the one from the bald hill. At the question, "Why didn't you fly away?" his neighbor shook his wing, and Andy saw a scar that was scabbing over on the membrane. That's how it went with them—questions and silent answers, although sometimes the dragon growled.

The time Andy didn't spend on one-sided conversations, he used to study his magical potential and abilities. A few methods remained in his mind that had been transferred to him from the now deceased Alo Troi. The despised shackles of notrium would not let him really get down to business since they almost cut him off from the source of his energy, but he was still able to gather and accumulate crumbs of mana. When the square was empty, and the guards had retired to their booths, Andy would experiment. The best ways to heal from his wounds after being bombarded with the rotten stuff were determined by the "Three F" method: finger, flame, flight. He learned to light little fires between his fingers and control them according to his will. In their first conversation, he asked the dragon whether mages in this world could create lightning and got a no for an answer. Andy was disappointed. He had studied very meticulously the nature of electricity, which had so lovingly touched him on Earth, and carefully read everything there was to read on that subject. He had wanted to know why he was obliged to stay away from computers.

The previous evening, Andy had come to his first result in this field. The little lightning that came from his finger singed a fat mosquito that was sucking his blood. All the accumulated mana was spent in order to finalize the skill. Another dozen bugs were zapped. He impressed even his black friend in the adjacent cage.

The street sweepers crossed over to the center of the square, collecting garbage near the enclosure.

"Oh! It happened faster today," Andy commented to the dragon, breaking the muteness spell. The dragon blinked in agreement.

"No talking!" the smelly supervisor cried, leaning over the railing.

"Cut it out, scumbag! If you squawk, I'll yell and tell them you're robbing the treasury!" Andy answered lazily. He was tired of their nightly bickering with this thieving miser. The vendors constantly complained that the supervisor wasn't giving them their cut, and he was a royal civil servant.

"Quiet, speak more softly!" the supervisor waved his hands in a quieting gesture.

"Get out of here, don't bother us!" Andy finished his apple and threw the core at the annoying eavesdropper. His shackles didn't allow him to fully chuck it, so it didn't reach the man, but the two-legged rat flinched all the same.

"So, what were you saying?" Andy teased the dragon, making big innocent eyes. The gargantuan creature beat his tail in protest. "Okay, okay, don't get upset. Why don't you tell me, can your chains be removed by magic?"

The dragon shook his head from side to side, meaning no.

"Okay. And you can't break them…"

The dragon tugged with his right front paw, rattling the thick chains.

"And what if you just get one foot free?"

There were energetic nods and blinks. He'd settle for that. They were discussing and working out their escape plan for the third day already.

"And can you fly away?"

The dragon rustled the ends of his wings and blinked in affirmation. Then he stopped blinking and growled, staring off somewhere behind the phony freak of nature. Andy turned around. Surrounded by a whole crowd of admirers, the green-eyed woman from the orc hunt approached the cages.

\*\*\*

## Raston. Andy.

Andy's chest swelled with hatred and rage. *Just let me get at you, you lowlife...*

"Two weeks have gone by, and nothing has changed. The same words. Remove the mongrel's chains and deliver him in one hour to the executioner's chambers," the dandy turned to the obsequious caretaker.

The pungent man rushed to the guards' booth. The other man turned to Andy and smiling, said, "It's time to teach you submission. I'll see you at the chambers, wolf-boy."

He turned sharply, the tails of his cloak whipping at Andy's face, and left the enclosure.

"He seems really mad," Andy told the dragon. The giant nodded. His eyes showed compassion. He knew very well how visits to the executioner's chambers ended.

"It's okay. We'll break through."

The supervisor came back, bringing with him five chain mail-clad guards and the burly blacksmith. A few sturdy hits with the hammer and chisel, and the first rivet came undone. The second one followed equally quickly. The guards pulled the chains, freeing Andy from his tether. Perhaps, he hoped, they would take off the shackles on his wrists and ankles as well. but no such luck. The blacksmith caught the silver coin the supervisor tossed at him and walked away, mumbling into his beard and spitting. The petty miser was again showing his greed.

"Don't pull!" the head guard warned; Andy didn't pull. *What is the point in digging in my heels like a mule? I can't best five guys, and I will yet need my strength.*

The guard poked him in the back with the tip of his spear. "Move!"

Andy got an aching, foreboding feeling. He felt he certain he might die. He heard the loud clamor of chains behind him and glanced back. The dragon was standing in his cage looking at him.

"I'm with you!" the black winged creature's eyes seemed to say.

"Thank you," Andy whispered. He felt a bit better.

"What are you waiting for? Get going!" A new prick with a spear head made him walk faster.

\*\*\*

"Where is he?" a voice came from the street. The dandy appeared just then.

"In the third cell. He was delivered a half hour ago!"

Andy was always surprised by how loudly and clearly the guards spoke, shouting out their answers as if reporting at a parade.

"Get that barbarian to the gallows in the smaller courtyard in fifteen minutes." There was a silence, and in a few seconds, the dandy's voice spoke again, "Why the bulging eyes? I said let's go!"

"Yes, sir!"

*Why does he have to yell like that?*

The guards burst into the cell. Four to one—apparently, they respected and feared this Nirel character. In a moment, they tied Andy up and dragged him to the smaller courtyard where Alo Troi had taught him, and where he met the king. A pair of sullen workers—the ones who had taken away Alo's body ten days before—looked at the sky with cold eyes before extracting a couple of special racks from a barn.

"Nir, the whips?" a broad-shouldered guy with a protruding brow asked the dandy. "Perhaps you should herd the little wolf first with the whips?"

"I'm feeling fatigued, today, Migur." Nirel sat down on the steps of the platform and extended his long legs. "As the royal executioner, I have to deal with all kinds of riff raff."

"Can I do it?"

"Do you need that, Migur? You're an apprentice! Sanchez is just as capable of waving a whip around." Nirel pointed at the guard.

Andy followed the direction he was indicating and saw a barrel on two legs with a conical helmet on top. The guard was sitting on a small bench drinking beer from a large mug.

Migur frowned skeptically.

"But if you're just itching to, I'll let you get some practice," Nirel said.

Upon Migur's command, the gloomy men threaded a long chain into the rings on Andy's shackles and tied him to a tall post that was impounded in the ground in the middle of the courtyard. *Like a dog on a chain,* Andy thought, glancing at his fifteen-foot-long leash.

Migur undressed to the waist and took the light whip in his hand; the assistant planned to amuse himself a bit, but not beat Andy to death. The lashing began. Strike, recoil, strike, recoil. Andy covered himself with his hands and dodged, jumping to the side as much as possible with the chain and the shackles on his ankles. The burning blows from the whip rained down on him, and the guards began to bet out loud on whether the little beast would be able to dodge or not and where Migur would strike next.

Rage bubbled inside Andy. He hit his left side on the post and wasn't able to jump out of the way of a biting blow to his shoulder. Migur darted one way; Andy ran the other.

A plan in mind, he retreated to the post. The apprentice, who had been dashing here and there, lowered his guard. *Closer, closer now...* He needed an abundance of chain. The whip whistled and Andy, instead of dodging, jumped forward. Migur had gotten carried away with beating his defenseless victim and therefore had no time to react to the lunge. A loop of the chain encircled his thick neck. Andy's body fired forward and sharply downward. The leash didn't let him get very far away, but he wasn't really trying. He lay on the trampled dirt and looked at the dead apprentice.

The guards, Nirel, and the gloomy men leaped to their feet and stared at the dead body in stunned silence. "Grab that boy! Put him on the racks! Look alive!" Nirel's sharp cry broke the silence. The frozen people sprang into action.

They lifted Andy up by kicking him, took the chain off, and in less than three minutes, he was lying on a rack. The guards brought a ramp on wheels and removed the apprentice's body. Tough luck, Migur.

"Tear the wolf's fur off of him."

Someone's hands ripped the fur off of Andy, making him cry out in pain; the glue was quite strong.

"To my chambers, NOW!" Nirel ordered, causing the skinny guard to bolt upright. "Bring that valise. Find the blacksmith, I need him to remove the shackles. Notrium dulls the effects of the spell."

***

The executioner's chambers were a flurry of activity. The blacksmith appeared—the same bearded man from the enclosure. "First cuff him, then uncuff him...," he said, mumbling into his beard and swearing. He began to beat at the rivets. He held out his hand when he had finished the job.

"Get out of here!" Nirel exploded at him. A pair of guards practically kicked the hammer-and-anvil-wielding man off the premises.

"I hope everything goes wrong for you!" he yelled back from beyond the fence.

They tied Andy down by his arms and legs. What a relief now that the notrium had been removed. The world, full of energy, opened up before him. Latching on to the external replenishment, he missed it when Hurga the orc appeared, and the enraged executioner began his witchcraft. Nirel grabbed a small box from inside his valise and handed it to the humongous orc.

"Put the powder from the black mushroom spores here, and the dried poisonous Birim flies. I'll beat, you pour!" he explained after Hurga's questioning *moo*. The orc's eyebrows crawled upward. A whip with a black handle made of bone appeared in Nirel's hands. Runes decorated the handle all around. He whispered quietly, and the whip blazed with a living flame. There was a quick whistle, and Andy's back burned with unbearable pain.

"Pour it!" Nirel cried. Andy's scream of insane pain could be heard in the yard outside. Another blow. "Pour! I'll teach you, wolf-scum, to obey! Does it hurt? Pour!"

The orc held out the empty box, and Nirel stopped, grabbed Andy by the chin, bloody from biting his lip, and smiled a shark's smile. "Well, didn't pass out. A strong little wolf you are."

"I'm a wolf, and you're a dog. That's a good name for you. Nir-Nir, come 'ere, boy, lick the king's boot. I'll die a wolf, free at heart, but you'll croak like a dog on a chain," Andy wheezed, turning his head toward the cloudy dark stain on his blood-red back.

"And they'll bury you in the backyard, spitting in the grave. The king has lots of dogs on chains! No one'll notice one less flea-bitten mutt in the pack." Andy wasn't afraid. He mentally prepared himself to die as his torturer laughed mockingly.

"Do you know what a delayed-action spell is? No? You will! Tomorrow, I'll start opening your scabs and scars. Slowly, one scar a day. I don't need you to die right away! I won't even have to touch you. Magic is a terrifying thing in capable hands."

Andy said nothing. If he guessed correctly, this process would be long and torturous. The black dust and fiery whip have to mean something, but what? The orc, when he was told about the flies, widened his eyes. That meant his future sessions would be linked to today's mutilation.

\*\*\*

Irina had liked to read all kinds of fantasy fiction. Sometimes, for Andy, she would print out some of the books she dug up online and liked. He had read one once; he didn't remember the name or most of the plot, but he remembered that there was a part where the main heroine had to undergo some peculiar psychological training in which she was humiliated, abused and pushed down to the very rock bottom, then brought back up to a normal human state. When he read it, Andy found it truly fantastic.

Once broken, people don't become normal people again. Fear remains in their eyes to the end of their lives. Once they let themselves go there, there was no coming back; the human person was gone. He had seen enough of those whining creatures in the cells with him to know.

A breeze of fresh air blew by, bringing with it the booming sound of thunder. A storm was coming.

Nirel patted the silent Andy on the head and laughed a satisfied laugh. "I see you've realized what's going on. You understand what'll become of you?"

He squatted in front of Andy, who spat in his sneering face. Andy got a punch in response that knocked out a couple of teeth before Nirel extracted a batiste handkerchief from the cuff of his coat and wiped the blood spatter from his cheek. Then he hit Andy again; Andy spat again, with more bits of teeth.

"I see you don't get it yet!" Nirel said. "No matter! We have a lot of time. You'll understand yet. Why are you jerking like that?"

\*\*\*

## Raston. Nirel.

Nirel noticed how the little wolf jerked on the rack when the lightning struck. Next to him, Hurga the orc covered his head with his hands. Afraid of the storm, the orc bellowed and ran to the inner chambers. *What do they call that orc god of the sky and of rage, with arms of lightning, the one gray orcs are afraid of? The name was on the tip of his tongue, but he just couldn't think of it. Targ take it. The little wolf, raised by orcs, is afraid of lightning? I'll arrange for him to meet this feared heathen god of his!*

Nirel called the guards and ordered them to drag the boy to the observation deck of the Mages' Tower in the royal palace. There's a cage there, and he'd be closer to the sky. If their god of lightning killed him, then that would be his fate. Nirel could tell the King and the Princess it was the goddesses' will.

The guards removed his body, riddled with black scars, from the rack and took Andy toward the palace complex. The Mages' Tower made up part of the same architectural composition as the palace, although it stood off to the side a bit from the main buildings.

Nirel gave his last orders, packed his valise and went to the stables, deciding he'd had enough for the day.

\*\*\*

The doorman at the gates of his villa bowed low and took the reins. The whole way home, the elf had been bothered by doubts over whether he had made good decisions that day. *Something's off. But what?* He didn't grieve Migur; he died like a dog, but that was one less human in the world, and they were still multiplying like rabbits. *Why was it such an emotional shock then?*

He began to sort out the events one by one. He might have been in Migur's place if he had agreed to the apprentice's first suggestion. It would have been a stupid way to die, and the orc's brat had earned some respect. He was only a boy, but he held his own like a man. *He is straight as an arrow, more worthy than all my acquaintances from Rimm, with pure and unadulterated rage and contempt. It's a shame to break him, but I have to for Taliza's sake.*

"Your brother is here to see you, sir." The old housekeeper met Nirel on the front steps.

*Brother? I don't have a brother,* Nirel thought. *Targ take me, Radel? Radel's here? Has he picked up on Nim's trail?*

"Is he in the parlor, Eliz?"

"In the fireplace room, sir. I told the cook to heat some wine and make your brother a fruit salad. Let me remind you that dinner is in an hour, please don't be late." Eliz cast Nirel a strict glance, but changed the subject, "Something's going to happen. A dry thunderstorm at the end of the week is a bad sign."

Nirel, running up the stairs two-by-two, hurried to the second floor and stopped in front of an oak door to the fireplace room. His heart beat fast, his mouth was dry. Taking a deep breath and calming his upset nerves, he pushed the door open and stepped inside, activating a curtain of silence with a slight wave of his hand.

Radel leaped from his deep comfy armchair and took two steps to meet Nirel. His unfinished glass of wine rested on the mantle.

"Rad!"

"Nir!"

The brothers managed a choppy embrace.

"Something big has happened. Have you found a trace of Nim?" Nirel immediately switched to the matter that troubled him.

Rad didn't say anything, staring at the wall. But then Nirel noticed bags under his eyes and the gray, earthy hue of his guest's skin. With a foreboding feeling, his heart began to pound and ache in his chest. "What happened?"

"I found Nim." Rad's tone of voice as he said this was so full of bitterness that Nirel felt no joy at the news of his sister's discovery.

"She's...dead?"

"Yes."

Nirel's legs turned to jelly beneath him. The executioner dropped to the floor. A sharp, three-sided blade had struck at the chink in his armor.

Elves always take great care when it comes to their relatives; their long lives and the rare birth of children forced them to hold onto their family. No one had ever been closer to him than his sister. They were twins, such an incredibly rare phenomenon; their birth was quite the event. But it wasn't celebrated anywhere. No one would celebrate the birth of changelings.

Changeling babies, from inside their mother's womb, could appear human. They never knew love or care from their parents but were raised in a closed center deep in the Forest. They were brought up to be a secret weapon—spies, managing the interests of the perpetually green canopy. He and his sister knew no other life and believed everything that was taught to them as the sacred truth. They liked the same things and the same books, they never fought, and they understood one another without words.

Thirty years had gone by in the blink of an eye. They learned to be human but to remain elves faithful to the Forest, and they were sent out into a foreign world. Radel and Nim, playing the roles of newlyweds, were sent to the Patskoi Empire, while Nirel settled down in Meriya.

Ten years went by, and Rad and his sister had gotten married for real. Later, Nirel was sent to Rimm, and one year ago, Nim went missing. She had traveled to Ronmir, a city in the North of the empire. She was traveling along the passenger's diligence road when bandits seized the carriage. Rad organized search parties... Nirel lived in expectation of good news for a whole year, fostering hope that Nim was alive, that she was being held in a prison, and her captors were waiting for a ransom to be paid by her relatives, or—he tried to cast the thought out—she had been sold into a harem. It was his daily personal torture that made him bitter and hate-filled toward humans.

Nirel's world crumbled. "How did she die?"

"At my hands. I killed your sister, my wife." Rad was horrible to look at.

"What!" Nirel grabbed a knife.

"Listen to me! LISTEN TO ME!" His guest flung the weapon from his hands with a kick, grabbed Nirel by the lapels of his camisole and fell to the floor next to him.

"Speak..." Nirel allowed, in a hoarse whisper.

Radel began to tell the story, and the longer he spoke, the darker and gloomier the executioner's face became. He didn't want to believe what he heard, but his rational mind knew every word from the first to the last was pure truth.

"But His Lordship promised me he would put every effort into the searches!" he cried, his voice breaking.

"His Lordship is a politician. An hour later, he forgot you existed."

"Can it be that no one continued looking? She has the aura of a purebred elf!" Nirel continued to search for answers.

"Can you hear yourself? Who would continue searching for a living doll after she's been given a horse-sized dose of kolod and crossed the boundary of intellect? An obedient doll with primitive instincts, who can't keep a thought in her head and wants only to give birth? You can't imagine what I had to go through to break into the wolf preparation center and come back out alive! The guard there was rummaging around the entire territory with her nose, searching for her wolf-queen's killer! Guess who the project's curator is? Your own dearly beloved, His Lordship!"

Quiet reigned in the room, disturbed only by the choppy breathing of two elves, floored by grief, and the crackling of logs in the fireplace.

Nirel picked the knife up off the floor and cut a slit in his left palm with it. His life had a new purpose. "I'll get my revenge on His Lordship and the Forest for what they've done to us."

Radel's bloody palm clasped his. "I will avenge her with you. What do you plan to do?"

"I don't know yet. You should go back to the Forest and find out anything you can about His Lordship Ratela. Gain his trust and try to get into his inner circle. He has a daughter, we can strike at her. Let him feel what I am feeling now!"

There was a knock at the door; the curtain allowed sounds from the outside in, just not the other way around.

"Sir, dinner is served." Eliz, as always, was punctual.

The elderly housekeeper had not yet finished speaking when there came a loud pounding sound of fists banging on the door.

"Sir! Sir! The palace!" it was the gatekeeper's voice.

"What about the palace?"

"There's a fire! The central complex is burning!"

"Quickly saddle up Vulcan!"

The brothers ran out to the balcony to a view of the royal residence. Against a backdrop of gray clouds and flashing lightning, pillars of black and white smoke arose from the palace.

***

# Raston. Andy.

They shoved Andy into a cage. The lock clicked loudly. Scoffing merrily, the guards descended to their look-out posts. He was left on the small square alone. *How nice it is to lie on cold stone sometimes…*

He had been carried like a sack of potatoes on the guards' shoulders all the way there. They hadn't shackled him; there was no reason. The prisoner was no more dangerous than a kitten in the state he was in. In the middle of a spiral staircase, the guards tapped out and threw their load on the floor. The second half of the way, they dragged him behind themselves. Some walkers on that staircase fell off to the side and tumble down head over heels; he was fortunate enough to make it to the top of the stone steps, counting them with his rear end and with his striped back.

It was pleasant in the cage. It was cool, and a fresh breeze was blowing, carrying away the stench Andy bore. He had lived ten days in wolf's clothing without being able to wash. He was flea-bitten, and suspected fleas weren't the only ones chowing down on him. He dreamed of a hot bath with a leafy birch branch to help him exfoliate... and tried to forget how the rain on his wolf's fur made it stink like urine. He wished he could eat a piece of fried beef with a thin crunchy outer layer and a sweet juicy center, or even a piece of bread, rye, which smelled like home. *Where was home, anyway?*

Two of the exhibits in the menagerie never got fed—the dragon, of course, and him. For him, they just pointed to the scraps all around, saying, "Choose what you like. If you don't like these, wait until tomorrow, and they'll throw others at you." True, they weren't stingy when it came to water. They put the enclosure near a fake stream, but that was the effort of the builder, not the supervisor.

Andy carefully turned over on his back. He pressed his elbows to the ground as a safeguard. The cold stone placated his burning back a bit. Lightning struck, followed by a deafening clap of thunder. There they were, the bolts of energy breaking through, one tiny little bit of lightning would be more than enough... Andy covered his eyes and concentrated.

*I don't get it! The sources of mana are right there, nothing is overarching the energy. It's just that something troublesome has crawled onto the outer edges, something annoying like the buzz of a mosquito in my ear. Forgetting about the pain on his back, he turned over to his stomach again and, stretching out his knees, crawled over to the bars. It was the familiar gray metal, gray as a rainy day, but they weren't blocking his magic. Did they forget to cast the spell?*

A blinding flash and a clap of thunder close to the ground jolted on the floor; the lightning had hit the tall metal spire on the other side of the square across from the cage. Tiny discharges of energy ran down the bars. *Now that's something!*

"I love thunderstorms at the beginning of May!" That's why the notrium wasn't hindering the magic; the electricity in the atmosphere had destroyed or countered the spell.

Andy wanted to smother the black cloud with kisses. A burning thirst for action took possession of him. He had to strike now. With a silent prayer that the capricious lady wouldn't turn her back on him once more, Andy began to go into a trance. Remembering what he had done in the wagon, he bathed himself in the familiar energy waterfall, but this time, he didn't limit himself in any way. Energy flowed throughout his whole body. His magical reserves began to replenish within him.

Without leaving his trance, Andy approached the bars and carefully examined all the places where they were reinforced and where the bars were sealed. The black barn padlock was the weak spot. He slid his right hand through the bars, concentrated, and let the potential come about... A small, short bolt of lightning came from his pointer finger. *Don't stop!*

*More, more!* The curved part of the lock began to glow red-hot. *Better not touch the bars.*

"Aaaah!" leaning against the door and burning himself until he blistered, Andy continued to pummel the lock with bolts. *More, more!* His eyes watered, but he knew he mustn't stop. Clinking briefly, the curved little bar broke and fell down. *I did it! I'm free!*

Andy darted over to the fence around the square and looked down. Below, pairs of guards paced back and forth. There was a guard in the tower, too. It was too soon to rejoice; he had to think of something. A hot little flame began to tremble between his fingers from the sudden frenzy. *That was it! He had to scorch something.* The hulk of the palace towered before his eyes. *Hmm, wouldn't that be a nice gift for the king and some work for the guards to do? How do they put out fires here? By magic or do they call in firefighters?*

Andy ran back and forth along the edge of the square. He wasn't afraid of the guards; they wouldn't be back until the storm passed. They had run from the square painfully fast, and the elements were in no hurry to tone it down. Andy created a small flame, took shelter behind the spikes of the fence, and sent it toward the closest palace wing. The flame flew toward the building and went out when it hit an invisible defense. *That's bad, very bad. What now? Send it crawling through the chimneys? Yes! I can enter through the chimneys.*

"You're a genius!" Andy praised himself. A new spot of flame flew toward a chimney pipe and plunged downward unhindered. In a few minutes, unnoticed against the backdrop of lightning, a dozen encapsulated spots of fire were flying toward the main palace complex.

"Hey, Alo! Why did you give me so little? But for what you did give, thank you!" The spots flew into the chimneys, steered by Andy's will. Then it was time to let the salamander loose. Nothing happened for five minutes, and then he heard screams coming from below. It was burning well and had engulfed a third of the closest wing already. Thick black smoke tumbled out the windows where people were tearing about.

Andy tore off toward the staircase. His energy-filled body required movement, but he could feel that it was only temporary. Soon the recoil would come, and his wounded back would call attention to itself with a redoubled force. He would have to pay for everything.

Then, racing from the top down to the second platform, Andy ran into an old mage coming up to meet him. The man had a thick white beard and a strange metal rod in the shape of five clawed fingers in his left hand. Andy grabbed a torch from the wall and went at the head of the old mage with zeal. The mage was knocked out cold. The rod fell onto the stairs. *I'll take that; could come in handy.*

Andy's decoy worked. The palace was going up in smoke in several different places already; dozens of people were rushing around and yelling like mad. It was a true panic, with all that entailed. It was also fortunate that the staff and the mages left the palace for the city at night. No one was there to notice his part in the disaster, and the king wouldn't be able to count on putting out the fire by magical means.

Andy ran to the menagerie. He could feel his time running out. As he passed the stables and the blacksmith, he stopped for a hammer. A horseman came galloping by from behind the stables. Andy let loose a flash of lightning that struck the rider in the chest, then bashed his face with the clawed rod, leaving several stripes in its wake. With a moan, the rider crashed from the saddle to the ground, and Andy rushed over to him. *Nirel!* Before Andy could deliver another blow, Nirel's stallion rose in front of him, defending its master. Andy grabbed the hammer and ran.

The dragon's face showed such surprise at the sight of naked Andy with a hammer over his shoulder that Andy involuntarily glanced down at himself. "I said we'd break through!" he called joyfully to the scaly prisoner, and with a few blows, knocked the pin from the anchor of the first chain. "Get your wings in gear, in the meantime, we'll have to skedaddle as fast as your wings can carry us!" He finished the other pin; one paw was free.

"Don't wiggle, I'm gonna get your other leg out," Andy turned to the dragon. People were running toward the menagerie from the palace. An arrow pierced the ground right next to him. Another couple of blows with the hammer. *That's it, the paw is free!* "Break the chains, we've gotta scram! His peacock majesty won't forgive me for burning his house down!"

Suddenly, Andy was hit with excruciating pain as arrows with green feathers whistled all around him; the watchmen from the wild park appeared at the latticework fence around the menagerie. A strong blow to the back just above the waist floored Andy. He wanted to dart out of the way, but his legs weren't working. He couldn't feel his body below the waist at all. He stretched his arm around his back, touching the shaft of the arrow buried in him.

With a loud cracking sound, the dragon's cage burst into pieces. Pieces of the powerful chains flew into the watchmen and guards, maiming and killing some of them. A long tongue of flame swept the remaining men away.

"Get on!" the dragon cried in a strong bass. He put out his right front leg for Andy to climb on. "A-rei, what's wrong?|

The dragon's head appeared over Andy, pouring his back and legs with dark blood from the broken chain. The dragon carefully pulled on the arrow. The shaft easily parted with the leaf-shaped tip which remained in the wound.

"Hold on!" he shouted to Andy, right in his ear, and carefully lifted him from the ground. His gigantic wings spread open, and his back legs pushed him off the ground. The dragon took flight, gently squeezing the fragile human body to his wide chest. "Hang in there, A-rei."

"My name is Andy. Don't call me a wolf."

\*\*\*

## The Marble Mountains, No Man's Land, the Valley of a Thousand Streams.

The mighty beating of enormous wings sounded above the house, and the earth shook. "Jagirra! Jagirrr-aah! Are you home? Jagirra!" Karegar's deep voice called.

Jagirra placed a large bottle of extract of arachnid on the ledge, wiped her hands on a towel and went into the hallway. *Finally!* Her heart beat joyfully. The elf wiped away a tear or two. *I'll let him have it now, I will, the old black fart! I'll teach him to disappear for three weeks!* She thought she would lose her mind from the waiting.

"Well, look what the cat dragged in! Yelling my name... Why don't you fly back to wherever it is you've been all this time!" the herbalist scolded, opening the door. The smell of wet dog assailed her elven nose, along with a whole bouquet of other scents; she got queasy. "What garbage dump have you been hanging out in? Go clean yourself up!"

Jagirra slammed the door, which was immediately smashed into splinters by the dragon's claws.

"Are you crazy!?" the enraged woman dashed out the door. A fireball burned in her right hand, lighting up the field in front of her house. "You asked for—."

The bright fireball lit up the dragon, and the herbalist was taken aback. Karegar had turned into a sorry sight with shabby scales on his legs and neck, his whole face covered in dried blood, and in his right paw, close to his chest, he was holding some human.

"Help, Jaga..."

\*\*\*

Surrounding him like a tight cocoon, some sort of whitish cloud swirled around Andy. Breaking the silence, he heard two voices, as if a far-away echo. He knew one of them—the dragon's resounding bass. The other belonged to a female.

"Karegar, you know he'll perish; there's nothing we can do to help him!" the woman said in a pleasant alto.

*The dragon's name is Karegar. It suits him. A black dragon. Who'll perish? Me?* Andy thought. *I want to live! I want to go home!*

"He's still alive and is not ready at all to face Hel's judgment."

A cool palm laid on Andy's forehead, the white shroud dissolved; he opened his eyes and saw an elderly woman.

*A queen! Someone like her must be a queen from a fairy tale. You could tell.* She had an oval-shaped face, a long thin nose, curved brows and big, dark blue, almond-shaped eyes. She was extremely beautiful, her silver hair swept into a tight braid. Topaz sparkled in the tip of her pointy pierced left ear. *An elf, the queen of the elves!* Behind her, Karegar looked at Andy with a worried look.

"Like what you see?" she asked, reading all his emotions. She offered him a warm, open smile.

"Yes. You're very beautiful." Andy didn't try to evade the question and asked right away, "Do I really have no chance at all?"

The elf turned away. She extracted a white handkerchief from the waist of her simple linen dress and, wiping her hands, answered.

"Your spine is broken. The tip went right between two vertebrae. I've blocked all your painful sensations for now, but not for long. That's not the worst of it. Your scars are traces of a delayed-action spell. Whoever tortured you added poison from Birim flies and black mushrooms into your wounds. You don't have any immunity against any sickness now. Do you know what immunity is?" Andy nodded. It was another word in Alat, a different one, but he understood it to mean just that.

"Your body can no longer fight illness and even the simplest little cold would be fatal to you. We've removed the arrow tip. You've lived this long because dragon's blood got on your wound, which neutralized the Watchmen's poison. Karegar, why didn't you remove it right away?"

"With what?" the dragon boomed. "This?" he showed his claws. "I would have pulled it out along with the boy's soul. No blood would have helped."

The elf leaned toward Andy once again. "Was it an elf that tortured you?"

"No, a human."

"That's strange. Forest elves use that torture method, and I'm willing to bet it was actually an elf. It's a spell interweave too complicated for humans. The low-life. I see you're not at all afraid of the word death, which I find quite troubling. Young people, your age should think differently about mortality. How old are you?"

"Sixteen. I'm not afraid of death. Something happened to me, and I changed; I can't explain it. Three weeks ago, I couldn't have imagined that I could kill someone, and now there's been so many deaths at my hands, I can't count them right away. But I don't feel any pangs of conscience. That's strange for me...it was strange.

"I'm not afraid to die, but I really want to live. I have a lot going on and…." Andy fell silent, not knowing whether to speak up or not. Karegar and the elf said nothing, respecting his decision. "I really want to return to my world; I'm not from here. And I want revenge on Nirel. One thing makes me glad; I zapped some lightning in his chest."

Karegar snickered, picturing it, and the elf grew pensive. His words about being from another world had no effect on them at all.

"I just can't accept it, Jaga. I can't have death on my conscience twice! Please understand!"

"Lightning?" Jagirra asked after a long pause, ignoring the dragon. "Show me."

Andy relaxed, slipping into a trance in his already familiar fashion. He extended his arm to the side, and a short bolt of lightning smashed a low tree trunk five feet away into small bits and dust.

Jaga once again turned thoughtful, periodically casting quick glances at either Andy or Karegar, who paced in circles.

"I could be wrong, but when he went into a trance, I saw all the elements in his aura. We could try the Ritual," she said, drawing out the last word a little.

The dragon stopped in his tracks and jerked his tail sharply, knocking down two young birch trees. His long claws came out and cut up the turf he was standing on.

"You know about the incarnation Ritual?" Jaga nodded. "All right, let's!"

"What incarnation ritual?" Andy asked.

"It's a Ritual—" Jagirra began, but Karegar interrupted her.

"I suggest you become a dragon! You'll be the first person in three thousand years to complete the incarnation Ritual!" Karegar began dancing on the spot. A slap to the paw with a towel made him stand still. Andy smiled watching them. Jaga's cheeks became flushed as if she had been caught kissing the dragon.

"You could…eh…" Andy couldn't formulate his thought.

"You could die…" The elf understood him without words. "There's a fifty percent chance of that, but without the Ritual, you have no chance at all."

"How does the incarnation work?"

Jagirra asked about what knowledge Andy had of the human body. He explained that his grandmother had been a doctor—a healer in their world—and he had been looking at medical textbooks for several years already. Thanks to Alo, he was fluent enough in their language to translate his previous knowledge.

Jagirra nodded. "The point of the Ritual is to infuse the human with a special extract taken from a special gland in the dragon. There are some other ingredients, too, that you don't need to know about. What's important is that you meet two conditions: a lack of immunity and the ability to accept external energy streams.

"During the Ritual, nature and magic come together to infuse every part of the human with this special mixture. The human begins to change, every cell in his body rewired by the elixir until his human body is transformed into one of the winged creatures. There must be no immunity within the human body to fight the transformation.

"During the ritual, the person repeats all the dragon's stages of life— outside the womb. As skeletal and skin changes take place, he won't be able to move from the spot. An influx of energy and constant monitoring by others are required at all stages. Dragons' beings are half-magical, and if the person can't take on external energy, well, you understand... The problem is that no one has ever performed the incarnation with humans or elves older than five years old. That is, they performed it, but..."

"Why not?" Andy asked.

"Older children cannot take on external energy, and if they can, they generally can't control most of it, and with their larger bodies, most can't endure the pain. When incarnation takes place, the person undergoes horrible, excruciating pain. The older the person, the more the body fights the change. You're a match for almost all the main parameters, except age and weight. Morally, you're prepared to die, but you want to survive even more. You don't have any immunity, and your physical reaction is suppressed. Do you agree to try?"

"I agree!" Andy had decided during the lecture. He wanted to live, regardless the form.

"I'll get ready and prepare the ingredients. And you," she pointed at Karegar, "take the boy to the hot springs and wash him and yourself well. He needs to be ready in five hours."

Jaga leaned over Andy and ran her hands through her hair, her fingers parting the gray locks.

*** 

Karegar was groaning in the meadow in front of the cave; Jaga had cut off a couple of scales at the base of his neck and stuck a magical silver tube with a collection instrument at the tip under the scruff of his neck. Another "prick" had been done at the base of his tail.

On a silver tray near the plank Andy was lying on, Jaga laid syringes with silver needles. Only instead of little tubes, they had specially formed intestines. In silver-plated flasks covered with a magical glimmer visible to the naked eye, dragon's blood mixed with extracts from his glands and brain.

"Are you ready?" Andy closed his eyes. "It won't hurt when I insert the tube; I'll block any unpleasant sensations. But later on.... The most important thing is to endure and live through the recreation of your nervous system. The pain will be terrible. If you can survive that, consider yourself a dragon. The process of building the body is a long one."

Jaga lifted the "shot."

He felt a slight prick at the base of his neck and the middle portion of his spine, and then an injection into the vein in his left hand.

\*\*\*

The pain swept over him in waves, with each wave higher than the last. He was drowning in an ocean of pain, and in order not to lose himself in that hellish world, Andy created a point that he called "I" and held on to it as to a lifesaver. He didn't know how long the painful torment lasted, but at some point, the red ocean disappeared and he opened his eyes.

It was as if he were viewing the world around him in a fun-house mirror covered in tulle. The elf leaned over him. She had bags under her eyes, red capillaries showing in the whites of her eyes, and wrinkles from fatigue on her face. She stroked Andy's forehead and smiled.

"You've done it. We've done it. Happy birthday, dragon. Now, rest."

# PART 5: WINGS ON MY BACK.

## The Marble Mountains, No Man's Land, the Valley of a Thousand Streams.

"Are you awake already?"

"I wasn't asleep." Andy looked at Jagirra. Judging by her appearance, she hadn't been sleeping either. The same fatigue that was written on her face a few hours ago was still there. The one thing that had changed was her dress and hairdo. Her hair was now braided into several braids, intricately intertwined. Instead of yesterday's dress, the elf wore a colorful jumper and apron. Karegar slept at the entrance to the cave. His noisy breathing called to mind a blacksmith's bellows.

"Now you'll need to sleep as much as possible."

"The life of a lazy cat. Eat, sleep. Sleep, eat. A depressing prospect."

"Get used to it. There's no way to change anything now. You'll have to live that way for a couple months." Jagirra rolled a wide block of wood over to his couch and sat down beside him, resting her hands on her knees.

"I can't get used to the fact that I'm turning into a dragon." Andy shrugged and stared at the cave roof, which was supported by stalagmites.

The elf laughed, threw the blanket aside and turned him to his left side. Andy was surprised by the strength of her elegant little arms. Jagirra examined his back, disfigured by scars, and touched the injection sites with her fingers. She squeezed the pink scar from the where the arrow had entered.

"Progress is visible. Toward dinner time or late tonight at the latest, you'll feel your rear becoming sinewy. Remarkable regeneration is taking place. Honestly, I just about buried you. The changes in the nervous system should go on for not more than twenty-four hours, and it's been four days. What was I supposed to think? But Karegar was always by your side and didn't allow me to walk away for a minute. He…he believed in you." Jaga went silent and looked at the sleeping dragon.

Andy tried to remember her description of the process, but when he asked her questions, she didn't seem to understand some of his terms for the body.

Jagirra soothed him and said, "Think for a minute and say them in Alat. You can't, can you?" the elf saw his struggle. "I could tell right away that your knowledge of the language had been planted through unnatural means, but the one who did it was a true master of his trade. My mentor was a pretty good sharp wit, so I know a thing or two about this. Unfortunately, the Ritual robbed you of that mage's hard work."

"What should I do?" Andy asked in alarm.

"Nothing. Just read good books, have conversations in Alat more often, and in a year from now, everything will be different for you, all by itself." Jagirra smiled.

"I have another question."

"Ask."

"Karegar said I was the first person to undergo the Ritual in three thousand years. Why? Is it so hard to find candidates for this? It worked on me…"

"You know, I didn't expect these kinds of questions from a teenager." Jagirra tucked the blanket under him at his chest and said nothing. Andy waited patiently for her to answer. It was impossible to find anything out from the look on her face, but he suspected she was thinking hard about something because she avoided eye contact.

"It's harder than you can possibly imagine. Even if you don't count the limitations I was telling you about, there's a whole pile of other barriers. Like the existence or lack thereof of a mage who can perform the preparatory work; there are no more left after certain tragic events three millennia ago. I suspect I'm the last that kind in Ilanta. Second, the recipient should be a mage who unites all the elements within himself. Do you know how many fully universal mages there are? One in thirty thousand! Both you and I am incredibly lucky to be a part of that infinitesimal percentage of people capable of carrying out the incarnation."

"And what happened three thousand years ago?"

"Let's be done with questions for today, okay? I promise we'll tell you about what happened, definitely, because your life will be directly connected to all of that. Now, what you need to think about is how to learn settage as fast as you can. The physical changes that will begin in a day or two are part of a long and painful process, interconnected with several unpleasant aspects, and a lot depends on your ability to immerse yourself in your inner space and control your body functions. We'll begin lessons after you get some sleep."

The elf suddenly recalled something and pulled a dull metallic coin-shaped object about as big as her palm from the folds of her jumper. "It's a kran and allows you to record your memories and keep a diary. I'll show you how it works. You'll need it. Now, sleep." Jagirra touched Andy's forehead ever so slightly, and he collapsed, melting into a soft, cozy fog where pain and suffering did not exist.

*Jaga spoon-feeds me! So awful! 'Take a bite for Mommy, take a bite for Daddy. Don't spit it out. It's such yummy porridge, I'd eat it myself!' Ugh! I would never eat porridge flavored with a good portion of crushed chalk, bone flour, and charcoal ashes if it weren't for this beastly appetite of mine... I'm gagging, but I'm eating. The bodily changes she was talking about didn't start two days later; sooner than that. Jaga was wrong. All my joints are breaking and turning, my back's getting wrung out like a wet rag, my elbows are swollen to the size of my knees, and my fingers are like sausages. It hurts to move my jaw. They attached the kran to my temple; Jaga gave me her coin. Now, I'm like an autonomous module; I lay on this block of wood and think...*

*Regarding my complaints of this beastly, hellish itching at my tailbone, Karegar said, "It's nothing. You're just starting to grow a tail." Oh geez, if only I could scratch it. But my arms won't budge. "It's an unpleasant part," he said. Kill me now!*
*Just deal with it. Good things come to those who wait. My skeleton is being rebuilt. Soon, all my organs will be rebuilt, and then... I'm afraid to think what it'll be like then.*

*It's day three of Jaga getting me into a state of settage. It's awesome! It's a cool thingamabob; you look at your own insides. There are rivers of blood, everything around you is burning, moving, it's as if the energy channels are glowing with high-voltage power lines. I thought the channels follow nerve cords, as Jaga says, but I'm different from other dragons and mages. I have a separate system complete with loops and distribution of currents. The channels connect to the cords through thousands and millions of tiny capillaries; it's like a whole galaxy lighting up. Really neat. The points of energy accumulation and my magical reserves, well, they look like gigantic cisterns. True, they only contain a small drop. My granny elf is amazed. What do I need such a container for? As if I know? On the other hand, who couldn't use some extra for a rainy day? Having some extra ammunition just in case won't hurt.*

*Every time I dive in, she breaks the trip down into stages and makes me memorize the sequence for how to do it. She doesn't believe that I already remembered everything from the second time and have been taking dips of my own. "That's impossible! The changes facilitate an improvement in memory, but not to that extent!" But whatever. She promises that, in a week, she'll explain and show me how to use my body. I wish it were sooner; I can't take it anymore.*

*It's getting cold out. I thought it was summer year-round here. It turns out there is a winter, but probably the kind they have* in tropical countries. It's cooling off and starting to rain often; there's a little snow up in the mountains. But it doesn't bring me any relief. My body is breaking and twisting beyond belief. It's like living in a meat mincer every day. How long can this go on? A month has gone by in a flash. Settage is good, but I can't be there all the time. You alleviate one nerve ending, another starts acting up, and it goes on like that for hours. And yet, I rush into it very quickly and easily now. But there's no point to it.

Yesterday, my pelvic bones cracked, and my ribs started to chatter. My last teeth fell out three days ago. We've cut out the lessons for now; I'm training myself. Before I lost my voice, Jaga showed me a couple techniques for using true vision. That's another thing; I spent two days getting the hang of the simplest technique. Today it finally worked out. To make it stick, all day today, I've been using only true vision. It's like looking at the world through snake eyes. You see heat and energy contours. All objects glow in a unique way, and there are these strange pulsating lines around things. Jaga says those are the world's energetic connections. I believe that because outside the cave I think I can sense a magnetic field. You could send me to Canada now like a goose, I wouldn't get lost.

It's interesting to look at Dad's aura; it's big and glows with all colors of the rainbow. Will mine be like that? Too bad I can't ask for the time being. Karegar doesn't know that's what I call him in my head. I never thought a dragon would act like a soccer mom—always buzzing around me and fussing over me—but he does. Jaga looks at my four-legged nurse and laughs, but I can see it in her eyes, it's as if her heart's being ripped out and she's full of longing. It's impossible to tell anything about her from her aura, just like Daddy. Jaga's constantly covered with a dark cocoon. She keeps her defenses up.

We're studying the Younger Edda. She brought a thick folio and said, "Any self-respecting dragon ought to speak Edda, and you need to keep your brain occupied with work, so please commit this to memory." She started reading the words aloud and translating them. It turns out I know a lot of words, which I'm trying to tell them, blinking a lot and growling. Karegar realized what it was I was saying and told the elf. Idiot. I should have kept it to myself. "Ahh, that's even better; we'll study writing then." In an hour, a blackboard stood in front of my face. If you understand, nod. If not, blink. Now, I'm blinking and nodding, nodding and blinking.

For the third day in a row now, my old skin has been cracking and breaking. A sticky fluid and slime is constantly pouring out. My insides are burning. A new skin is starting to grow in the form of little coins. It's beginning... For a week now, I've been either too hot or too cold, but my body's not breaking anymore as it was. It's all mixed up, but calmed down a bit. I'm constantly in settage. Otherwise, I start whining and growling. Dad runs around, jerks his wings and looks into my eyes wanting to help in any way. Jaga has grown thin. My neck's stretched out five feet, my tail even longer. My skull and face are transforming into a dragon's snout, my lower and upper jaws are extending forward, and my eye sockets are moving to the sides. My nose and ears have simply fallen off, like a syphilitic. Behind my head, on my skull, the collar of bone is cutting into my skin. I mustn't jerk my head. Jaga says tendons are forming, and I'll just have to stand it. They feed me beef bouillon, porridge made of ground-up chalk, charcoal, and some sort of stone through a tube made of intestine. I already weigh 650 pounds. I'm like a hero from a horror film, oozing slime. I'm so freakin' cold I can't stand it. I hope my voice comes back fast. I'll freeze to death, and no one will know what I died of!

I'm lying on my stomach. They turned me over yesterday and holy moly; they ripped a third of my skin off in the process. The old, the new? Who knows? Both. Now, you could take me to a senior-level anatomy class and use the bare spots to study muscles. I'm looking at what used to be my arms. Thank God they finally let me turn my head. My long ostrich's neck lets me look at my own back. My fingertips are swollen; claws are coming in. It's just peachy. You could say the main changes in my limbs are pretty much coming to a conclusion. My butt's stopped making loud crackling sounds, but my insides are still like a furnace. I'll be able to talk soon. Jaga inspected my mouth and throat. She says my vocal cords are almost all the way formed, but I'm not sure. I check it through settage a hundred times every day. In the past couple days, my heart has gotten a lot bigger and moved to the left; I think another one is forming on the right side. New capillaries are coming in around my lungs, and they're changing themselves or doing something I can't quite understand. On my chest, along my ribs, some sort of muscles are growing, it's strange... I can't figure it out yet.

*I'm so incredibly sick of the cold from my external environment, and the burning furnace inside doesn't help. Wings are piercing my back; I can feel the tendons and muscles forming along my spine and on my sides. The shoulder blades on my front paws are tugging horribly; they're moving backward, freeing up space under the shoulder blades of my wings. On my back legs, the joints that attach them to my pelvis are changing. I weigh about 1,000 pounds at this point, maybe as much as 1,100. Jaga's concerned I'm gaining weight too quickly. The organs should form first, and for me, it's all happening at the same time, in unison. Not a trace of my human face is left. Hello, two-foot-long dragon snout! I'm waiting in fear of the day my teeth start sprouting! We've studied all the runes, now working on writing words. I blink, and I nod, I nod, and I blink... Soon my head'll fall off...*

*Hooray! I spoke! Now, I won't shut up! It's bursting forth from me incessantly. Judging by Jaga's face, she's fantasizing about how to keep me quiet. I'm constantly changing voice modulation. Now, I can sing in falsetto and bass; dragons' vocal cords are surprisingly flexible and are made up of several stages, yielding the full sonic palette, from ultra to infrasonic. Finally, Jagirra's not holding back anymore and swats me on the horns. I expressed my great desire for something that can warm me. After all, feeling like you're freezing alive for yet another week wouldn't be very pleasant. Jaga slapped her forehead and said, "How is it I forgot about that!" and got after Dad to take her out to the countryside. It's been three thousand years; no wonder she forgot something. Two hours later, (I can now sense the passage of time exactly), I heard the beating of wings. They were back and had brought along someone else. Jaga asked the guest to wait for a few minutes while she ran into the cave to throw a veil on me. Now, I can see magical spells, or magical interweaves, as Jaga calls them. Sometimes, they look like lace, sometimes, like strange geometric constructions. Jaga squeaked, "You can come in!" Two short men walked into the cave, and I swear their hair glowed.*

\*\*\*

"Come in!" the Mistress called.

Gmar straightened his jacket and gave Glir a little push. *It's supposed to be a "good" dragon, but it's still a little scary entering its lair. The lady of the house doesn't mind; she's not afraid of anything.*

"Come on in already, we won't eat you," came the dragon's bass. Gmar remembered flying on his back, and how his knees knocked. *Holy Gorn, please don't let me ever go through that again, not for any price! Better a rusty nail to my foot!* He'd go home on foot, he decided; it was more comfortable—and not so high. *The Mistress flies on him, and let her! That's her business. But me, never! May my anvil crack if I ever set foot on a dragon's back again!*

"What do you…Your Selfness, need? A wall put in? Er…somethin' else?" Gmar found the courage to say, and, pulling his brother along with him, stepped into the dark gaping mouth of the cave.

The inside turned out to be not as scary as he had imagined. There were limestone stalagmites and a large fireplace with a kettle. There were a couple of magical lamps under the dome. There were blocks of wood instead of chairs, obviously for the Mistress; they were no good to Karegar. He had a stone couch. He wasn't a dragon, more like a house cat. He twisted and twirled around himself, then plopped down, curling up into a ball as big as two covered wagons.

"What do we need a wall for? We need to build a fireplace here and a chimney for warm air, and here, we need to put up a partition made of animal skins." The elf emerged from a strange veil and indicated where everything should be. "Don't come closer," she stopped Glir, who had stepped toward the veil.

"Eh…I need to see what kind of support material that is," Glir said, embarrassed, and couldn't help but ask, "What's back there?"

"A young dragon."

"What, another one?" Gmar looked at the elf.

The Rauu explained. "He's wounded. Hunters stripped him of his scales, you don't need to see that. He's the reason we're putting in the partition."

A loud coughing sound and wheezing could be heard from behind the veil. Gmar felt sorry for the young dragon. *How could they? Taking his scales from a live dragon! That's like skinning him alive…*

"Take your measurements, but don't go behind the veil," the Mistress warned and disappeared behind the grayish wall.

"What are you just standing there for? Hand me the ruler!" Gmar tugged at his brother's sleeve.

Glir snapped back into the moment and started fumbling around in his pockets for the long rope marked with knots. Noting his curiosity, Gmar shook his fist at his brother, making sure he wouldn't think of breaking the Mistress' rule. He shook his fist, but he was at the same time drawn toward the cloudy wall.

They went about measuring for 15 minutes, calculating and estimating the best way to install a curtain of animal skins and run the flues for the fireplace, and how to install the fireplace itself, and finally thinking about the chimney. The Mistress was discussing something with the dragon behind the veil. His voice sounded pleasant, velvety, and not at all childlike. Gmar pulled a piece of leather from his pocket and a short lead pencil and made a sketch indicating the measured dimensions.

"Okay, got it. We have bricks, and it be better not to hang skins, they'll stink. We'll let the gals know today; they can sew curtains from triple sackcloth, and we'll lay the masonry in about two days." Gmar carefully rolled the bit of leather into a little tube and tied it. "Let's go."

"Fine." Jagirra stepped into the light. "Karegar will fly you back."

"No!" Gmar said, frightened. "We'll walk. It be not far. We'll stretch our bones."

***

*"They're gnomes. Gnomes' hair always glows." Jaga explained. That woman, a watchman, the one who sold me, apparently was a gnome, too. I have to admit. Honestly, I imagined little people to be something else entirely. I shouldn't have read so many stories and watched so many movies and cartoons. I told Jaga my doubts, and she went into fits of laughter for 10 minutes from my description. Well? I pictured them as bearded, pot-bellied little guys as wide as they were tall, gripping axes. They dig up the earth, they forged metal, they hid gold in their stashes. Here that's not correct. But why does their hair glow? I don't buy the line about not getting lost in the dark. Dad's explanation—that they're different—doesn't clear things up for me either. I'm not gonna worry about it. I'll figure it out later.*

*I had a fight with Dad this morning; he called me A-rei. I asked him not to call me that. That stupid name; it reminds me of the enclosure and the cage. One thing led to another... Jagirra lifted the partition, and we both got caught. Now, we're thinking about what we've done. I was wrong to get so steamed, probably. They don't want to call me Andy because there is no such name in dragon; there isn't and never has been. That name existed for sixteen years, and now it doesn't anymore. I don't want them to call me Andy like Mom and Irina used to call me back home. Andy means "frog" in Alat. Little Frog, Mowgli, the Jungle Book! I unexpectedly cracked up at that. In the novel, Mowgli's name means "frog" in the wolf language, because of his lack of fur. Dad asked me the reason I was laughing so hard. Apparently, he's stopped sulking. I explained to him about the Kipling story. I surprised myself in how carried away with it I got. Mowgli was sitting in my memory so exactly that it was as if I were reading from the book.*

*The gnomes are Gmar and Glir. Jagirra told me their names yesterday. They finished building the partition and laid the foundation for the fireplace, then sat on a block of wood and listened to the story with open mouths. I stopped on the Bandarlogs, (monkey people in Hindi) when they stole Mowgli. It's time to eat. Broth and bone meal. I'm so fed up with it! I want meat, fresh, bloody meat, perhaps still warm. Now, that sounds like my new obsession. I close my eyes, and I see a sheep, which I then sink my teeth into. My teeth have come in all the way now, by the way, and everything's great. My chompers have taken up their rightful places, but my upper and lower fangs are still pretty short. It's just a matter of time. And I was right about my heart. I have two of them. Jaga didn't believe me at first... and for a long while afterward. She came up to me ten times and listened to the double pounding and looked at me with true vision. Dad was just interested in whether it was dangerous and then calmed down.*

*I always want to scratch my head with the fingers on my ha— my wings. They grew up literally in one night. They don't have the membranes yet. For now, there's a very thin pink layer of skin with transparent patches, but I think of them as hands. It's interesting to raise them above my back and move my loooong fingers. If you look at a wing as a human hand, then the thumb and pointer fingers can grasp, are small, and are located in the middle of the wing. The other three are three meters long, and the membrane is growing right between them, and between my arm and the upper edge of my back.*

*Today the gnomes got here a lot earlier than they have been. They brought bricks on mules and a special clay. Gmar's daughter came, too. He introduced her to me as Dara and tried to peek behind the veil while doing so, then immediately got a scolding from Jagirra.*

*** 

"Granny Yaga, Granny Yaga!" Dara threw herself at Jagirra. "Is it true you have a baby dragon? Can I play with him? Will he tell me a story? Papa told me a story about Mowgli yesterday, and Uncle Glir told him that that wasn't right at all and that he had got it all mixed up. Was Mowgli really raised by wolves? And Shere Khan is like a sul or a mrown?"

The little girl rattled off with the speed of a machine gun. Her ponytail glowed with an amber flame and seemed it would ignite for real at any second.

*Granny Yaga?* Andy couldn't help laughing to himself. It sounded just like "Baba Yaga," a classic character of Russian children's literature. She was a witch with a hut that stood on chicken legs. He snickered again. This morning, nothing hurt, nothing burned, and nothing itched. He was in a super mood, and the girl's words made him smile, then laugh out loud.

Jigarra made him explain what was so funny. Dara, clinging to the hem of Jagirra's dress, stuck her tongue out at the veil.

"Granny Yaga! There's a fairy tale about you? Maybe the little dragon can tell it?" Dara immediately started in. "There aren't any tales about anyone, and there's one about you!" Andy once again broke into a silly, completely out-of-place laugh.

"Granny Yaga" glanced at the gnomes, tapping away with their trowels, pretending they weren't there and never had been. She turned to the veil, and the nice little dragon realized he was going to get swatted on the horns and in the face that evening. Karegar pretended to be asleep. As soon as Jaga took her eyes off him, one of the dragon's eyes opened and winked a mischievous wink at Andy.

"Yes, he can. But let the little dragon finish the story about Mowgli first," the elf allowed, and again looked at the dragon. One more peep out of him, and she wouldn't beat him in the face; she'd cut his tail off! Andy could feel her intentions and tucked his tail in under himself; it had become as dear to him as his memory. He saw Jagirra's and the dragon's glances as beams of light; the dragon's was red and sparkling with merriment, Jagirra's not so much.

The gnomes wanted to hear the story of Mowgli, too. Gmar gathered up his courage and asked if they might not begin without them. They worked like machines, and the tapping of trowels never ceased for a minute. Dara helped her Granny Yaga cook soup for the "wounded" dragon, grinding up chalk and charcoal in mortars. Karegar stubbornly kept up his sleeping facade. He was not threatened by any towels now, but it was such a long day.

\*\*\*

When they finished their job building a fireplace, the gnomes ran to the stream to wash up. Then, entering the cave one at a time, sat down on wooden blocks.

Andy began the story. This time, he portrayed all the characters by acting them out, trying to imitate the voices from the cartoon version. Dara jumped up and down and ran back and forth from Gmar's arms to Glir's.

The gnomes booed at times and fidgeted in their places, worrying about Mowgli, wrapped up in the story. Jagirra's countenance grew warmer; the cold blue ire and offense melted away. Karegar heaved a heavy sigh when the story finished with Mowgli leaving the jungle for the human village.

"Are there other tales?" the dragon pleaded. The elf's and the gnomes' eyes sparkled.

"There are," Andy answered, "but I'll tell you another one tomorrow."

"Why? I want to hear it today!" Dara began to pout.

"Because Uncle Dragon isn't feeling very well, and he can't tell anymore." A wave of cold rushed over Andy. He saw little stars floating around in front of him.

The gnomes packed up quickly, thanked him for the interesting story, and promised to double-check their work the next morning before leaving.

"Why am I so cold?" Andy asked Jagirra.

"Because it's warmer in a mother's womb than it is outside!" she answered, dipping a huge ladle into Andy's dinner. "Tomorrow, we'll heat up the fireplace and wall-off your corner with a curtain. It'll be warmer then."

The tale of Mowgli caused a stir among the village people. In a world without radio, television or movie theaters, the new story was met with rave reviews. And just like that, village inhabitants began to gather in the cave for story hour. Jagirra stopped preparing his porridge since compassionate peasant women brought mountains of various edibles with them for the "poor, unfortunate" little dragon. They could not care less about the elf's insistence that none of it was allowed, and snuck over to Karegar, bombarding him with cakes, biscuits and other homemade delicacies. The kind soul in black scales quietly passed the presents over the cloudy wall. Andy scarfed everything down quicker than you could say "dragon's feast".

"You're stuffing yourself so much, your wings'll start flapping!" Dad joked. Jaga worried that her patient was gaining weight too quickly. He sized himself up at over a ton and was still gaining by leaps and bounds. His awful internal itching had stopped, his skin was no longer cracked and got covered with scars, and the membranes on his wings had begun to roughen, but a dark bandage still covered his eyes. Andy did quite well without them. The mandatory blindness had so promoted the development of his true vision that he could scarcely tell the difference between them anymore.

"Quie-e-et," came from the cave entrance. "Gmar, if you keep laughing, you know what I'll do?"

Duke the tanner was looming over the small, bushy-haired, redheaded gnome, shaking his enormous fist. The gnome was strong, despite his short height and scrawny build. No less so than Duke, but Duke lorded his authority over him, as well as his Herculean dimensions.

"Ow!" Someone's toe got stepped on; mumbled swearing followed.

People were gathering for the evening show. The gnomes had amassed a few benches for the comfort of the audience, and then a few more, and then more. Everyone living in the nearby villages who wasn't occupied with work or housework gathered at the entrance to the cave. The new myths and fairy tales were unusual and exciting, full of adventure and danger, and there was a new story every day.

Andy threw the last bit of pie with rabbit filling into his large hungry mouth and peeked around the veil. There was literally nowhere for an apple to fall on the benches; each one was so packed. The listeners fidgeted in their places, bumping elbows and whispering to one another. They were discussing J. R. R. Tolkien's eternal *The Hobbit*, or *There and Back Again*, which had been told the previous day.

Andy hobbled to the second veil Jaga had put up near the entrance to the cave and lay down on the ground. Dad covered him with several horse-cloth blankets. Andy had begun to walk right away, as soon as all the bones and joints of his pelvis and legs had formed, ignoring Jaga's forbidding it. For now, his walks were confined to the cave, but that was sufficient to help him work his way up to full ability. He took a deep breath and began to tell the story. Silence fell on the audience from the very first sound of his voice. Only Duke shook his fist at Gmar and also at a gnome who turned to him and said, "Shhhhh!"

Modulating his voice freely, Andy told the story using the voices of the various characters. He tried especially hard to relay all the characters' personalities.

"Maybe tomorrow you can do one that's not so scary?" Gmar asked, arranging the benches after all the listeners had gone home. "Now, I'm going to be afraid of my own shadow! What if all a sudden some nether creature jumps out and bites me in the buttocks? Hammers on the anvil, they might suck me into the bellows!"

Andy lay in the cave alone. Logs crackled happily in the fireplace, filling it with warmth and a sense of the comfort of home. Five minutes before, Karegar had taken Jagirra to a distant farm. Rum the hassan's wife had gone into labor. She had climbed up onto Dad's neck, holding on tight to the hassan's son, a boy of seven, who had run for an hour through the woods to fetch the herbalist.

For a long time now, Andy had wanted to conduct a certain magical experiment. He wanted it so badly the tip of his tail itched, but the elf's constant presence and control hindered his plans. Whenever he would shake up mana from his magical sources, he noticed that beyond the thin barrier behind which his magical subsistence was found, he could sense yet another one that was thicker and sturdier than the first. His attempts to gain access to what lay beyond were fruitless, but he would not give up the undertaking. The waves of an entire ocean of energy sparkled and lazily billowed beyond the last barrier. The temptation to "attach himself" to the source was very great.

Falling into a trance, as usual, Andy overcame the barrier leading to the mana. Ignoring the energy splashing all around him, he came closer to the barrier that separated him from that ocean. He tried to cross it head first, but that didn't work. The barrier bent backward as if it were made of rubber and then returned to its original shape. The magical reaction to the would-be trespasser forced him out of his trance. Andy shook his head from side to side. His ears were ringing, and his nose was bleeding. It was a good reminder of the formidable response he would get if he tried to force his way to the "forbidden fruit," but the prize called to him like cheese always did to Monterey Jack from *Chip 'n Dale, Rescue Rangers.*

*What now?* He could draw only one conclusion, he must solve the problem by means other than force. He needed a different strategy, a subtle, deliberate approach. He needed to learn to be as flexible as that barrier, magically speaking—to become the barrier. Andy clung to that last thought, *Become like the barrier. What if I try approaching the barrier, but not piercing it, hmm? What if I could meld with it and get to the other side that way?*

Intuitively, Andy felt he was on the right path. He dove into settage and began checking his body's energy channels and evaluating his reserves. All right, that should be enough energy. Now, he had to quiet his breathing and concentrate on his senses. It was a short trip inside himself, and the usual entrance into the world of mana. Mana would come in handy, but not yet. He imagined himself as the barrier, sensing its structure. His consciousness spread out along the endless film that separated that energetic "something" from the rest of the world. The barrier became a thick gel. He calmly immersed himself in the jelly-like substance and gave himself time to dissolve in it. *Yes, here we go.* Slowly and carefully, he built a bridge of consciousness between the two worlds of energy. He felt as if his "I" were the head of a sharp pin, and he pricked the tenacious film, which popped suddenly like a bubble.

A powerful rush of energy swept over Andy. It was tens, hundreds, and thousands of times greater than the puny trickles of mana he had previously known. Andy wished to be back on solid ground. The energy rushed in a raging stream over the "bridge" he had built. Everything Andy was made of twitched under the pressure of the unlimited power that side held. The channels in his body simply couldn't handle the load. His reserve containers filled to capacity, and the borrowed raw mana flowed freely throughout his whole body.

An incomprehensible force took control of him and began to whirl him into a mad dance. Multicolored flecks and bands flashed before him. Any more of this, and he would burn away without a trace.

*Nooo!* He lunged back, destroying the bridge and putting up an indestructible dam in his consciousness. Twirling with him in the dance, pressing with unbelievable might, a force knocked him back across the barrier with a powerful blow. It was over.

Andy fell out of his trance and happily took a deep breath of cool air. He was shaking all over; it had been a while since he took a big gulp of adrenaline. He was alive. Andy walked away from the results of his experiment, which had almost sent him to his grave. Despite his expectations, he felt completely fine. Nothing hurt, and the energy channels in his body were lit up with an even light. His internal magical reserve containers were filled to the brim with mana. The intricate glow of his scales made him quite happy. *It can't be!* Not trusting settage, Andy felt around his chest and side with his right paw, meeting firm scales everywhere, which hadn't been there even two hours ago. And that must mean… He ripped the blindfold off his face and opened his eyes. *Yes! I can see!*

The sun was shining brightly, its golden rays peeking into the cave and splitting into fragments when they touched the polished sides of the stalagmites. His internal clock said 12 in the afternoon. Karegar and Jagirra were running late, it seemed; apparently, the Rum's wife's labor was a difficult one. The fireplace had burned out, but Andy did not feel the cold at all. He caught a warm ray of sunshine on the tip of his nose and, following it like a trail, left the cave.

A nice, cool breeze played with the tiny hairs on his wings and refreshed his flushed body. From the height of the cliff's edge, there was a breathtaking view of the valley, fading into a bluish haze and surrounded by white-capped mountains. To the left, a brook babbled with pristine clarity and freezing cold water. The creek had its beginning at the foot of the alpine glacier and, oddly meandering along the gentle slope, flowed to the bottom. Near the cave entrance, the mountainside took a sharp plunge, and the brook cascaded downward from the height of 300 feet in a flurry of rainbow sparkles. The brook flowed into a wide lake that began in the mist hundreds of feet from the ledge and disappeared into the shroud of vapors. A tiny fishing vessel flashed once, just for a moment, and then was lost in the foggy haze. Beyond the brook, tall pines crowded in the distance.

To the right, a comfy, well-trodden trail climbed to a wide, flat area that went from the cave to an age-old pine forest. There, it disappeared into the shadows of spreading pine boughs. Dark green pine tips stretched upward for miles, gradually growing sparser and giving way to even squares and rectangles of cultivated fields. Beyond that, the peaked roofs of village houses could be seen.

"So beautiful! Sooo nice!" the young dragon said to himself, noisily taking the air into his nostrils. He opened his wings to their full width and lifted himself up onto his hind legs. The dark stone was lit up with a thousand colored highlights reflecting off his scales. Little prisms flashed in the centers of his wings. The young dragon turned his head a hundred and eighty degrees and stared at his own back. The rays of sunlight played on the notches of his scales and the translucent membranes of his wings as on faceted crystal, dancing here and there, flashing with brilliantly colored light.

Whimsically twisting his neck, Andy examined his new self. Despite his impressions, he looked different from the outside than what he had gathered from settage and true vision.

He liked his new look. The main color of his scales was gold. A design of blue, green and black scales wound along his whole body like a harmonious floral ornament or an intricate, colorful tattoo. The design was full of whorls. The colors intertwined, alternating. Two black stripes ran symmetrically along his chest, covered by large, diamond-shaped scales to the left and to the right. Little crests ran along his neck, disappearing toward his back and then reappearing near the base of his tail, where the one row turned into two. He wished he had a mirror or at least a sheet of glass to see his reflection. His snout required a thorough examination, head-on and in profile. It occurred to him that he could check out the shadow of his face on the ground. Andy looked down. *The lake!* That was as good as any mirror. Humorously hopping with impatience, he scurried down the well-trodden path below.

It wasn't in the cards for him to make it to the lake. Halfway there, his sharp dragon's hearing picked up the frightened bleating of a sheep. A large griffon flew overhead, turned on the tip of its wing, and rushed behind a low stone ridge to Andy's right. From behind the heaps of stones and boulders, came the scream of the flying hunter, some choice words in a melodious boy's voice, and the hysterical bleating of the frightened sheep. *Meat. Juicy mutton. What could be better?* His stomach growled loudly.

\*\*\*

Danat picked up a stone from the ground and threw it at the horrid creature. The griffon turned around and kept flying circles over the frightened flock. The poor scared sheep ran around in every direction.

The striped "winged wolves" were very bright creatures, sitting on cliffs or hiding among the foliage of the trees. They watched their prey. All it took was a chicken's yawn or a lamb getting separated from the flock, and the loud flapping of their wings could be heard in the air. Next thing the owners knew, some of the animals would come up missing. But the "bobtail" surpassed them all. He appeared in the valley six months ago and immediately made his presence known. This bold vulture, who lacked even three feathers in the fan of his tail, not only constantly stole small lambs, but also flew over the sheep's very heads and chased the most frightened and careless ones into a deep ravine or onto cliff edges. There, they would break their legs or tumble from the precipice and become his meal.

He never hunted in the same place. For weeks, they wouldn't see him in the pastures or near the villages. After each successful hunt, he would spend a few days hidden in the mountains far from the humans' outrage. All attempts to catch or kill the elusive beast were fruitless, but as soon as people let their guards down, the griffon would strike again, attacking where they least expected it.

Danat was almost to the point of tears. The vulture had chased one ram and one ewe into the ravine, from which he then heard a heart-wrenching bleating. And it wasn't at all ready to stop at that. The winged bandit wasn't afraid of stones. He simply squawked mockingly over the boy's futile attempts to hit the half-feathered wolf. The little shepherd leaned over the next stone and froze, amazed.

A small golden dragon climbed up to the boulders, waved his right front paw, and the griffon tumbled to the ground. Unlike Danat, his willing helper hadn't missed. The gigantic boulder he pitched had hit the bobtail right on the head.

"Got him!" the dragon's voice was velvety and pleasant. "Well, are you just going to keep standing there staring?" he asked Danat.

"What?" The boy forgot about the sheep, forgot about the griffon, and stared at this new entity with wide-open eyes. The dragon's question confused him even more.

"You've never seen a dragon before?" The young shepherd shook his head in such a way that it wasn't clear whether he had seen dragons before or not. "All right then. Go ahead; look. I don't charge for looking!"

Danat almost choked.

Yet another pathetic bleating sound came from the ravine. The little dragon crouched and turned to the sheep. The yellow vertical pupils in his blue eyes narrowed to thin slits. His toothy jaws clicked loudly. The boy's blood went cold. *May the Twins forbid it; he's going to strike! Targ, don't let him chase the flock over that slope!* He knew very well that the Master, Karegar, could fly in at any moment. Catching the scent of a large predator, the sheep ran toward the village, but the golden dragon managed to keep hold of himself. His tail flung from side to side a few times, and it was with visible regret that he turned away from the fleeing bits of fresh meat and looked at Danat. The boy was so relieved. It would have been impossible to explain to his father that some sheep had been eaten by a dragon. The Master didn't touch the flocks and preferred hunting in the mountains, while the young storyteller was supposedly sick. The shepherd had already guessed who this helper could be.

He didn't seem much like the invalid storyteller. Honestly, he didn't seem anything at all like him. The village people had constantly been asking one another what he looked like and asking Gmar and Glir to tell the secret, but they reported that Jaga had covered the wounded dragon with a veil and they could only hear his voice. Dara, who had been in the Master's cave, was proud and self-important as a peacock. She told various tall tales with wide eyes. The humans and gnomes who came every evening to hear the stories couldn't catch a glimpse of anything either. Jagirra had hung the second veil at the entrance to the cave, and the people remained as curious as they had come. The old dragon accepted bundles of goodies on the storyteller's behalf, but strictly rebuked any attempts by the old ladies to stick their noses where they didn't belong.

Danat was excited and happy; he was the first village dweller to see the storyteller. Now, he would be able to rub Dara's nose in it. And a fine handsome dragon it was...

"Helloo... Can you hear me?" The dragon's snout appeared right in front of the shepherd's nose.

"Yes?" Danat snapped out of it. He had been mesmerized by the dragon's scales, sparkling with every color of the rainbow.

"I suggest an exchange," the dragon said and licked his lips. The boy felt a cold shiver along his spine at the sight of the sharp, triangular, inward-pointing teeth lining the storyteller's smile. An iridescent charm of crystalline flecks scattered in all directions on the dreadful picket fence lining his mouth.

"What kind?" the shepherd asked, gathering his strength.

"A ram from the flock for the griffon. You can tell everyone you hit him with a stone. I never laid eyes on that creature. Swear to God!"

Danat looked at the dragon holding the dead bobtail in his claw and considered his options. His fear had passed, but an unpleasant chill continued to run down his spine. The golden dragon was offering him a deal. He could justify himself to his father, rub that little brat Dara's nose in it, and all the guys would die of envy. "Agreed!"

*** 

No matter how hard Andy tried to stop shivering, the treacherous tip of his tail kept making the outline of a pretzel. He handed the dead griffon over to the shepherd, broke a long branch off the nearest tree and flew down into the ravine. There were a ram and a sheep. *A double portion! But his deal...* The doomed animals, whose legs were broken, smelled the dragon and began to squeal. His appetite only grew from the sound of their squealing. Spilling thick saliva on the ground, Andy leaned down and struck the ram on the head with the thick end of the long homemade baton. Once he had knocked his prey out, he carefully snagged the senseless ram's body with the branch and pulled it upward, pinning it to and dragging it along the steep wall of the ravine. He removed the sheep in the same manner and gave it to the boy.

"Thank you!"

The shepherd, who was staring with wide-open eyes, mumbled something incomprehensible in reply. The sight of the ram in the dragon's mouth had made a lasting impression on him.

Carefully carrying his lunch in his mouth, Andy climbed over the boulders and trotted to the cave, with all his strength fighting the temptation to break the tender flesh on the spot. The end of his tail and his wings were trembling; they had a life of their own. *Quickly now, faster!* Suddenly the animal came to and bleated. He pressed his jaws together tighter, squishing the livestock that had started to move at the wrong moment. His teeth broke the skin, and his mouth filled with warm blood. The next thing he knew, the bones were crunching as he ate them. *Oh!* His tail drummed an intricate beat against the ground.

Somewhere far away in the background, Andy, the human, deliberately shook his head in a condemning fashion, not approving of this behavior and this blood lust, but he didn't interfere because he understood very well what was happening to him. The intelligent winged predator he had become as a result of Jaga and Dad's efforts would not be eating just grass and porridge. His specialized set of teeth was built for a different menu. His obsession with tasting fresh meat, which had taken possession of his mind for the second week now, was finally satisfied. Ripping the ram's coat off with his sharp claws and casting aside the giblets, he pulled a back leg off with pleasure and took a big chunk into his mouth. *It's better than ice cream!* Half the ram had been eaten to the accompaniment of a guttural growling. If he could have seen himself through the eyes of a bystander, he would have been surprised by the feverish glint in his eyes and the wide wagging of his tail.

Andy saw a dragon in the sky approaching fast. He grabbed the unfinished ram's body with his teeth and dashed away under cover of the cave roof, now like home to him. With the flapping of wings and the clatter of claws on stone, he landed.

"Don't go near him," he heard Dad's bass voice speaking to Jaga. "It's his first blood...let him finish it."

"Where did he get a ram? What has he done? Where has he gone with his scars open like that? He's going to get it all right!" the elf was upset at the loud cracking of bones coming from inside the cave. But she did not enter.

Karegar chuckled. "I saw more than you did. Believe me, you'll be surprised," he said to Jaga and grabbed the ram's guts and skin. "I'll throw this to the griffons. Come out already, enough licking yourself!" he cried to Andy, who was grinding the last morsel.

Guiltily hanging his head to the very ground and licking his bloody snout, Andy came out of the cave. Jaga took a breath, ready to let loose a tirade. *S-s-s-s-s...* she exhaled, and Dad stuck his tongue out.

"Well I'll be a griffon's uncle!" he said, breaking the long silence.

Jaga walked up to Andy and ran her hand along the scales on his side. Tears welled up in the elf's eyes.

"Open your wings up," she asked and gently touched the shining dragonfly inserts on his wings with the ends of her fingers. Her warm palm slid over the colorful scrollwork of his scales. Jaga hugged his neck, thin compared to Karegar's, and stood for a long time admiring the flashes of color on the young dragon's back, lit up by the sun. Karegar lay on the edge of the cave floor like a silent mountain. He was bursting with parental pride. The elf took a few steps back from Andy and, looking him in the blue eyes with yellow vertical pupils, said, "I've thought of a name for you."

***

*Wow, everything hurts so bad... I never imagined that once I became a dragon, I would get dog tired. A horse can be ridden to death, and sometimes, I feel the same fate is befalling me. Dad's taken it upon himself to seriously train me, teaching a full class of "young dragon," after which I ought to become a full-fledged flying dragon. He'll most likely chase me into a funeral pyre, then I'll rise up into the sky as smoke, not by the power of my wings. Jaga completely and totally supports Dad's initiatives to wipe me off the face of this planet, me who he's designated the "crystal" dragon.*

*"Kerr, you became a dragon when you were already almost a full-grown person! Your new body is trying to catch up with your adult mind. That's why..."*

*That's why shut up and quit whining, or I'll send a red-hot fireball up your tail or come up with something else particularly nasty. Run, faster, Kerr, move those paws!*

*"How many laps did you run around the village? Fifty? Only fifty? Kids, who want to take a ride on a dragon? Everyone? Well, climb on, and you, stand still and don't wiggle. What do you mean too many? Too many kids? You've only got ten little tots on your back! Twenty laps for complaining! Go on, move it! Are you a dragon or what?"*

As Dad and Jaga say, the goal is to get closer to the people, and I have been chosen to be the bond that brings us all together. And the people are glad to do their part. They've thrown an entire kindergarten on me while they sit on their benches and munch sunflower seeds. They discuss among themselves which lap I'll be on when my legs give out. It's just plain awful.

After my laps, the children stay on my back, and I begin the exercises designed to develop my wing-flapping muscles. Wings forward, resting against the ground a-a-a-and, do a push-up. In order for life not to seem too sweet, I have to start out with one hundred push-ups to the happy cries of the kiddos.

"Have you done the exercises? Change your position. Open your wings, let the children crawl up onto the ends. Slowly bring them up, now down. If you scare any of the dozens of kids clinging onto you, the number of reps goes up twenty times!" The nimble little babes unhook their hands and plop to the ground all by themselves, but Dad's pretending not to notice their cleverness and is increasing the number of repetitions. It's cruel. I wouldn't put it past him to make me sweep the whole village, just to make sure I know how it feels to clean my own spit off the hard ground. I can't go into settage; Jaga watches me like a hawk.

"You should train your wings by yourself, not through magic!"

It's a festival! A merry fair for children! "They're tired, the poor things, of holding on to your wings. Drop and give me twenty! Oh! What's that? Dad pressing on your back with his tail, pushing you down? Why are you kissing the ground? Push up!"

All, while he talks about the harvest with the village people, about prices in the city, even about the women! Ahh! I can't take it anymore! Hello, dirt in my face...

"Oh dear me. Your wings are tired? Ki-i-i-ids! Where a-a-are you? Get on his back! Twenty laps around the village, crawling on your belly!" I've plowed all the land around the village with my belly! "No big deal, you'll keep on plowing..."

By evening I look like a squeezed lemon and crawl into the cave with trembling legs and wings, wanting to collapse and sleep the sleep of Napoleon after the Battle of Waterloo. But it's not meant to be. With a snide smile, Jaga tells me it's time to train my brain a bit...and it begins.

I gave the elf a pleasant surprise when it comes to numbers and math, but that only encouraged her. I don't even know which of them is worse. Herbs, herbs, herbs. Names, where they grow, *healing and magical powers. When to collect them and how to store and prepare them. Which can be used with other herbs and magical ingredients. Multi-component teas and potions. How to make poisons.*

*I don't remember what the mountain climbers' names were, who completed a trip with no safety nets across steep slopes using just their hands, but it doesn't matter. All that matters for me right now is not to let myself fall from the 500-foot height of the steep slope a half a league (a mile) from the cave. Dad has a new obsession: chasing me up and down the wall. I have to crawl up and down it using just the fingers of my wings. The elf's attached to my back in a special harness and is telling me the history of Ilanta, and I'm memorizing it as we go. She promised to tell me the tragedy of the dragons, and now she's keeping her promise.*

***

"Three thousand years ago, dragons and the embodied ones ruled western Alatar, and there were many thousands of them, not just a few loners here and a tiny handful there, scattered through the quiet nooks of the mountains.

"There are four continents in Ilanta. Alatar is the largest and resembles a stick with a crossbar at the top. Rold is located beyond the Azure Ocean, to the east of Alatar. Radd lies beyond the seas to the west, and Aria is the smallest continent, located in the north.

"Dragons came to Ilanta 30,000 years ago from another world called Nelita, which was the night eye of the goddess of Life, Nel. A network of spatial portals built by the dragons connected both worlds and allowed free travel between them. The secret of building portals was lost some 20,000 years ago when a group of builders researching dragons was killed, every last one of them, while activating a portal to another world. Not only did they die; but only melted ruins remained of the big city that was home to dragons and other intelligent creatures.

"In those long-ago times, there were no humans, gnomes or elves in Ilanta, just a few tribes of wild orcs roaming the steppes of Rold. Dragons brought elves with them and planted the first Mellorny trees, which were the start of the Great Forest and the Light Forest."

Andy asked about gnomes and humans. Jagirra poked him in the spine and told him not to interrupt; she would get to humans and gnomes. "Be quiet please; it's difficult to speak while pinned to a steep cliff wall, trying to feel out the smallest cracks in the granite monolith."

*Jaga's fine, sitting there knitting away!*

"Gnomes and humans both came to Alatar of their own accord. Fifteen thousand years ago in the Stone Mountains, a portal opened, and thousands of gnomes entered through it, refugees from a war in their own world. The gnome mages who opened the portal remained on the other side and passed away, once they had given the rest of the gnomes' time to save themselves.

"The half-dead refugees were allowed to settle in the Marble Mountains. Twelve thousand years ago, in the center of Aria and the south of Alatar, practically at the exact same time, the gates to other worlds opened. The dragons didn't explain their reasons for opening the gates and didn't say whether or not this was the result of the highest form of magic. No one could say. But humans came to Ilanta and later to Nelita through the dragons' portals. The gates that united worlds stood open for ten years, then disappeared. The dragons decided not to tamper with them. They set reinforced posts around the magical gates and removed all conceivable characteristics from the passages to the other worlds. The people who had settled in Aria and the north of Alatar became known as Ariates. A lot more people came through the southern gates and weren't all of one tribe or nation, like Aria. There still isn't a single name to describe them all."

Daddy swung his head in from above and added, that during his youth, experiments had been conducted in Ilanta and Nelita on building and opening gates to other worlds. "Characteristics were taken from the Ariate gates for settings, and they were somewhat successful, but I had not had time to take an interest in the university news; there were more important things going on that were a lot more interesting..." At these last words, his eyes glazed over, and he fell into a bought of reverie. He grunted softly, and his black head disappeared.

Now, this was getting really interesting.

"Well, how did the dragons discover the possibility of incarnation?" The question made Jaga fall silent. For 10 minutes, Andy beat his wings on the cliff in total silence.

"There were experiments on elves and humans," Jagirra finally answered.

"Okay. Experiments. That means...interesting, how many two-legged guinea pigs were dismantled by these doctor Dragonsteins?"

"Not sure what you just said, but I get your drift. In the end, they found out that dragon's blood contains a lot of special hormones and when harvested during their molting period or during a time of stress, there is a universal healing balm that also counters the effects of aging in both humans and elves. In order to keep their research pure, orcs were brought in to work on the project. The potion had the same effect on the fanged ones. The gnomes didn't take part in the tasting because they were different. But, in the university in Irga, the capital of the dragons' state in Nelita, some interesting discoveries were made on the mutation of the human body. A few years later, the first embodied dragon flew into the sky."

*And how many never got to fly?* Andy wondered.

"Problems began on Alatar 8,000 years ago," Jaga continued. "There were fewer and fewer dragons. Many moved back to Nelita, while humans and elves populated the entire south and west. The Ariates built cities on their snowy expanses and in the north of Alatar. Green and white orcs from Rold settled in the east of the continent. For about 300 years, no one paid them any mind, until the good-natured residents of the west and the south noticed that the east was overtaken with fanged savages, called 'The greenies,' constantly attacked their neighbors, posing a threat to the peace of all the states that had formed in the west. In one fine instant, hordes of 'greenies' advanced on the west. They had been whipped by the 'whities' in the southeast and the 'grays' who came to their aid from the islands. The 'mountaineers' of Aria, who lived beyond the Marble Mountains and had never engaged in battle, were completely wiped out. The dragons had to get involved. They stopped the 'greenies' in the foothills. War had encroached upon the dragons' peaceful world. They needed warriors, post-haste."

"It was then that the dragons created the Snow Elves. The Rauu became the first warriors who managed to cast the orcs off the eastern foothills," Karegar put in.

*I can't say I was surprised.*

"How did they create them?" Andy asked.

"By magic, of course! How else? They took volunteers from the Forest Elves and the Ariates, added magic and got a new kind of being. Strong and fast, they resembled Forest Elves, with silver hair and light skin, and they could live in any part of Ilanta, not dependent on nutrition from Mellorny, as Forest Elves are," Jaga said simply, but Andy could tell something was eating at her.

"Only, the Forest Elves didn't recognize the Rauu as full-fledged elves and refused them the right to reside in the Forest. By that time, such snobs had come to power among the 'woodies', and even the dragons were nauseated. Naturally, the dragons pressured the 'woodies', who set aside some land for the Rauu on the edge of the Great Forest. Underneath the shadow of the Mellorny was no place for the Ariate degenerates. The first Rauu had a hard time tearing themselves away from the greenery of the woods, and the dragons took them under their wings. Then the first black cat ran between the two elven races."

Daddy's head once again appeared over Andy. "Here, too, they call those poor creatures monsters, bearers of bad news! And I'd always liked black cats. Five thousand years ago, the Rauu were asked to leave the

Forest. The 'woodies' had refused to listen to the dragons. Then, they had to burn them to ashes..."

Playing with his wings, Andy almost lost a thought that had been bothering him since he turned into a dragon.

"Wait a minute. You talk about people becoming dragons, but have there been cases of the reverse incarnation?" Oof. *If I hadn't blurted that out then, my nagging thought would have escaped me again.*

"Yes, there were," Jaga replied. "It's a different mechanism, but there have been such operations. In Nelita, among dragons at one time, incarnation was popular. For them, the change isn't painful, and the nervous system doesn't change. The entire process depended on magic. Incarnation in humans and elves can change the substance, the hypostasis; in dragons, it's more complicated than that. Humans are not magical creatures from the start, and they have a harder time taking on different elements, but without doing that, you can't become a dragon, and you can't change the hypostasis.

"It's all a matter of bodily memory. In those who were human first and dragon second, the human is not erased completely, and the two combine and they become a kind of third entity as it were. If the personal magic power permits, then the hypostasis is changed. It's important to maintain the balance between the hypostasis and not stay in one of them too long, or uncontrollable switching from one body to another can result."

Andy almost fell down. What! His tail twitched completely of its own accord, and his jaw hit the cliff wall.

"How can it be, what do you mean...?"

All of his thoughts seemed to whirl down a pipe; there was a tornado in his head. He was hanging on one wing and remembered where he was after the painful blow of a little fireball to the back of his head.

"Climb up to the top!" Jaga yelled.

Andy couldn't remember at all how he had gotten up on the cliff. *I can be a person again!* He just couldn't think of anything else.

"Daddy! Why didn't you tell me this before?" Andy attacked him. "Well? Dad? Jaga?"

"Because you should become a real dragon first!" Jaga jumped from his back and tapped him on the nose. "You should have the ability to control yourself and your feelings, not giving in to the instincts of a predator, like with that ram in the cave! You should learn patience and be able to separate yourself from the world. You forgot about that too quickly once your changes were complete. You should be able to control your new body as if it were the one you were born with, or you risk becoming a horrible monster.

Jaga and Karegar fell silent. Andy was sprawled on the platform. He spread his aching wings and digested what he had heard.

"And 3,000 years ago, the dragons' and embodied ones' power over northern Alatar became pretty tentative," Jaga went on, picking up the interrupted lecture. "In Nelita, the ruling dynasty changed. A portion of the dragons and embodied ones went back to their native worlds, and in Ilanta war broke out."

"I'm going to the top ground," Daddy turned to us. Somehow, I knew deep in my heart that he couldn't stand hearing this part of the history. "Kerr, when Jaga's through, come up and see me."

Jaga's eyes followed him for a long time. "The 'woodies' killed Karegar's daughters, cut their heads off. Dragons can get their paws, wings andtails cut off and lose half their body mass and grow it all back later. It takes a long time; it hurts, but dragons will return to their normal life. But they can't grow their heads back.

"The elves beheaded the dragon elite, which consisted of embodied ones. Disguising their trap as an invitation to a great feast, His Lordship and some human kings sought to cast off oversight from the skies. The lordships of the Great Forest headed the conspiracy. War broke out; the carnage was terrible. In the end, the embodies went back to Nelita and sealed the portals behind them, and the elves attacked the dragons' settlement, finishing off most of the women and children."

Jaga spoke facing no one; her voice sounded like she was speaking from inside a barrel.

Andy lay on the hay listening to the elf, but he knew without a doubt that Jaga was not telling the whole truth. There were other reasons for the war besides the Lordships' dissatisfaction, and she knew it. But she wasn't talking about them, and Andy got the feeling it was exactly what was left unsaid that made up the main driving factors for the war.

*Why didn't they tell me about reverse incarnation and about turning back and forth like a werewolf right away? Why is it that Jaga and Daddy pin such importance to real dragons' changing form?*

"After that killing, the dragons destroyed the Great Forest along with all its inhabitants," Jaga said.

"I would have done the same thing."

"And they put a spell on the Mellornys. These sacred trees no longer bear fruit. Since then, it's been hard to find a dragon who doesn't hate Forest Elves or vice-versa. The portals between Nelita and Ilanta haven't opened once in 3,000 years; it's safe to say they've forgotten about us. The north was demolished, and the orcs struck through the mountains. The Rauu and the gnomes were able to stay in the mountains, and the Ariates retreated to their ancient lands. The 'greenies,' who had been forgotten by everyone, seized all the northern steppes from the Marble Mountains to the western seas. Two centuries later, a horde of gray orcs settling into the coastal areas forced them to relocate. And in the south, the Empire of Alatar came about, named after the continent. The emperors invested a fair amount of effort into conquering the neighboring lands.

"Two thousand years ago, the Imperial fleet with troops on board was sent to conquer the Ariates, who flooded all the vessels and used the highest magic against the Imperialists. Due to that uncontrollable release of energy, all the Imperial ships and the island were swept away. A portal opened in the sea, and a dozen ships with humans came into our world. They called themselves Norsemen and Vikings. The Vikings settled on new, far-away lands, and soon, a dozen shiploads of humans had become hundreds. After the news that the fleet had been destroyed, there was a coup in the empire, and a new ruling dynasty came to power. As is always the case with these things, a civil war broke out, and the empire collapsed. Imperial legions were called in from the wild provinces. The Rauu, the gnomes and the 'woodies' remained unconquered. Special squadrons of warriors created by mages from the Rauu remained in the foothills of the Marble Mountains. They became the ancestors of the vampires."

Then she told Andy that the far-off provinces became kingdoms and principalities; the borders were regularly re-drawn depending on the winners of these wars.

"And human mages made attempts to conduct incarnation?" he asked.

"They tried, but the most serious thing they ended up with was monsters that killed everyone in their path. The other mages like me who knew how got their heads cut off in the castle where they staged their trap.

"Now, go to Karegar. We'll continue the history lesson this evening; then you can ask your questions." Jaga patted Andy on the neck and sent him to the very top of the cliff. She sat down on a big boulder and stared into the distance. She didn't notice Andy hadn't left...

"One more thing?" he asked.

"What is it?"

"Jagirra, how do you know all this? Your knowledge of thousands of years?"

"I was born in Nelita and studied at the University. Go on now."

*Wow! How the heck old is she?*

\*\*\*

"What is it, Father?" Andy asked Karegar, who was looking at something on the steep wall.

"Have you finished?" the black dragon turned his gigantic head toward his adopted son. He had been standing on the very summit for a long time, considering. This wasn't the first time Kerrovitarr—the Crystal Dragon as Jaga had named Andy—called him Daddy or Father.

Subconsciously, the boy was looking for his own father in Karegar—the one he had lost in his own world. The flexible psyche of a teenager, now a dragon, tail and all, simply switched the images. Karegar had dreamed of a son for thousands of years and finally had one. He was now justifiably proud of himself for what he and Jagirra had done. It didn't matter that a human woman had brought Kerr into the world with a human man; he had come back to this world through the efforts of an old dragon and a senile elf. "Come here. I want to show you something. You'll like it."

Andy walked up to the edge of the precipice. If he were to fly straight down, it would be 2 miles to the ground. Karegar stepped back.

"Look at the boulder sticking out from the left side of the wall."

Andy hung his head downward. A powerful blow by the tail sent him into a free fall...

***

"Have you got it?" Jaga was sitting on the bench near her home, keeping a glowing magical construction interweaving in the air.

"Yes," Andy replied lazily. It was a bummer to lift his head off the warm sun-soaked earth. He had memorized the formation nodules of the power constructions last time, but Jaga began each lesson by repeating what they had covered during the last one.

"It's a 'spider web,' a very simple and effective security spell. It has several positive aspects: you can use it on a certain area and volume in order to avoid the possibility of someone violating the perimeter through air or water. It unfolds and folds up in a moment. It takes on the function of a scanner interweave—the nodal response settings are set to the type and kind of external influence, and the size of the trespasser is determined upon deployment of the spell in a large area. Oh, and I almost forgot. It doesn't require a lot of mana."

"Excellent! We'll end on that." The elf put out the "spider web" and formulated a new construction. "Today, we'll study 'canopies.' A canopy is a spell that allows you to block sound, light, visual, tactile, and mental information. The veil you know so well is one of the varieties of visual canopies."

Jaga created and sent forth different un-activated canopy constructions and explained to Andy the ways they could be used. The diligent student consciously memorized the positions of the power nodules, the reinforcement points, and the spell activation points.

"Polana, come here," Jaga unexpectedly interrupted the lesson. A young lady in a leather marching suit with a birch bark box on her shoulders stepped out onto the field from the bushes before the herbalist's house. She walked up to the elf and bowed low. She paid Andy no mind. He was taken aback by that attitude; he wasn't used to being ignored.

He naively thought he knew everyone in the valley. He had circled it up and down several times over the last three months. Apparently, he didn't know everyone, and he hadn't circled everywhere. Cocking his head to the side, he examined the newcomer with interest. She certainly wasn't a local, he decided. The village peasant girls didn't dress like that. Her chestnut hair was in a tight braid under a scarf. Her large, steel-gray eyes looked over the dragon's figure and scales with polite interest. For an instant, a ravenous flame flared up and immediately went out in them, unnoticed by Jaga and Andy.

"Kerr, why haven't you put up the security 'spider webs'?"

"Because my 'spider webs' are more energy-packed than yours and they're screening the simple defense circuit. The free-tracking modules are not to your liking."

"They're fluttering around like moths in front of your nose. That means you have something to work on. You'll fulfill the activation of the spell using minimal impulses." Andy was only half-listening. Pretending to pay attention to the herbalist's words, he kept casting sidelong glances at the uninvited guest and was considering whether it was possible for a member of one biological species to arouse sexual attraction in a member of another. Judging by current events, apparently, it was. He hadn't yet seen local women in pants suits, let alone any like this. The newcomer's suit fit like a glove. The leather pants hugged her shapely legs and highlighted the curve of her tush. They joined with the jacket in an intricate lacing of colored hide. Coupled with soft boots of goat hide, the outfit allowed its wearer to move about the forest silently

"Kerr?"

"Huh?" Andy snapped out of his contemplation of the dark gap between her full breasts, peeking out from the unlaced top of her jacket.

"I said, go fly to the cave and fetch the almanac of healing herbs. It's in my chest near the fireplace."

"Sure... I'll head out." Andy took a couple of steps away from Jaga and Polana and strongly pressed his paws against the ground, waving his wings. "Geronimo!"

"Stupid brat," the elf said without a hint of anger, pulling some leaves from her hair and following the dragon's skyrocket into the sky with her gaze.

"He's showing off for you," she said to Polana. "Sit down, why are you blushing? And why are you dressed like a vampire? Did you want the peasant men to drool, and the young boys to fight? Don't even think of going into the village in that get-up. Shame on you... but it looks stunning. The dragons and the others won't be able to stand it." The girl smiled.

"Fine. Anyway, tell me, how are things in the wide world? Wait. Are there newcomers in the caravan?"

Polana nodded. "A new head of security."

"Has he been warned that he'll have to take an infallible blood oath?" The elf's gaze became as cold as ice. The air became noticeably colder, too. Jagirra didn't appreciate uninvited guests, and she really didn't like it when they'd been brought to the valley by tradesmen who had taken an oath, even if they were from the village. All inhabitants of the mountain nook—forgotten by the Twins—from the babes to the elderly, were under an infallible oath. The Rauu had taken precautions to protect herself; no one beyond the borders of the ancient mountain pass would know what happened there and the identity of the Master of that valley. Anyone who found out would take the oath on the spot or go to Hel's judgment.

At home, they could chat about dragons all they wanted, but as soon as they crossed the border of the first mountain gates and went down to the gnomes' tunnel, the spell worked its magic and put a taboo on any mention of the valley and its inhabitants. Unfortunately, it wasn't possible to isolate the valley from the outside world completely, but it was possible to cut down on the number of people in the know. She never refused to help those in need and allowed them to stay as long as their hearts desired—sometimes a lifetime—but sometimes, in bringing strangers there, people posed a threat to the quiet life, albeit unknowingly and unwittingly. In 2,000 years, that had happened a couple dozen times. A dozen foreign guys had lost their lives, and five times, they had to bury their own valley-dwellers.

"He was hired under that condition."

"Good. This evening, he'll take the vow."

"Um..." Polana began.

"Kerrovitarr, son of Karegar," Jaga answered the question before it had been asked.

*** 

Andy caught an updraft, spread his wings and slowly flew away from the cave. His cheekbones, the tiny whiskers on his snout and the down on his wings caught every movement of the incoming air and the oscillation of the wind, upstream and downstream.

Two months had gone by since that memorable moment when he first flew. During that time, he had been able to feel all the delights of molting and to make almost a pound of gold on his old scales. Gmar, when he found out about the molting, ran from the dragon's cave—with fire in his eyes—to the herbalist's house and convinced them that burying these beautiful things in the ground would be a crime. Andy could not care less about it. The elf, pacified by 50 vials of dragon's blood potion clinking in her basket, waved her hand and gave the go-ahead to proceed with the commercial operation of selling the scales. That evening, she and the gnome came up with an entire legend to justify such fantastic wealth in the hands of an unassuming mountaineer.

For days, Andy trudged around behind Jagirra among the most hidden corners of the mountains surrounding the valley, helping her collect herbs and serving as a means of transportation. They devoted four hours a day to the study of magic and the elements. Jaga complained that she had no experience in teaching and she couldn't even give him a basic education. The elf knew and could do a lot, but often couldn't explain the essence of some spell or another.

What she did know, she drilled into him. They studied the microcosm hidden in the mountains, front to back, from the heights of the mountain peaks to the last shell on the bottom of the lake. Jaga cruelly exploited his mage's abilities and forced him to put thousands of security modules up on the mountain frontiers.

The constant flying and busying themselves in the fresh air helped develop his muscles. The young dragon's voice became deep, he could cry out from his chest, he grew taller, and he packed on 1,000 pounds. His father refused to fly with him and lamented that he had kicked him off the cliff too hard; he should have let him fly a bit more slowly and carefully then, but now it was too late.

*** 

Papa Karegar's kick off the mile-long cliff had forever united the crystal dragon with the sky. At first, he screamed some perfectly choice words at the top of his lungs as he was sent plunging to the ground. He forgot about his wings entirely. The ground was getting closer with frightening speed.

"Wings!" Daddy yelled, rocketing down behind him.

Andy recalled his third pair of appendages, better late than never, and tried to flap them. Things only got worse. His body started to spin around its own axis, and he was flung to the side. Panic took over, and he could no longer think rationally. Strong paws grabbed him, stopping the chaotic spinning.

"Look at me, and do what I do!" Karegar cried, releasing Andy from his claws.

Daddy stretched his neck down and corrected the spikes on his tail. His wings were pressed tightly against his back. Andy stopped all attempts to move his wings, quickly flattened them to his back and stretched out his neck. The speed of the fall immediately increased.

"Come on!" Karegar sharply spread his wings and curved his neck upward. Andy copied the maneuver. The approaching air stream blasted him upward. The fall speed decreased; he was no longer losing altitude.

"Wings!"

A simultaneous flap of both wings, another one; it was indescribable. He had flown in his dreams so many times, but the dreams couldn't compare to the real thing. As he pushed the last traces of fear out of his mind, powerful, ancient instincts awoke in him. He could read the slightest movement of the air, and those winds awoke his perceptions of the world through his dragon cheekbones and the sensitive vibrations on the end of his snout. His wings caught every vertical upstream. The plates of his tail spikes tilted outward and stabilized his flight, similar to how a bird's tail feathers do.

Jaga had sat on a hot stone and watched the two dragons frolic in the sky, her hand on her forehead shading her eyes.

*** 

Andy was so engrossed in fondly reliving recent events that he almost flew right past his home cave. Clicking his claws against the stones, he ran to the chest like a whirlwind, got out the old almanac, and dashed toward the exit. He could admit it; he wanted to see Polana again as soon as possible.

Andy ran out of the cave and folded his wings, preparing to jump off the rock shelf. Instead, unleashing his claws, he stopped suddenly and remained on the platform. Clouds of smoke were rising over the village, which he hadn't noticed earlier for all his thinking and remembering. He put the almanac back into the chest and decided that Jaga and Polana could wait. Pushed forward by a strong wind, he flew toward the human dwellings.

Gmar the gnome's haystacks and house were burning. The barns' roofs blazed in hot flames, the second-floor windows of the house emitted black smoke, and the roof tiles flew off with a whistling sound. It was clear that, without Jaga's magic, the fire could not be put out. Andy himself couldn't control the elements as the elf did. Gmar's house was quite robust; they had built it with several generations in mind. Half the village's population was fussing around the fire. People were trying to stop it by passing buckets of water to one another taken from a stream that flowed near the house and the smithy, but the hot flames wouldn't allow the firefighters to approach the source of the fire, and most of the water missed its mark. The ravenous red flames attacked the logs of the second floor from all sides. A strong wind gathered up burning hay and carried the fire toward the village, which upset the boys keeping watch at the gates and made them grab their ready buckets of water. Several humans and gnomes were holding Gmar and his wife, Nired, by the arms and legs so they wouldn't run into the house.

"Dara's in there!" the gnome, pinned to the ground, cried in despair to Andy when he saw the dragon.

"What?" Andy didn't understand.

"Dara is in the house!" Gmar cried once again, tearing himself away from those who were holding him down. To stop him from doing anything stupid, Andy brushed him back with his tail and put a spell on himself that he'd learned from Jaga. The "water shield" gave him immunity from fire for five minutes. He dashed into the flames.

Many people think dragons are clumsy creatures on the ground, but they are profoundly mistaken. An adult dragon, despite its six- or seven-ton weight, can run far at a speed of 20 leagues an hour or speed up to 30 leagues an hour and maintain that for three or four minutes.

Clumps of dirt and little stones flew from under Andy's feet, and he knocked a good-sized hole in the wall with his shoulder to stick his head inside. Dara was there. She was lying down near the staircase on the second floor, her arms out to the sides. The girl's aura was glowing with a weak, greenish light; a little longer, and it would go out completely. Apparently, she had tried to run downstairs, but had breathed the poisonous smoke and passed out. A burning ceiling beam collapsed from overhead, crashing down on his head and almost breaking his horns. Another one fell on his neck and blocked his way back. Now, his horns wouldn't allow him to go back, and there was too small a hole to move forward. His water shield's time was running out; the defense was losing power. His wings started to bake from the outside heat. *Why aren't I human? Dara was so close! I could certainly go get her if only I were human. Oh, why aren't I a human!*

"Aaaaah!" he yelled at the top of his lungs. He jerked his head down as hard as he could, broke the wall to pieces and plunged forward, scooping the girl up in his arms.

Suddenly it seemed as if a large-caliber missile had been fired into the two-story house. The blast blew the roof off, luckily not injuring anyone. The beams of the second floor and the bricks and masonry of the first floor were blasted dozens of feet away. People were knocked to the ground. Slowly turning and leaving smoke trails behind them, beams, boards, and pieces of furniture of the blown-up house fell to the ground after the people. The explosion knocked the flames from the barns and the hay that were still burning. Pressing the girl to his chest, Andy left the ruins of the former house. He didn't understand what had just happened. The village-dwellers picked themselves up from the ground as if in slow motion.

In a fog, he went over to the gnomes and gave Dara to Nired, who was standing staring at him with an open mouth. Before Andy could ask why, the loud sound of beating wings came from behind him. The ground in the courtyard trembled. Karegar landed. Jagirra and Polana jumped down from his neck.

The elf ran up to Nired and looked the girl over.

"She'll be okay. I turned her faint into a deep sleep," she said after her examination. "Who was it that was trying so hard with your house?"

Nired stepped to the side and pointed at Andy. The herbalist's lips formed an "O" shape. Behind her, Karegar sputtered loudly, and his jaws clamped shut. Polana's cheeks became flushed. The young village women giggled. The elf walked right up close to him and pulled an apron embroidered with protective charms from her belt. In her extra-large eyes, besides the reflection of the still-burning flames, he saw amazement, disbelief, admiration, and a whole gamut of other emotions.

"Cover yourself up!" she handed him the accessory.

Andy looked at her quizzically.

"Oh, what a pain you are!" Jaga sighed. "Lift up your arms!"

Andy obeyed the command and found himself staring at his human arms. After that, he no longer heard or understood what was happening around him. He returned to reality when Karegar unloaded him onto the ground near the entrance to the cave.

*\*\**

In the cave, Jaga met Andy with an absolute interrogation. She passionately demanded to know what he was thinking about and what he had done in Gmar's home. In response to all questions, the person of interest only shook his head, shrugged his shoulders and asked for a mirror. Sufficiently convinced that she was getting nowhere with the stunned poor excuse for a rescue worker, Jaga spat and postponed the interview until a better time. She pulled a silver mirror from her chest and handed it to the were-dragon. One glance in the mirror and Andy immediately knew: he wasn't a person. No, the face in the reflection wasn't the face of the Earth boy he used to have. The blue eyes with yellow vertical pupils spoiled the view. So did the sharp fangs in his mouth. The whole set was in place: the five or so front teeth Nirel had knocked out had grown back in. Even his wisdom teeth decorated his upper and lower jaws.

"I was right. You were tortured by an elf," Jaga said, examining the horrifying scars on his back and sides. "How nasty. The delayed-action spell isn't reversed with incarnation. What a wretched villain you have to be to use that. Better to just kill someone right away, than…"

What it was better than, she didn't say. The scars interested her, but they weren't her first priority.

"Have you tried turning back?" she asked the young non-human, who had torn himself away from the mirror. Andy shook his head. "Try it. Imagine you're a dragon—"

Jagirra hadn't finished speaking when Andy began imagining. He heard a scream from the elf as she darted away from his sudden dragon's mass.

"You almost squashed her, you idiot!" Daddy laughed and immediately hushed upon seeing Jaga's strict glare. "Now, back again."

"Yes, of course! Where's the apron?"

"The old one's in tatters. Just cover up with your hands."

"Again!" Karegar cried.

"Yes, you can do it again. There's no apron, and who cares? Now, turn back again. Incredible! If I hadn't seen it with my own eyes," Jaga went on, "I would not have believed something like this was possible. Turn human again."

"I'm sick of this," Andy whined.

"It's the last time. I need to compare your aura in different hypostasis."

"Well, for science's sake then," Andy answered.

"Karegar, you see, his aura hasn't changed. The shape and color are like that of a pureblood dragon. I need to think."

*Fine, let her think.* Happy to be left alone, Andy made a beeline for his corner by the fireplace and collapsed onto his stone bench in a fog of exhaustion. His eyelids slammed shut.

He dreamed of his father, with his arm around his mother, sobbing over a small granite slab in the city cemetery. There was nothing written on the black slab, not a name, not a portrait, but he knew that they had buried him under this slab. Papa barely managed to take Momma away from the grave and drive her home. Andy was riding in a long black car with his parents, trying to tell them, yelling that there was no one in the grave, but they couldn't see or hear him.

Olga and Irina met him at home with red eyes swollen from crying. Bon came in, claws clattering on the parquet. Andy let out a happy growl; his sisters suddenly noticed him and squealed like frightened piglets. Momma and Papa ran from the room, and he, with a dragon's face, tore the howling Bon to pieces.

"You're not my son!" Momma said. "My son died."

Then he woke up. Both his hearts were beating frantically, the claws on his front paws were stabbed into the stone of his bed. A muffled growl came from his chest.

"What is it?" Karegar's eyes glowed in the dark.

"I have to send them a message..."

There was no need to explain further.

\*\*\*

Earlier on, before he changed form for the first time, it was easier. He divided his life into several stages: before he was struck by lightning, from the lightning to when he landed on Ilanta, from the time he came to Ilanta to the time he underwent incarnation, and from incarnation to his first flight. He had made his peace with and gotten used to his new appearance, stopped thinking of himself as a human and understood that his birth family would never believe in a winged beast. Andy openly called Karegar his father, and Karegar likewise publicly pronounced him his son. A fun holiday celebration had been arranged in the village to honor the new Master, although no one called him that; Kerr was more than enough. There was a last name attached to the name Karegar: Gurd of the High Nest. That meant something, but they never explained it to him.

He supposed he was entering a new stage in his life, starting from the fire and the change in hypostasis, which turned his well-established way of life upside down. *Where will these new abilities take me, and what will they lead to?* Already they had resurrected his long-gone desire to get back home, or at the very least send some news. He thought about that idea for the rest of the night. Was it worth venturing to search for information about building gates to his home world? It was possible his desire to see his family would result in his ending up in some top-secret research center on Earth, where they would... *Well, what wouldn't they do to me there? Probably bake me. Is this idea worth risking my life or freedom for? Is it worth risking Jaga or Karegar? Polana...?* She had captured his heart in one day. It was a hard decision, but he had to decide.

Andy's adoptive parents met his request to go traveling in search of information on inter-world gates with hostility. They said he wasn't ready. They said he didn't know the customs, ways of life, the religion practiced there. They began counting on their fingers, listing everything he needed to know and to be able to do. *How could they not understand! I need to find a way to get news to my family! Or else I'll never get rid of the nightmare that woke me up last night.*

All Jaga and Karegar's objections shattered at the look in his eyes. He was staring in one direction, silently declaring that he would do this with or without them, whether they helped him or not. Jaga grew tired, slowly sat down on a block of wood and folded her hands in her lap.

"It's you he takes after," she said to Daddy.

"And I thought it was you! You're just as stubborn," the dragon retorted. "Have a chat with the Hermit. He might be able to help."

"I will." The elf stood up and walked over to Andy. "Perhaps you'll change your mind?" Andy said nothing. "I see it's useless to try to talk you out of it. You're a real dragon. What are you just standing there for? Let's fly!"

"Where to?" the stubborn dragon asked in surprise.

"To the Hermit!"

***

The Hermit had moved to the valley twenty years before. No one knew where he came from, and he had immediately gone to Jaga's house. How he managed to get by the security periphery and the traps unnoticed would forever remain a secret. But after a long conversation with the elf, the valley's population grew by one. No one knew his real name, and everyone just called him what he asked them to—the Hermit. The old man settled down in an out-of-the-way place, far from the others. On the slope of the Broken Mountain, he built himself a wooden frame house and hired a couple of guys from the village to help him bring his belongings from Gornbuld, ninety percent of which were books and ancient tomes. There were manuscripts and scrolls in three chests, protected from decay by a preservation spell.

The Hermit agreed to help Andy. The little man had snow-white hair, a long white beard, and fuzzy caterpillar eyebrows over wise eyes. Through his potato-like nose, he informed them that he would turn this good-for-nothing into a real human.

Andy now had lessons with the Hermit in addition to his lessons with Jaga. There were dozens of disciplines in his "young nobleman class, from ethics to riding tricks on hassback. There were only three horses in the valley, none of which was available for teaching purposes. The one thing the old man did not allow him was sword fighting, talking his way out of it by saying that he had been occupied with other things since childhood and he had simply missed learning to use this weapon. Andy returned to the cave around the time Nelita rose and fell like a dead man onto his bench. The old man had squeezed the very last energy out of him.

The little old man underscored all his words and actions with reminders of the sacred circle and the switch, which had "kissed" Andy more than once while he underwent his lessons in human hypostasis. The hardest thing was rehearsing the various dances a nobleman must know. Not able to think of anything fancy, the Hermit invited several young women from the village, assessing their abilities with doubt and rolling his eyes, taking the One God's name in vain. He shook his head and taught Andy the dances, along with his partners, who constantly blushed and pressed up against him at every chance. Andy blushed no less than the girls. Through willpower and settage, he managed to decrease the flow of blood to his crotch and wished that the tradesmen would arrive in the valley as soon as possible; Polana was set to arrive with them.

In his time not taken up by lessons, he gutted the old man's library and practiced his "will shields," which covered and masked his aura. He got pretty good at them. When he had somehow put up a shield, he asked Jaga to reverse the effect. The elf scrupulously examined his work with true vision and remained satisfied, noting that when he put up shields, his pupils disappeared completely. It was too bad Jaga couldn't apply cloaks with a subtle, point-specific interweave. Hiding his non-human eyes was a very attractive idea. A simple magical masking didn't last long on them.

In a short time, the Hermit helped him to know all the manners and customs of all the different branches of elves, Forest Elves, the "Dawn-bringers," and the Rauu, and of the humans, gnomes, and orcs that populated Alatar. During one visit by Jaga, the old man said, coughing, that only religion was left; Andy had bled him dry on all other subjects. He had never had such a capable student. If it weren't for a couple of hairy circumstances getting in Andy's way, he might achieve great success in the field of serving the One God and, who knows, even sit on the Patron's throne.

Today, the old man didn't have his switch handy. The Hermit swayed from toe to heel, stared at Andy with his white, faded eyes and ran his hand over his gray beard.

"The Gods should be closer to you than they are to anyone, but you continue to deny the divine beings. No matter what happens, today, we're going to talk about religion. Jagirra asked me to educate you in a manner that is complete and comprehensive. I intend to honor her request as best I can. But on the question of faith, I'll deviate from my principles for the first time and just give you the bare bones. Surprisingly, I have standing in front of me a dragon who doesn't believe in the Twins. On the other hand, you don't believe in the One God, either. Pity."

Andy set aside a fat tome with a description of the historical events of 400 years ago on the siege of Orten, the second-largest kingdom of Tantre, by a horde of green orcs. He heaved a sigh. *The Hermit is in his element; let him have some room to work. He won't give his sermons a rest until I've heard him.*

As Andy suspected, his mentor had previously been a religious servant of the One God, and pretty high up in the ranks. He could sense in the Hermit an unbending streak of stubbornness and a strong will. The breadth of his views was astounding, as was brilliant mind. The Hermit could speak of any subject from various perspectives and then would immediately analyze his speech and show the listener where, in his view, he was right, and where there was work to do and further clarification necessary.

"I'd like to begin with Alatar's ancient faith," the old man began. "The Twins symbolize Life and Death, Order and Chaos, and are the symbol of the struggle and unity of two universal opposites. Faith in the Twins came about long before the Empire of Alatar. I'm inclined to believe the ancient legends, which state that dragons brought this faith to the world. Your existence supports that version, but anyway, back to religion. The symbol of the Twins is a circle of light and darkness".

"The Twins do not symbolize good and evil. They are higher than that, neutral, and maintain a sacred balance in the world. Sometimes, life is so unbearable that a person will gladly take on death and search for peace in Hel's embrace. One could call the goddesses a symbol of balance and harmony. There is a belief that the souls of the dead go to Hel's judgment. She'll weigh a person's life and deeds on a scale of black and white stones and decide where to send him after death. If the cup of white stones is heavier or the scales are even, the soul will have a light afterlife and may be reincarnated a hundred years later as a different person. If there are more dark stones, horrible torture awaits the soul, because dark stones in a human soul are evil and throw off the world's balance. Dark souls will be sent to eternal suffering and oblivion. Currently, this ancient belief has been preserved in the north of Alatar in all the branches of elves.

"The coastal orcs serve goddesses. The Twins are revered in Tantre, Rimm, Meriya, the dukedom of Taiir and the principality of Mesaniya. The Norsemen or Vikings revere their own gods, the principal of which is Odin the one-eyed, but dwelling alongside the Dawn-bringers and the free barons made its mark on them. Most of the northerners believe in Hel and Nel, which does not prevent them from slaughtering a chicken on an altar as a sacrifice to their gods or sacrificing a slave. The gray orcs, who were strongly influenced by the northerners, believe in Odin, the Twins, and in Khirud, their god of the sky with arms of lightning, along with an entire pantheon of pagan orc gods.

"The gnomes are an exception from all the others with their belief in Gorn the Fiery, ancestor of all gnomes, who gave them fire of the soul, which is why their hair glows. Besides Gorn, the gnomes have a few other gods. Grom is the god of earth and metals, who gave his people the ability to see iron in earth. Nirada is the goddess of beauty and fertility, but in essence is their version of Nel. Targ is similar to the Vikings' god Loki, the god of deception. Targ gives trash instead of minerals, floods mines, and mocks the foothill tribes in all kinds of ways. To recall Targ's name as something unpleasant, to think of him as bringing misfortune, spread from the gnomes to all the peoples of Alatar. Rad is the god of honor and military prowess, an incorruptible judge, equivalent to Gorn, a witness to vows, and a great warrior with a heavenly flaming sword, and there are a few more lesser gods.

"Let's go back to the topic of the Twins. Over thousands of years, people distorted their understanding of the harmony and balance of the goddesses. Dark cults of Hel appeared, the priests of which drew their strength from wicked human passions and made sacrifices to Death. By their efforts, the fair goddess was slowly transformed into a cruel monster that requires human blood and death. The Servants of Death are acting illegally in all nations. In the empire, they're executed without trial. The One God, through the hands of his servants, is battling the darkness."

The old man fell silent, scooped some water out of a bucket with a carved wooden ladle, slowly drank it, and turned a couple pages in his tome. A new image unfolded before Andy's eyes. It was a symbol similar to that for the Twins.

The Hermit went on. "The One God. Briefly, and based on the knowledge that came about with the dawn of the empire, the world around us was created by a Great Intellect that unites all the elements and beginnings of the universe. The pagan gods Hel and Nel are the essence of one Creator-God's manifestation. This God unites the entire universe unto himself. Everything begins with him and returns to him. The Creator doesn't have a name, he is One—the God that unites all names, Light and Dark, Order and Chaos, Good and Evil. The black and white circle in the center of the sacred circle is a person created by the One God in his image and likeness. Not in his external appearance, as you might think, but in the likeness of his soul, which contains dark and light sides. The light and dark halves of the One God struggle with one another for human souls. If the dark half wins, and the human circle becomes dark, the world will come to eternal chaos. If the light half can win, and people's souls become light, then a golden age will come, an era of complete prosperity. The faults and virtues built into humans cannot be in balance. People are weak, and doing dark deeds comes easier to them essentially than rejecting dark deeds. Their faults will soon master them. The Holy Church is called to help the light side of the One God and send people down the path of truth."

The next part Andy only half listened to, although the Hermit was singing like a nightingale. Andy relaxed and started to doze with his eyes open, then the Hermit switched to the structure of the church, and that was serious. Spiritual authority was a powerful tool of political influence on the continent.

"The Sacred Church is headed by the Patron, the anointed sovereign of the One God in Ilanta. The Patron's throne is located in the center of the Great Temple, built 2,500 years ago in the small city of Pat, which became the capital of the Second Empire 1,500 years later as a result.

"The church is divided into eparchies, each governing a certain territory, headed by Patras, who are chosen at the Patron's conclave. The church stands on three pillars. The first is the pillar of Light. It's made up of white or light clergy who bring the light of true faith to the people. The second pillar is the pillar of Knowledge. All the spiritual schools and seminaries are subject to the pillar. The Great Master rules according to the pillar. Besides schools, all the book and newspaper printers of the Church are under the control of this pillar. The third pillar is the Pillar of Purity, called to keep the thoughts and deeds of the clergy and the parishioners clean. It is designed to root out heresy."

Andy frowned. *An inquisition, of course.*

"The pillar of Purity is the most serious and dangerous for the enemies of the Church structure. It entails not only an investigatory division but knightly orders. There is the Order of the Sword, the Order of the Purity of Light, and the Order of the Sacred Circle.

"The Great Masters of the orders are elected at their General Chapter and confirmed to the positions by the Patron." The Hermit went on to describe the structure of the knightly orders, the "Circlers," the common name for the Order of the Sacred Circle that served as internal guards, the Sword-swingers, as they were called, engaged in joint military tasks, and then there were the pure ones," the punishers in service of the Sacred Church.

"What relationship does the Patron have to the Government?" Andy asked during one of the many pauses in the Hermit's monologue. "I can't imagine the Emperor of Pat simply tolerating the presence of the Church's armed forces on his territory."

The old man was silent. The white hairy caterpillars over his eyes did an intricate dance. He tugged his beard a couple of times. "The Patron occupies the position of being the Emperor's first advisor," he said, finally.

"So the Sacred Church fused with the state apparatus of Pat, and for the most part, supports imperial politics or implements its goals, and in return receives tax breaks and some state perks. The knightly orders can be viewed as extra army reserves, only they've been brainwashed by priests into killing for a lofty cause in order to create a small circle in the center of a big white one. The Church itself allows for centralization of power in the emperor's hands. Excuse me, Hermit, but I have one more question. Is the Patron chosen at the conclave, or by direct order of the Emperor himself?"

"Jaga told me I'd have to watch my words with you," the old man sat down on a bench and looked at Andy anew. He twitched and moved his eyebrows for a long time and muttered under his breath. "What do you think?" he asked, instead of answering.

"Class dismissed."

\*\*\*

A surprise awaited him at the cave. Flying up to his home, he saw two female figures arranging bundles of herbs. His hearts beat joyfully. *Polana has arrived!*

"Land over there, to the side," Jaga called to him. "You're going to put all the herbs away for us!"

He flew over to the platform near the ravine he had plucked a ram out of, landed, changed hypostasis, quickly got dressed, and ran back up. He stopped for a second right before the platform, caught his breath and casually stepped out into the open, raising his will shields just in case. If Polana looked at him with true vision, he wouldn't want her to see him glowing unevenly toward her.

He helped sort wild herbs and wrap them up in bundles until dusk. His conversation with Polana went awry; he didn't know what to talk about with the girl and constantly got embarrassed. *Where was that loquacious little Dara when you needed her?*

"Where's Dad?" Andy asked the elf, only just noticing Karegar was gone.

"He won't be back 'til tomorrow or the day after."

Andy lifted his brows. "Flew to the lake," she answered his silent question. *I get it, when a dragon's angry and annoyed, he's no sweet treat to all those around him, plus he just wants to be alone.*

In half an hour, they finished with the herbs. They were tied in little bundles, wound up again in dry rags and placed in birch baskets. Andy flew the yawning Jaga home and went back for Polana and her baskets of herbs. The girl laid them on him and climbed on his neck.

"What a smell!" Polana said when they flew over the deciduous forest. "The Nightbloom is in bloom; now's the time to gather. You have to get them at night. Will you come with me?"

*She's actually asking me!* He went breathless with excitement.

The tradesmen had set up camp on the edge of the village. There was a small caravan of five wagons and two carts. Andy landed far from the horses. Scaring the animals and having them wake everyone up was the last thing he needed. Polana quickly took the herbs inside and came back with a small basket behind her shoulders.

"Let's fly!" she "commanded," and Andy chuckled to himself.

***

"You know, when I was small, my mom told me a story," Polana said when they landed in the meadow with the Nightbloom. Andy didn't change hypostasis. In a rush, he had forgotten his clothes in the cave, and walking around naked in front of a girl he liked is a faux pas.

"What story?" he inquired politely.

"About dragons. My mother said that at night, when Nightbloom is in bloom, a heavenly fire in the form of a golden dragon comes down to

Ilanta. He flies over houses, cities, and villages. Only pure maidens can see this fire, and the one who notices him first can call him to come with her to a meadow of Nightblooms and experience the love of the Lord of the Sky, who turns into a beautiful youth. The lucky girl, with the love of the dragon, gets heavenly beauty and prolonged youth." She dropped the basket from her shoulders and took a blanket and a red ribbon from it. Andy got a sweet feeling in the pit of his stomach, and the tips of his wings trembled. "I have an intended fiancé, but I want you to be the one to tie the first matrimonial ribbon on me. You're my dragon from the fairy tale. Turn around."

Andy turned around like an obedient child. His wild imagination drew several frivolous pictures of what was happening behind him. The tip of his tail was drumming against the ground like a wind-up toy. He could hear the slight sound of untied laces behind his back. He couldn't stand it and turned around. Polana saw eyes glowing with a blue light and slowly, deliberately pulled the lace at her chest.

"What about your fiancé?" Andy tried to step back a bit; he was suddenly scared. He had dreamed of this moment, but he had never been with a woman before. Naughty dreams and daydreams don't count, and... he was afraid he'd goof it up.

"Silly," the overalls fell to Polana's feet, and the nighttime nymph was standing before him in all her naked glory. "He doesn't know. You keep our secret."

Andy turned around, took a step toward the object of his passion, changed hypostasis in an instant, and awkwardly dug into her supple, warm lips...

***

Polana's father had given her the task of walking around the merchant rows of Gornbuld and finding out the prices of goods. She assessed the variety and quality of the goods. She hadn't been in a gnome city in six months. Trading was noisy, barkers were shouting, and cunning salesmen grabbed the pretty girl by the hand and offered valuables and jewelry. Not paying their promises any mind, she turned to the dealers. They had taken a dozen hasses from Rum in the valley to sell, and it was worth it to find out the prices of the four-legged goods so as not to get in a bind. In the rows with hasses, she suddenly came upon the tent of a zavis and wanted to keep walking, but a redheaded woman stopped her.

"Hey, beautiful, do you wanna know your fortune? The old lady never lies."

Polana was interested. "How can your clients tell whether the old fortune teller is lying or not? Or do they just wait for the third moon to rise?"

"You don't have to pay any money, Granny will tell your past and present first, and then you can decide whether to pay and find out your future or go away with nothing." The redhead smiled.

"All right then," Polana decided. She could do a thing or two with magic, herself, and she wanted to see the charlatan, or maybe not a charlatan. The hasses wouldn't run away in five minutes.

The redhead lifted the tent flap and stepped behind Polana. "Granny!"

A hideous old lady came out from behind a curtain in response to the call. Her whole face and wide hooked nose were furrowed with deep wrinkles. Black stumps of teeth stuck out from her cavity of a mouth. Her thin hair fell in greasy locks.

"Charda, leave the tent and don't let anyone in here!" she ordered in an authoritative voice and raised her head. Polana grew a little cold. The old woman's eyes were completely white. She extended her hand with its long knobby fingers.

"Give me what you're hiding in your bodice."

Polana became even more frightened, but she dares not disobey and took out her matrimonial ribbon. She was already convinced that the zavis wasn't a charlatan. With a sharp movement, the ancient zavis grabbed the ribbon and stood swaying back and forth for a few minutes. Suddenly, her toothless mouth opened, and she asked with the hiss of a snake, "Were you his first? Answer me!"

"Yes," Polana answered. She had chills.

The old woman laughed a cackling laugh. "You hussy! Read too many ancient legends, have we? Decided you would get the power by trickery? You tricked one love-struck dragon and ran away before the Mistress caught on? Oh, yes! Jagirra would tear you apart with her bare hands! How did she miss such a liar as yourself? For deceiving a dragon once, you ought to be quartered three times over!"

"Who are you to talk to me like that!" Polana cried and grabbed the ribbon. The crazy old woman grabbed her by the arm. She was unbelievably strong. Polana fell to her knees.

"A Seal. A white Seal. Have you heard scary stories about Seals?" The girl nodded. Tears came from her eyes. "They're ugly witches who can tell the future and have a terrifying unknown strength. It's too late to cry. Do you know how we became Seals? No? You should have read the whole book."

She shoved the crying client with her foot. "You deceived a dragon and got his love. And not just love, you got a magical power. The fairy tales are true. Your youth will be long, a hundred years or more, and then, in one fine instant, you'll turn into an old crone like me, and you'll live a thousand years, unable to die. That's exactly why virgin dragons must not meet with virgin girls! Their first night in the arms of a virgin is truly magical, and the power and magic splashed with ecstasy are transferred. They try with all their might to keep their first love. And they keep it..."

"What about you, old hag! Must be hard to bear a stolen strength?" Polana cried, fighting her fear. The Larga grabbed her by the hair and dragged her out of the tent.

"Get out!" The old woman hobbled back to the tent. Her strength had suddenly left her.

"Charda!" In response to the cry, the redhead ran into the tent with a worried look. "Get me a pen and paper, quickly."

The girl brought what was asked for. The old lady grabbed the writing materials and began to scribble something in Edda. When she was done with the letter, she wrapped it up and slid it into a small tube.

"Take all the gold and ride to Karegar's valley. Give this letter to the elf that lives there. Don't come back here. Now, listen to how to get there." The old zavis told her helper the way to the protected little corner of the world and handed her some purses full of gold and precious stones. Then she closed the tent flap.

***

Some time, a long, long time ago, the old Larga's name was Enira. The daughter of a royal magnate had fallen in love with a Lord of the Sky, and he returned her sentiment. They got married. Enira wasn't afraid to become a Larga. Life with her were-dragon rid her of the curse of someone else's power. But on the second day after the wedding, Ratigar flew off to a banquet and never came back...

Largas live long, and cannot end their lives by suicide. The slightest thought on the subject, and they undergo terrible pain. They can die from another's hand, but in 3,000 years, no one had lifted a hand against the ugly old woman. They can trip and fall into a hole, but no unfortunate accidents had crossed the clairvoyant's path. Or, they could die by passing their power on to another Larga, who was marked with the seal of the magic and power of a dragon. Enira had read the pretty girl's dirty soul and transferred her power to her without any prick of conscience. Even more reason to, since the girl wouldn't have time to use it. Largas truly can see certain people's future, and Enira had seen the girl's death. In three days, the trade caravan would encounter a gang of robbers, and a bolt would pierce the sleeping deceiver's heart. The power of sorcery only awakens after seven days. And, holding the ribbon in her hands, she also saw the dragon's future. Blood, pain, and war—another war; he had so little time.

The Mistress, Lady Jagirra, ought not hold the wind in her hands, for her own sake, for his sake…

Her last strength left her, and the old woman's white eyes turned clear. The soul, finally free from the body, ascended in a wisp of smoke.

# EPILOGUE

Crouching clumsily and nodding from fatigue, Charda jumped down from her mule. The fog, thick as soup, rose from the river to cover the cliffs all around with a cloudy curtain. The sounds of a mountain stream bubbling along the sandbars faded away into the impenetrable milky cloud.

The girl took the mule by the bridle and stepped along a narrow trail that ran along the embankment, carefully navigating the wet stones. Her eyes were heavy, closing all by themselves. Her granny had described everything exactly. It would take three days to get from Gornbuld to the hidden passageway to the protected valley. Charda hadn't slept almost that entire time. During the day, she rode Teaser from one landmark to another as described by Granny, and during the night, she kept the fire going all night and kept her mule close to her. He wouldn't have run away anyway. He snuggled up against his human, sat down on his hind legs, and flicked his ears attentively whenever he heard a rustling nearby or the far-off howl of a predator.

"Ah!" Charda slipped on a wet stone and almost fell. Someone's hand grabbed her by the elbow and kept her upright.

"Thank you!" she said to the unknown helper. Something sharp dug into her back. Sensing a stranger, Teaser tugged on the reigns and brayed. Her sleepiness disappeared in an instant.

"You should be more careful," a creaking male voice came from behind. An acrid, stinky smell assailed her nostrils, like from the leather-tanning district of a city. "Don't move an inch!"

The milky haze dissolved, and she saw a short guy in a cape with a hood on his head and a loaded crossbow in his hands standing in front of her.

"Duke, step aside," he said, and the sharp metal point she could feel pressing into her back relented. River pebbles gave off a muffled rustling from under the bulky body. Charda didn't dare move. Her gaze was fixed on the glint off the tip of the bolt aimed at her.

"Where are you taking this path to, dear?"

"To Karegar's Valley."

"Well, well now!" the little man said and moved the crossbow slowly side to side. "Don't you move a muscle! And what business do you have there?"

"I have a letter for the elf." The girl tried hard not to cry and not to bolt. She was so upset, she was on the verge of tears. After making it all the way through a wood full of ravenous predators, she was caught by bandits at the very end... Maybe they would leave her alone if they knew she was just a messenger.

"Give it to me. I'll take it to her." The crossbow shifted its aim away from her; the bowman held out his hand. The cape moved, and the hood fell from his head to reveal a gnome's fiery locks.

"Take it," Charda pulled the small tube out of her bodice. "I don't think your hands can be sewn back on; if you don't get your head cut off, that is," she bluffed recklessly. "Only the elf can open the tube. That's what my granny said."

"And who is your granny?" she heard someone say from behind.

"A zavis from Gornbuld."

"Seriously?" The gnome thought for a moment. "Glir!" he cried, turning a little, but still not taking the crossbow's aim off her.

"What?" the sound of the unseen Glir's voice came as if through a haystack.

"To the village, quiet as a mouse. Let 'em know there's a letter for the Mistress." The sound of hurried feet scurrying away was the reply. "You can relax, dear. You can put your hands down, too."

Charda realized they weren't going to rob and kill her and calmed down. The villagers were defending the path at any cost. The girl glanced around and noticed a large flat boulder, sat down on it, and wrapped her arms around her knees.

Twenty minutes later, the loud sound of flapping wings came from above, and a golden dragon landed near the messenger. Charda, with good reason, considered herself a brave person, but when she saw the tooth-filled mouth a foot away from her face, she went breathless and started to tremble. She curled up into a ball and awaited death by the ancient monster. Teaser brayed and rolled his eyes wildly, tore away from the lead, and galloped up the trail. The mule didn't get far. After a few seconds, a blinding light flashed under his feet, and the animal was ripped in two, drops of blood dousing the crossbow-yielding gnome.

"Wait!" The dragon grabbed Charda by the shoulder, who had tried to run to Teaser's aid. "Are you through with living? You want to run over the cutting stones?"

"Teaser..." Charda sobbed, and without realizing what she was doing, hugged the dragon's surprisingly warm neck.

"Gmar," he said. "Take our guest to the village and come back. I'll guard the trail in the meantime."

The gnome nodded in compliance. Judging from the way Kerr's eyes shone and his nostrils widened when he smelled the fresh blood, it was clear, the girl ought not watch the "clean up." With complete tact, Gmar unhooked the redhead from the dragon's neck, took her by the hand and—carefully avoiding the traps—led her along the narrow path.

When he had given Charda over to the care of the old ladies of the village, Gmar hurried back. His watch wasn't over yet. No need to worry about the girl anymore; the grandmothers would clean her up, feed her, give her something to drink and not let her out of their care. Glir saddled up on a hass and rode to fetch the Mistress in Karegar's cave.

***

A dark shadow covered Charda for an instant. She was dozing in a wicker chair in an apple orchard. The loud beating of wings made her lift her disobedient eyelids. She was very sleepy after the filling porridge with spices and chunks of boiled meat she had eaten.

*The golden dragon has landed,* she thought, but another one landed next to the garden, black as tar and as big as a house. *How many of them are there here?* She'd heard only one tale about the Lords of the Sky in her life, and now she'd seen two with her own eyes today. A stately female figure lightly slid from the giant's neck. *The elf!*

"Hello, my child." The Rauu regally sat on the edge of a second chair that had been brought by the members of the household while the elf walked through the garden. When they set it down, they immediately disappeared, as if they had never been there. The black dragon carefully navigated his way through the trees behind the elf.

*A real Mistress!* Charda thought to herself, standing up from the chair and bowing low and respectfully. She had seen hundreds of highborn noblewomen but compared to the Mistress, they all paled.

"Sit down, there's no need to get up. What is your grandmother's name? It's indeed she who sent you?"

"Yes, Madam." The girl bowed again. She couldn't make herself sit down. "My grandmother's name is Enira, but she doesn't like that name."

"Enira..." the Rauu clasped her hands together with interlocking fingers and turned to the dragon. "Do you remember?" In reply, he closed his eyes. "That means old Enira is still alive. Give me the letter."

Charda pulled the letter out of her bodice and gave it to the elf. Taking a thin piece of paper from it, the Rauu concentrated on reading it carefully. A winged shadow flashed in the sky. The golden dragon landed on the edge of the orchard, his scales sparkling in the sun with a thousand rainbows. Folding his wings, the bright image immediately faded. He started to follow the black dragon's tracks, but halfway there he wheezed, suddenly got up on his hind legs, opened his wings and collapsed to the ground on his back, like an epileptic having a seizure and knocking down several young trees with his tail. The elf jumped up from her chair and darted toward him, dropping the letter on the ground. The black dragon turned around, breaking several more apple trees with his powerful tail.

"Polana!" the young dragon cried, as he stopped his thrashing and spat out some black clots of blood from his great mouth. Ignoring the woman running toward him and the black dragon razing the apple trees, he turned over on his stomach and pushed off the ground with all fours, rocketing into the sky. "I'm off!"

"When was the girl with you?" the Rauu ran back to Charda. The elf's almond eyes flashed like lightning.

"Three days ago. Granny threw her out of the tent, and immediately sent me to you."

"Targ!" the Mistress of the valley swore, grabbing the paper and in one smooth motion mounting the black dragon's neck. "Karegar, fly to Kerr! I put a tracker on him!"

"What's wrong with him?" Karegar's deep voice inquired.

"What? He was with Polana, understand? That wench! She wanted to receive the power and became a Larga! Enira writes that she'll be killed today; it seems they've killed her already! Kerr felt it all—that cursed connection—he knows where she is!"

"What!" the dragon roared. A strong gust of wind from the beating of his gigantic wings knocked Charda to the ground, overturned the chairs and sent grass and leaves flying. The garden was empty, with a third of the trees now broken. The dragons had flown away.

*\*\**

Vigrel kicked the corpse of the caravan guard with contempt. Stupid tradesmen didn't want to surrender and fought as if they were hauling stones for Hel's balance. No matter. The goddess would weigh their souls anyway. The Rauu rubbed his right cheek where a tattoo had been removed. The outcast didn't have a clan marker and wiggled the toe of his boot under the lifeless body of the young boy who had shot Mig Three Fingers with a crossbow bolt. The traders had killed four of their men and wounded two; nine people were left standing. It was too big a trade-off for taking a caravan of seven carts and killing ten tradesmen with guards…

While the ringleader went to check the posts of the watchmen on both sides of the road, the caravan had traveled on; five robbers cleaned out the carts and wagons.

"Hey, look at this beauty!" Ming, a big, one-eyed man scarred by a sword's swipe from his left eye up to his left earlobe, dragged the pretty body of a girl out of the last cart by her feet. She wore a leather jumpsuit like a vampire-ranger. A crossbow bolt with a red feather on the end stuck out of her left breast. Vigrel realized he had work to do.

The dead girl's face was calm and peaceful. Hel's cold breath hadn't touched her, and death hadn't spoiled her beauty. The elf took a curved knife from the top of his boot and, squatting, ripped up the laces on the dead girl's chest. He hadn't yet made the cut that would allow him to retrieve the bolt when a cross-shaped shadow covered him.

"Watch out!" Ming screamed at the top of his lungs. In the next instant, a dragon appeared out of nowhere and with a punch from his front paw, struck the man into the ground, breaking his bones and spine. The last thing Vigrel ever saw was the great, gaping, tooth-lined mouth.

***

"It's not worth it," Jagirra held Karegar back by the tip of the wing. "He's not going to listen to anything now."

The elf and the dragon, not interfering, observed Kerr, silently laying human bodies on the carts. They had been piled up for a funeral pyre. Lastly, the little dragon laid Polana's body, wrapped in silk. He held her for a long time and rocked her just like a baby. Setting aside his load, Kerr took several steps back from the carts, opened his mouth, and spat fire lighting the pyre.

The bandits' dead, mutilated bodies lay as they were, where death had overtaken them. Kerr had singed the guards along with the trees. Jaga and Karegar flew in when it was all over. The old dragon simply couldn't keep up with his adopted son. The little dragon pulling the wagon was a horrible sight to see; his golden scales faded and turned gray. His paws, chest, and wings were covered in other people's blood. In a fit of rage, he had killed everyone. Kerr sputtered loudly and showed Karegar his fangs when Karegar silently offered to help pull the carts. He took the reins from his adopted father and chased him away from the place of slaughter. Taking the hint, his adopted parents stepped aside.

"This is bad, very bad," Jaga whispered, glancing at the Snow Elf's mangled body on the ground. "I had heard of a band of outcasts headed by a Rauu, but I didn't think Vig the Handsome would attack this caravan. I'm afraid Kerr may lose his trust in the Snowy race."

"I'm afraid of something else," Karegar turned his head toward her. "He might not want to be a dragon anymore."

"That won't happen," she assured him. "Look at him. He's acting like a dragon and isn't attempting to change his hypostasis. Kerr doesn't want to be a human. That worries me more than anything."

"Why?"

Jaga paused for a long time, collecting her words, but then decided to speak directly, without any delicacy. "We need to send him to the humans as quickly as possible. Kerr needs to study magic. Time is of the essence."

"What happened, did you fall from a Mellorny?" the dragon's eyes sparkled.

The elf jumped down from Karegar's neck, made her way through the furrows left by the wheels of the multitude of wagons, and sat down on a thick oak root sticking out of the ground by the side of the road. Jaga got the letter out of her clothing and, running her eyes over the even lines, glanced at the dragon.

"There will be a war, my honorary husband." Karegar's lower jaw fell.

"It's pointless to deny the obvious. A great war will envelop the entire north, but that's not the most important thing."

"What is?" Karegar asked. He had lost his train of thought from the revelation in Jaga's last words.

"Enira writes that Kerr will be the stone that causes all the stones to fall. I don't know how he'll be connected with all this, but the world will once again be full of dragons. That's how it will be; the old white Larga has never once been wrong."

"How are you planning to convince him to study?"

"I'll send him to Orten. In a month and a half, they'll be recruiting new students in the Orten School of Magic. Tell him that there are ancient books and manuscripts in the school archives on building gates to other worlds. He'll most probably be interested in that, and he can get to the archives if he's wearing a school badge."

Kerr, tearing himself away from the pyre's fuming flames, approached the pair. They dropped their discussion.

"I want to be alone. Don't follow me," he uttered and flew away toward the east.

\*\*\*

Andy had been flying for a long time. He left sharp-tipped, snow-capped mountain peaks and gorges behind him. Redwoods and cedar forests changed to the deciduous woods of the foothills. He felt quite somber inside. Polana's death had torn the main waif from his soul, and there was nothing to fill that empty space. When the small star in his chest had suddenly exploded, and his left heart had skipped a beat, he knew. With complete clarity, he understood that his love was no more; Polana had left the world of the living. The foreign pain, as if his chest had taken the bolt, threw him down to the ground. Along with the pain came an awareness of the loss he had incurred. In that moment, Andy had seen the caravan road and the robbers stalking the guards. They had knocked down several trees, cutting off the tradesmen's path to retreat. Later, he had found all the thieves and made them scream in horror, but he wondered who could make him forget.

Andy suddenly snapped out of his reverie as if someone had called him by name. He looked around and below. It was a familiar place. There, he had been thrown into the world of Ilanta. There was the cliff wall and the ledge he had spent the night on. Further on, he saw the bald hill. The call rang out once again. Certain that the mysterious call wasn't just in his imagination, he began to circle the hill in wide circles. He heard another call from below. *The hill!*

A huge opening appeared at the top of the hill, and he could guess how the dragon got inside. Casting aside all his fears and doubts, he laid his wings flat and made a B-line for the inviting open entrance to the ancient structure. In a year and a half, nothing had changed inside. The broken bones and dragon's skull with its fangs extracted were still laying there. The amulet was sparkling with gold, its ruby shining near the altar. The dark bas-reliefs still told their tale, the cutout images continued to live their life. Changing hypostasis, Andy squatted on all fours before the mutilated skull.

"Forgive me." Andy carefully touched the arches above the eyebrows and ran his palm over the dead horns. The quiet call of the amulet sounded like the voice that brought forgiveness. "So it was you who called me?" he leaned over the circular object. The ancient structure was filled with the melodious call.

Curiosity got the best of him. Turning back into a dragon, Andy touched the golden chain with the tip of his claw. The chain stuck fast. Andy pulled his paw to no avail. *You burned yourself once, didn't you, and now you're tempted to do it again? Haven't you had enough rotten adventures? Isn't it better to cover your tail?* With the next quick wave of his paw, the medallion swinging on the end of the chain struck his chest and—melting as if made of mercury—it soaked right under Andy's scales. In the center of his heart, he got the feeling of a happy cat lying on top, purring with bliss.

"What? You've found a new master?" Andy knocked at his chest scales. The medallion responded with warmth and satisfaction. The image of Bon appeared before his eyes, licking his chin. It didn't mess with anything inside. "To heck with you," the new master of the golden circle said, quickly calming down. "Just don't bother me, okay?" A new wave of comforting warmth was the answer. "We have a deal then."

Andy carefully scooped up the broken bones and in a few trips took them up to the surface. He couldn't leave them lying there as they were, again. Obeying his mental request, the entrance to the interior of the hill closed. Every trace of the fact that a few seconds ago, a dragon could easily enter in, disappeared.

After catching his breath for a few minutes, Andy dug a deep hole and laid the bones of the former hill resident in it. Thoroughly trampling the bit of land, he was about to fly off, when the wind suddenly brought the smell of death and put him on his guard. Pressing his entire body to the ground and turning his head to meet the direction of the wind, he crawled to the wall of the wood.

The thick trees parted and revealed the field he remembered as the place where he had had his fight with the bald guy in black. In the center of the field, there were steaks dug into the ground, and tied to them were the remains of people in torn Watchmen's uniforms. One broad-shouldered guy's head was cut off. Shooing a few unhappy mrowns off the field, who were clearly not satisfied with this turn of events, Andy went out from under the branches. It was a scary execution; couldn't be anything else. Apparently, the men had been tied to the stakes several days ago and left to be eaten alive by predators, who didn't fail to take advantage of the opportunity. Only one of the watchmen was still alive and relatively whole—a yellow-haired female gnome. Gnomes aren't on hungry predators' menus. Cutting the ropes with his claws, Andy caught the limp body.

Once he had wanted to kill her, but with time, the thirst for revenge had burned itself up like so much straw. It left behind black memories and the knowledge that the watchman had not sold him all by herself, but in company with her fellows and under order from her commander. Perhaps, she personally had not sold him at all. Carefully taking the woman by the right paw, he carried her to the nearest stream and doused her with cold water. He had two versions of events prepared for her. She could stay on the field, and when Andy flew away, run in all directions, but he highly doubted the weakened, naked woman with no weapons could make it to a human or gnome dwelling from there. Otherwise, she could take a blood oath, and he would carry her to the valley. Glir, who was single, might get a bride....

The gnome woke up and, to her credit, did not writhe in his grip or scream at the sight of a tooth-bearing dragon. Andy made a mental note of this as a positive on her part. When she heard the options offered to her, she chose the latter.

"My name is Dorit," she told Andy after taking the magical vow. "I am forever in your debt."

"Call me Kerr. Are you going to ride on my neck or in my paws?"

"In your paws; I won't be able to hold onto your neck."

"What did they do that to you for?" Andy indicated the field with his paw.

"The hunters got back at us," she answered, falling silent.

Over the course of the past few events, his heartache had dulled a bit, but upon reaching the valley, Andy felt despair once again overtaking him. At home, everything reminded him of Polana. Targ, get under his tail, he didn't want to stay here. Flying to the village and handing over the gnome he had saved to the gnomes' care, he headed toward the cave. Dad and Jaga were home waiting for him.

"I want to finally start looking for information on building a gate," he announced from the entryway. "Whether you're for it or against it, I'm going."

Jaga and Karegar glanced at one another.

"Okay," the elf said calmly. "Karegar, is there anything you'd like to add?"

Dad lifted his giant head off the stone floor and shook it.

"Wait a minute," he said, suddenly stopping. "If you're going to look somewhere, it should definitely be Orten. There's a school of magic there where all the ancient archives that weren't stolen by the Forest Elves were taken 400 years ago. One old Rauu told me about it. The only thing is, Son, you'll have to put on a student's badge. No other way."

"Fine," Andy responded without hesitation.

***

The entire following week was taken up with preparations for Andy's trip. As it turned out, he had to run a zillion errands and take a pile of stuff with him that someone messing around with magic simply couldn't live without. The village ladies sewed him some suits. There were a couple made from a sturdy, practical material something like denim for everyday use and a couple of the most expensive material, for special occasions. Andy moved to the village that week and occupied the guesthouse, as per Jagirra's request. He was to go out among the people only in human form, but the Mistress' rule was constantly broken. The elf took Charda in, rightly assuming that after living for several years with Granny, she wouldn't betray her or play any underhanded dirty tricks. She hadn't even the slightest magical gift, but Jaga promised to make her the best herbalist in the region.

Dorit's eyes were a sight to see when Andy flew into her and Glir's engagement party and changed hypostasis in front of half the village. He no longer needed to take clothes with him wherever he went; Jaga had worked for a long time on a spell on a pair of pants, and now they didn't rip when he changed hypostasis, but simply disappeared, returning to his waist when he changed back into a human. The gnome's large eyes got even bigger, her jaw dropped, and she began to tremble.

"It's you?" she whispered, falling to her knees. She held her dagger out to Andy, the handle toward him, which she took from the sheath on her belt. "My life is in your hands."

Andy took the dagger and handed it to the clueless Glir. The guests looked on wide-eyed in surprise.

"Your life is now in Glir's hands. Remember that."

"Yes, sir."

"Take care of her," he told Glir.

Dad worried the most of everyone. He shut himself in and became anti-social, never left the cave without reason, and flew to Andy in the mornings to take him for an "air walk."

***

Jaga and Karegar discussed how to take Kerr to Orten for a long time. The future student put an end to any doubt on the issue with one sentence.

"Since I can't fly, I'll ride a hass. I don't know how to ride horses. I'd make a fine horseman, plopped on a horse's back like a sack of potatoes."

Once the question of transport was settled, the three of them headed toward Rum-bit's farm. The hassan, upon finding out the reason for a visit from such honored guests, began talking up his four-legged, toothy transportation and suggested making a gift of one of them, all of which were, according to him, quite stupendous. Andy, not listening to the owner, poked a male hass of a very rare white color.

"Handsome. Can I get this one?"

"You can try, but he's only used to me. Snowflake probably won't let anyone else on him." Rum made a face, sizing up Andy.

"I'll try."

Snowflake didn't have time to show any signs of the vicious temper that Rum had said was part of his personality. Andy changed hypostasis, hissed at the hass, pressed it to the ground with his paw, then quickly changed back again and sat on the jumpy animal's back. Demoralized by the show of strength, Snowflake feared throwing the rider off him. He still smelled like a dragon. Instead, Snowflake accepted his rider's authority. Rum bowed his head politely.

***

"Don't take unnecessary risks and don't go looking for trouble. Don't be a blabbermouth, and don't argue with the guards. Your fangs make you look like an orc, and in Tantre they don't like orcs very much; it's not worth ending up in prison," Jagirra added her last instructions. Karegar silently lay beside the road and sighed heavily.

Andy jumped off the hass, kissed Jaga on the cheek and hugged Daddy around the neck.

"Act like a real dragon. Use your conscience; I wouldn't want to be disgraced by my own son," the dragon said in his low voice.

"Don't worry, everything's going to be excellent," Andy tried to assure his adoptive parents and jumped back onto the hass. "Let's go, Snowflake! Gmar, Glir, keep up with me, come on."

Andy rode to Gornbuld accompanied by the gnome brothers. He had to buy a new bow and sword in the city and deal with the local banks and currency. The rest of the way, he rode by himself. There was just over a month until he would begin at the school.

Andy, as opposed to the gnomes, didn't look back at the two figures who had become family to him, standing in the distance, watching him get smaller and smaller on the horizon.

*** 

"Shall we fly?" Karegar asked Jagirra.

"Let's wait a bit," the elf answered, barely defining the white speck of the hass in the distance.

"All right," the dragon lay down on the ground and invited Jagirra to sit down on the curve of his right elbow. "What are you thinking about?"

"I'm worried about Kerr, whether he'll be able to live with humans. The boy's continuing to cling to his humanity, but he became a dragon a long time ago and already looks at many issues through the eyes of a Lord of the Skies. It'll be awful if he starts looking down on others. The future of Ilanta may very well depend on him. Perhaps, we should try to find a nice female dragon for him?"

"Aren't you overstretching things just a bit? Kerr and the future of the world?"

"No. I've begun to imagine more and more that Kerr's a true blood."

"A true blood?"

"Yes, it's the only way I can explain all the strange things about him. He was able to undergo incarnation at sixteen years old, grew in all his scales in only three hours, learned to change hypostasis without spending a drop of mana, without any long training sessions. There are many, many ways he distinguishes himself from all the other embodied ones."

"And in suggesting what you're suggesting, you sent him to Orten? We have to get him back right away!"

"I believe Enira. There will be a great war, our son should know magic. He won't have any other chance to learn."

*** 

The morning gradually became noon. The last dust from the hass' claws had long since settled.

"Let's go," Jaga grabbed the dragon's warm neck. Karegar folded his front paws into a boat, carefully flew Jagirra home, and went hunting. He always got hungry when he was worried.

Left alone—Charda had gone out to gather robin's petals—Jagirra took the letter out of her bodice. It now had holes in it. Her eyes lingered on the last lines written by the Larga, "Tell them the whole truth, otherwise, if heard from someone else's lips, it will kill them both."

"I can't, Enira!" the disobedient lips whispered, and an unwanted tear ran down the old elf's cheek. If someone had been standing nearby who could look with true vision, he would have been to see the woman's aura shining with all colors of the rainbow all around her, an aura neither human nor elf.

## End of Book One

Thank you for reading this book. Please leave a review of this book. Thank you.

# GLOSSARY

## Geography

*Alatar* – the largest continent on the planet of *Ilanta*.

*Aria* – a continent located north of Alatar.

*Empire of Alatar* – a state existing two thousand years ago that pursued an aggressive policy of conquest. Approximately sixty percent of the total area of the continent of Alatar was subject to the Empire. The continent itself was named in honor of the Empire. Northern kingdoms such as Tantre, Mesaniya, Meriya, and Rimm were at one time secluded barbarian provinces of the Empire. As a result of civil war, the Empire of Alatar was broken into separate states and ceased to exist.

*Ilanta* – a planet.

*Kingdom of Mestair* – a legendary human kingdom located on the territory of modern-day Taiir and the Great Principality of Mesaniya, which existed three thousand years ago during the age of the dragons. As an independent state, it was destroyed by the dragons and their allies during the war with the Forest Elves and few human states that had joined them.

*The Light Forest* – the state of the Forest Elves, limited to the growth area of the Mellornys.

*The Marble Mountains* – a large mountain range crossing the northern part of Alatar from north to south. From the north, the range is bordered by the North Sea. From the south, by the Southern Rocky Ridge and the Long sea.

*Mesaniya* – A Great Principality located north of the kingdom of Tantre.

*Nelita* – The second planet in a triple solar system: Ilanta, Nelita, and Helita. Nelita is considered the dragons' native land; it was named in honor of the goddess of life, Nel. The literal translation is "eye of the goddess of life."

*Ort* – the largest river in the north of Alatar, flows across the territory of the kingdom of Tantre.

*Patskoi Empire* – a human state with the capital at the city of Pat. The Emperors of Pat consider themselves the heirs of the Empire of Alatar.

*Rimm* – a human kingdom located east of the Marble Mountains.

*Steppe* – the self-designation of the kingdom of the white orcs. Located in the east of Alatar.

*Taiir* – a dukedom

*Tantre* – a large kingdom, second largest after the Patskoi Empire, located in the central part of north-western Alatar. Geographically limited by the Marble Mountains and the Northern and Southern Rocky Ridges. Has access to the Eastern Ocean and the Long Sea. Its capital is the city of Kion.

## Miscellaneous

*Alert-dert* – a military rank corresponding to that of captain.

*Asgard* – in Scandinavian mythology, the heavenly city is the abode of the Aesir gods.

*Book of the Guardians* – a book in which the dragons recorded the password spells to the inter-planetary portals. The guardians are the dragons (true blood mages), who stayed on Ilanta to guard the portals. At the time the events described herein took place, all guardians are thought to be deceased.

*Chucker* – a magical artifact that allows its user to throw balls of capsulized spells.

*Drag* – a flying lizard that can be saddled and ridden.

*Feather* – a junior military group of twelve to fifteen rideable animals.

*The Goddesses' Eyes* are what people call the planets Nelita and Helita. Helita, Nelita and Ilanta make up the system of planets that revolve around their sun.

*The Gray Horde* – the collective name for all the "gray" orcs residing in the northern coastal steppes; the strongest khanate of the "gray" orcs was also called the Gray Horde.

*Gross-dert* (gross- leading, dert- wing) – a military rank in the air units of Tantre's army, corresponding to that of colonel.

*Hel* – mistress of the world of the dead.

*Khirud* – the main god in the pantheon of the "white" orcs. Khirud the lightning-armed is the god of warriors and daredevils.

*"Knee" Prince-Khan* – that is, one who is bent at the knee, living in total vassal dependence on the king, unlike a "belt" prince or khan, that is, one who bows at the waist. Belt khans have a high level of autonomy, can mint silver and copper coins, and maintain personal militias, some of which are comparable to an army. They collect their own taxes independently on their lands, sending one twelfth to the king's treasury. In the event of war, "belt" princes are obligated to present one third of their troops to the king's army. "Knee" khans, most likely, are hereditary governors of the lands and take an oath of fidelity to the king.

*Loki* – the Scandinavian god of mischief

*The Lynx clan, the Dragon clan* – the strongest clans of the island Norsemen.

*nökürs* - elite warriors and bodyguards.

*The Northern Alliance* – an alliance of Tantre, the Rauu Principalities, and the gnome kingdoms.

*Odin* – a Norse deity.

*Pound, jang* – the currency of the kingdom of Tantre. Pounds come in silver and gold; jangs are a small copper coin.

*Rauu* – Snow Elves. The first artificial race created by the dragons for battles against the orcs.

*Roi-dert* – a junior officer's rank, corresponds to that of lieutenant.

*Rune Keys* – used for opening portals.

*Second-in-saddle* – the second rider on a large golden griffon. Usually armed with a bow, rarely with a magical chucker.

*Servants of Death* – helrats, priests of a cult forbidden in all countries which perverts the very name of the goddess Hel. Hunted dragons and actively promoted human sacrifice.

*Severan* – a cold northern wind.

*Taili-Mother* – The deity of the "white" orcs, representing the feminine, analogue of the goddess Nel.

*Targ* – the gnome god whose name took on a negative connotation in almost all countries. Occupies the niche of mischief-maker and prankster, analogous to *Loki* in some sense.

*Teg* – the polite form of address of a nobleman; *grall* – to a mage. *Teg grall* – form of address of a noble mage. *Tain, taina* – titles for high-borns, male and female, respectively. Professor/master/mistress [first name] Teg grall (tain/taina) [last name].

*True blood* – a mage who, unlike others, can work directly with the astral and consciously take mana from it. Other mages can extract mana only from the planet's magical field.

*Snekkja* – a row/sailboat of the Scandinavian peoples in the twelfth-fourteenth centuries. Predominantly used for raids. Held up to one hundred people.

*Valhalla* – a heavenly palace in Asgard for the fallen in battle, a paradise for the valiant warriors.

*Wing* – a regiment of griffons or drags consisting of one-hundred-twenty to one-hundred-fifty rideable animals.

# THE DRAGON INSIDE

The Dragon Inside tells the story of Andy, an average teenager from a small town who is transported to a new world by accident. Along the way, he meets dangerous wildlife and hostile locals. Battling to survive he is captured and sold into slavery. But after escaping, he is mortally wounded and must undergo the ancient ritual to become a Dragon to survive.

Once a Dragon Andy must learn to master his new skills and protect the innocent while taking revenge on those who have wronged him, which will lead him to take a central role in a war between planets including his old home....

**The Dragon Inside Series:**

Becoming the Dragon

Wings on my Back

A Cruel Tale

Three Wars

# WINGS ON MY BACK

Part 1.

**Orten. Near the western gates. Andy.**

The crowd at the gates stirred with anticipation. The tower bell rang 8 a.m., and the sound of the gate lifting mechanism came from behind the walls.

*It's time*, Andy thought and followed the peasants towards the narrow bridge. But it was not meant to be. Nobles on horseback of various stripes were the first to enter the city, parting the crowd like nuclear icebreakers breaking pack ice. Genteel and highborn. Surrounded by a dozen bodyguards, dressed in a light gray riding outfit, an aristocratic Taina[1] rode by on a tall bay stallion. Sitting in the saddle, with one hand she grasped the reigns; with the other she constantly lifted a perfumed handkerchief to her nose, glancing with contempt at the serfs and twisting her plump lips into a grimace. Her eyes lingered on Andy, who stood out like a bell tower among the short peasants. Her nose wrinkled up and her lips frowned once again. Her detest for the plebeian who had dared grow taller than a nobleman engulfed him from head to toe and then the feeling of her eyes on him subsided. *Douche-baguette!* Andy thought. *Stupid woman! It'll be tough for me at that school if there's even a couple of people there like that. I won't be able to stand it. I'll scarf someone for sure!*

The nobles' children, on horses, hasses, or in carriages made their way into the city first. Andy surveyed this variegated crowd indifferently. It was as multicolored as a parrot. Camisoles, dresses, and capes of various types and façons, feathers in caps, embroidery, and lace were intended to demonstrate a nobleman's place in society. With haughty and contemptuous looks on their faces, little kids and parents of the 'golden' youth accompanied their offspring to their preparatory experiences in the school of magic. And what great disappointment these lords of life endured when the occasional filthy serf was accepted into the school, as opposed to

---

[1] the word for an unmarried woman of noble class

another one of their own over-dressed, dolled-up prick-... progeny? True, the percentage of magically gifted people was significantly higher among the gentlefolk than among the rest of society. It was the result of hundreds of years of selective breeding and dynastic marriages, but real natural talents were born more often among the rest.

The city guards, exiting the towers over the gates, began to restore order with shouts, kicks, and spears. They couldn't let the people trample one another, all the more so since the crowd contained many future students of the Magic School, and mage guilds didn't appreciate disturbances and inconveniences created by their own, even future, members.

"Step aside! First, let the honorable members of the noble families through!" a fat untidy guard at the gates exerted himself.

"What about us?" Andy dropped the inappropriate question.

"The riff-raff can wait!" the sloppy guard's obese partner answered, smirking slyly. Spitting at Andy's feet, he pushed him away from the city gates with the tip of his spear.

The wide-brimmed hat intended to cover Andy's face, which he had really only donned for the purpose of this slight disguise, tilted from the sudden jerk and the brim flew upwards, revealing his bright blue eyes with no whites.

"If you're going to be insolent, freak, I'll keep you at these gates till next year!" the tubby guard guffawed, self-satisfied, itching his chain mail-clad belly. His fat sausage fingers scratched at the rings, not reaching the source of the itch. "You may have your traveling papers, but I still remember the king's edict! Got it?"

The chubby man's breath smelled of garlic and long-since un-brushed teeth. Plus, he stank of body odor and goat meat. Andy winced and thanked providence that it had prompted him to turn down his sense of smell; otherwise, he certainly would have vomited.

"I get it. I get it. What's there not to get," Andy turned away from the enforcers. Jerks. The guards in Tantre were like the cops back in Russia – looked just like them and were just as brazen. Hm, interesting, do they stamp them out with the same press or something? They were from different worlds, but their manners were the same, and their mugs were all vile.

Spitting on the bridge out of frustration, he made his way to the side towards the peasant carts. Not paying any mind to the peasants, who had begun to whisper to one another in fear when they saw him and make gestures with their hands meant to cast away evil spirits, Andy sat down on a log in the shade of a tethering post canopy, moved his hat a bit lower over his eyes, and began to wait until the bottleneck at the gates cleared and he could freely enter the city.

What did he expect? In the countryside, they frightened children at night, telling them scary stories of non-humans, and he happened to fit the description to a T. He was tall and broad-shouldered, taller than many of the nobles' children, ash-haired, with a strong jaw, a forceful chin, blue eyes with no whites and sharp fangs that stuck out slightly when he smiled. He looked just like the spawn of some wayward elf and a northern orc or steppe nomad.

The fact that elves and orcs didn't have eyes like that, that in them the blue didn't go beyond the iris, didn't concern the peasants. Orcs were indiscriminately gray or brown-eyed, and elf-orc mixes were gray-skinned or didn't differ from elves in appearance. But what the heck, what did he expect from peasants who had only seen orcs in pictures? No matter which village Andy might show his face in, the peasant men and women there would begin to wonder what kind of unnatural union he was the result of. Or they could imagine a lot worse! Apparently, the wild and war-loving orc raped the captive female elf during the raid, after burning down all the houses of that clan of elves and killing her unfortunate relatives! So that's why there was no mark of an elf clan on this blue-eyed freak's forehead! Who would want to take such an obscenity into their family? The guy gallivants around cities and all over, scaring people and playing all sorts of dirty tricks on honest folk. He might send down a curse here, poison the harvest there... but what else can you expect from such a half-blood? Only dirty tricks.

It was strange, but elves were esteemed and respected here. The pointy-eared race really knew how to appeal to people! Girls stared wide-eyed at each elven kite, and were ready to talk, flirt, and give them a chance. If any relationships came about, and if any of them were fruitful, they wouldn't consider the half-bloods that resulted to be freaks....

And then there were gnomes. As they say, they had hogged the whole banking sector and monopolized the trade of 'high-tech' weapons. The gnome chiefs had held Tantre's guilds of production masters accountable. Even the Royal Informants tried to stay out of the business of these masters of the foothills. They might refuse to make a loan to the treasury, and then the king would reward his servants with the rod.

"But yew not scawy. Hag tol' me thet non-humans aw scawy with big teeth stickin' out!"

Lost in thought, Andy hadn't noticed that a little girl of four or five had walked up to him and was standing a couple of feet away, examining his simple outfit and the visitor himself, not forgetting to pick her nose and wipe her finger on the skirt of her worn gray dress. He had lived long enough to get used to his second appearance and the feelings and senses it gave him, so much so that while in human form, he felt disabled. He hadn't seen her coming. But actually, the girl managed to walk up to him quite silently.

"And what if I'm very scary and terrible! I'm just pretending to be all white and fluffy?" he answered the little one.

"Nope," she began, and again brought her finger to her nose, but thought the better of it half way there and patting the hem of her dress, went on. "Yew fangs aw small and yew not foaming at the mouth! Besewks aw always foaming at the mouth. Aha!"


"My fangs are small but sharp, but I don't look like a berserk, since there's no foam. Where'd you come from? Are you an expert in berserks or something?" Andy looked at her face with interest. The girl pouted and looked down, lowering her toe-head, which gave her away as a native of the north. The old gray... no, at one time blue dress, re-sown in the shoulders, a hand-me-down. Her worn buckskin booties, the twisted copper coin amulet hanging from her neck, it all pointed to the far-northern isles of the Half-night Sea.

# BOOK RECOMMENDATIONS

I want to thank you for reading my book. If you enjoyed it then please leave me a review and look at the rest of the series. But I would also like to bring some other great authors to your attention.

Tabloid journalist 'Kif' must balance his real-world struggles with his role in an epic fantasy game. A must-read for those who love fantasy, games, and humor! Try the best-selling series Fayroll by Andrey Vasilyev.

I also want to recommend Realm of Arkon, a great series written by a friend of mine: G. Akella (Georgy Smorodinsky). He is one of the most popular and best-selling LitRPG authors in Russia. Book 1 is currently free on Amazon.

Also please join my Facebook community for the latest updates and news. Just search The Dragon Inside.

Finally don't forget to look at my publisher's website at Litworld to see other great series.

# ALEX SAPEGIN

Alex Sapegin is a popular Science Fiction and Fantasy author who lives in the city of Khabarovsk in the Far East of Russia with his wife and two children.

He trained as an electrical engineer working for the railway industry and tunnel construction. But he always had a flair for story-telling and enjoyed making stories for his classmates while at school. It was only a matter of time before he would write his first story.

In 2010 his first novel 'Becoming the Dragon' was published and instantly became a hit over Russia and Eastern Europe. These were followed up by three more stories.

When he is not writing, he enjoys spending time with his family, fishing and relaxing with a good book.

He has written numerous books in Russian which have all been popular amongst Russian readers.

CPSIA information can be obtained
at www.ICGtesting.com
Printed in the USA
FFOW02n0232110118
44447633-44222FF